NATHAN GOODMAN

Rendition Protocol

The Special Agent Jana Baker Spy-Thriller Series, by Nathan
Goodman
   Protocol One
   The Fourteenth Protocol
   Protocol 15
   Breach of Protocol

Rendition Protocol

On February 7, 1985, a DEA agent named Enrique Camarena Salazar was abducted while working deep cover in Mexico. To his friends, he was known simply as "Kiki." Agent Camarena was the first to propose that in order to stop the drug cartels, the US should go after the money, not the drugs. President Ronald Reagan, upon hearing of the abduction, became infuriated. He phoned Mexican President Miguel de la Madrid and threatened that if Agent Camarena did not resurface, immediately, he would order the US State Department to issue a code-red travel alert—the US-Mexican border would be sealed. The action would have destroyed Mexico's economy.

At the same time, the CIA was covertly involved in an all-out effort to finance the Contra rebels of Nicaragua. The Contras were attempting to overthrow the Sandanista government, and the United States was all too happy to assist. Secret funds were raised on two fronts. The first was in Iran. At the time, Iran was under an arms embargo, yet the CIA orchestrated the sale of Hawk and TOW missiles to the Iranians. It was an all-cash deal. The second involved CIA-protected shipments of cocaine from Mexico into the United States. Between the two sources of funding, the CIA secured the resources necessary to oversee the toppling of the Nicaraguan regime. But before that could happen, the scandal broke. It became known as *The Iran-Contra Affair*.

When Agent Camarena followed the money trail in Mexico

and discovered the CIA was running drugs into the United States, they orchestrated his abduction. His horribly tortured body was uncovered a month later.

This story is dedicated to the memory of Special Agent Kiki Camarena and all those who would risk their lives to make the world a better place.

1

Victim or Perp

Royal Police Force, American Road, St. John's, isle of Antigua.

"You're *not* going to fingerprint me!" Jana yelled.

The uniformed officer repeated his command. "Miss, *you are going to be fingerprinted.* You have no legal basis to refuse. If you do not comply, we'll force you."

She backed into a corner of the police station's intake room and then lunged for a door handle, but the steel door was locked from the other side.

The officer pressed a button on the wall and spoke. "I need a team in here right now."

Within moments, three officers entered and grabbed her by the arms. "Having a little trouble here, Charlie?" one said.

Jana thrashed against their viselike grips.

"Calm down, miss. Calm down," one of the officers said. But Jana slammed her heel into his foot. It impacted the lateral dorsal cutaneous nerve. He buckled under the blow but held tight.

Charlie, the arresting officer, lunged to take the man's place as a third officer circled behind and put a thick forearm around her neck then wrenched it tight.

"Assaulting an officer? Well, that's going to cost you another six months inside. Let's get her into the chair. We'll print her once she's secured."

"No!" she screamed against the choke hold.

The trio of officers yanked her into a metal rolling chair, then strapped her arms, hands, feet. The officers stood back a moment and caught their breath. The struggle had been brief but exhausting.

"She's strong as an ox," one said.

"Good God," another officer said as he removed his boot. "That hurts like hell. Hey, lady. What is wrong with you?"

"I'm not going to be fingerprinted," Jana returned.

"Well, I'm afraid that's not your decision."

She looked at them through eyes of steel. "I do not consent to this!" The bindings on her hands and feet brought back visions of her ordeal the year prior. The memories began to flicker and pop in her mind.

"Again, not your decision." He looked at the other officers. "Let's roll her to the table. She'll be printed alright."

"No!" she yelled as she thrashed against her bindings. Though the officers could not tell, Jana's right hand had begun to shake.

One said, "What's her problem? It's not like we're trying to hurt her. What did she do anyway?"

Charlie replied, "Busted a guy up pretty bad. He's headed to the hospital. Never seen anything like it. I'm not even sure he's going to make it. And she won't even tell us her name. Must not want us to know who she really is."

An officer said, "Tighten that wrist restraint. Good, now let's get the digital pad underneath one finger at a time."

She struggled and thrashed but could not prevent her fingerprints from being taken. Her chest heaved and the edges of her vision began to darken.

"Good work, boys," Charlie said. "Get her into solitary for now. And leave her in the chair. She needs a little time to cool down. I think the detectives are on their way."

"Hey, is she alright? Miss?"

Jana's eyes rolled into her skull until only the whites showed. Her body began to convulse.

"Oh, shit!" Charlie yelled. "She's having a seizure or something. Quick, call an ambulance and tell them to expedite!"

2

The Devil Within

In a cellar deep underneath the home of Diego Rojas, a young woman lay on a table, unconscious. When she opened her eyes, her head hurt. She could see nothing in the pitch blackness. The air was heavy and the table cold. She was disoriented and groggy, like one awaking from a drugged stupor. At first, she was calm; the drugs still coursed through her system.

She tried to move but her limbs did not seem able. She dozed off for what seemed like only a moment, but when she finally awakened everything felt different.

The drugs had left her body, and she discovered her hands and feet were lashed. Her breathing accelerated in earnest. She began to scream but found her mouth taped shut.

Just outside the room she heard muffled voices.

"Where is this one from?" a deep voice said.

"The homeland, Signor Rojas, as instructed. Villa de Leyva, to be precise. She has been prepared according to your instructions."

The cellar door swung open and light cast into the room, illuminating the table where the woman lay.

Rojas stopped and his eyes flared.

Only then did the girl realize she was completely nude. She

began to thrash and scream but to no avail.

A sickening grin peeled across Rojas's face. "Ah, yes. Villa de Leyva," he said with a distant gaze, "just north of Bogotá. The women there are beautiful." He walked into the room and closed the door. As it slammed shut, the room again descended into blackness. "We will get to know one another quite well."

The girl thrashed at her bindings.

His eyes widened further and his words sliced the air. "Yes, we will get to know one another quite well."

3

The Pinch of Truth

As a CIA operations officer, Kyle MacKerron was still green in terms of years of service. But as a former special agent with the FBI, he was allowed more than a little latitude. The typical two-year training window for new ops officers, which teaches clandestine operational tradecraft, had been shortened to eight months in his case, and after multiple successful assignments, Kyle was on his own.

He hadn't understood the reason for his current assignment at first. To gather intelligence on a drug cartel setting up shop on Antigua didn't fall under the typical CIA purview. But he accepted the assignment without hesitation. During training, his CIA handlers had practically beaten the charter into his brain. *Clandestinely spot, assess, develop, and recruit.* It had become like a mantra, but here on an active field assignment, the mantra was almost comical. Nonetheless it reverberated in his head.

But waking up tied to a chair, reciting it was hardly comforting. The shroud over his head was thick and hot and made breathing difficult. Not a sliver of light penetrated and carbon dioxide had trouble filtering out. Kyle knew the excess CO_2 had resulted in a condition called hypercapnia, and he experienced the full brunt of it: flushed skin, muscle twitches, and reduced neural activity—and these were just the early stages.

Kyle struggled against his bindings, and between decreased brain function and sleep deprivation, he had trouble processing rational thought. The fear started as a trickle, but had grown to an immeasurable state.

Muffled sounds were audible and Kyle struggled to decipher them. *Where am I?* he thought. His only defense was to joke with himself: *We're not in Kansas anymore, Toto.*

He tried to stay calm, but when a heavy metal door scraped open across the gritty cement floor and slammed into a wall, he startled. Two sets of footsteps approached. The first sounded like those of hard-soled boots, but the second were different. They sounded more like leather-soled dress shoes. The door slammed closed with a heavy bang that reverberated through the tiny room. Someone pulled at the base of the shroud and yanked it off.

Kyle gulped at the air but a hand grabbed his hair and yanked his head back, exposing his neck. He squinted in the low light at the man in front of him. He looked to be of Latin descent and was dressed in a double-breasted business suit. Kyle's head began to clear, but he still felt an overwhelming sense of heaviness, as if someone was standing on his chest.

"Welcome to my humble estate," the man said in an accent heavy of Central America.

"Who the fuck are you?" Kyle said, though his voice was hoarse. He coughed.

"My name is Diego Rojas, and yours is Agent Kyle MacKerron."

Kyle's heart rate soared as the terrifying realization struck home. *They know who I am.*

Rojas clasped his hands and walked a slow circle around Kyle. "You have been very busy," Rojas said. "Very busy indeed. And that is what brings you here."

Kyle craned his neck to follow the man but feared a blow might come at any second.

"You've gotten yourself in deep, haven't you?" Rojas continued.

"I don't know what you're talking about," Kyle said through a cough.

Rojas laughed. "How very in keeping with the United States government. Always sticking its nose where it doesn't belong." Rojas squared off in front of Kyle. "You have been very busy penetrating the Oficina de Envigado cartel. Yes, very busy indeed."

Oficina de Envigado was the largest and most aggressive cartel in Colombia, and had been the subject of Kyle's investigation. His brain raced to catch up. *Shit, I've been caught by Oficina de Envigado. But who is this?*

Rojas said, "And you are going to tell us everything you know about them."

Kyle thought, *Wait a minute. Tell you about them? If these guys aren't Oficina de Envigado, who are they?* But then it hit him. *This must be Los Rastrojos, the competing cartel.*

Two Colombian cartels had recently infiltrated the tropical paradise of Antigua in order to establish new drug routes. The new routes were set up to push product to the Mexican cartels, and from there to the United States. What the cartels didn't know was how deeply the CIA had penetrated.

Rojas reared a hand to punch Kyle, and Kyle braced, but the blow never came. Rojas laughed loud enough for the sound to reverberate off the cement walls. Kyle opened his eyes to find the man standing over him. "Ah, but in the old days, yes," Rojas said, his voice becoming deep and distant. "We would torture out anything we wanted to know. Those, my friend, were good

8

times. But as it is, I have other needs for you. And now there are better ways, more accurate ways, to find out what we need to know." Rojas nodded to the other man.

Kyle felt a sharp pinch in his neck as a syringe went deep and the plunger depressed. By the time the syringe was removed, Kyle felt a warmth unlike anything in his experience, and the feeling of heaviness in his chest evaporated. It was like watching the waters of a fleeing tide recede. His eyelids flickered and what he could only describe as complete euphoria overwhelmed his senses. His head slumped. He had been drugged and there was nothing he could do about it.

4

Inhospitable

Four hours later. Mount Saint John's Medical Centre emergency room.

"This is the one that shot our victim?" Lieutenant Jack Pence said as he peered through the window into the hospital room. Pence was new to the island and hadn't even had time to learn the names of the other officers.

"Yeah, won't say a word though," a junior detective replied. "Doc says she's checked out medically. He can't rule out a psyche evaluation though. Headshrinker will be down here from ClearviewPsychiatric Hospital later."

"What happened when they tried to book her?"

"Doc said she probably had a seizure or episode of some type. Brain waves are normal now."

"Christ, what set her off?"

"I don't know. I looked at the tape from the booking room and it looks like she fought them pretty hard. Once they strapped her in the chair, she went nuts."

"And she won't talk? Who is she?"

"Hell if I know, man. All I know is she got picked up by the uniforms two blocks from the scene. She had no ID and wouldn't disclose her name."

"The victim pretty bad?"

"Let me put it to you this way, the vic has a compound fracture to the left leg, broken collarbone, a face that looks like purple butter, and two gunshot wounds."

"Two GSWs and he's alive?"

"At the moment, yes. He's upstairs in surgery. One through the kneecap, the other . . . the groin."

The lieutenant rubbed his chin. "We sure she's the shooter? They find the weapon on her?"

"Yes, sir. Glock .380 subcompact."

"So what's that look on your face supposed to mean?"

"It's the gun."

"What about it?"

"Custom made. Never seen anything like it." The young detective looked at Lieutenant Pence. "The grip had been shortened to reduce the size of the overall weapon. And then there was the silencer."

"A silencer? You're kidding me. Where does she think she is? The Bronx? This is Antiqua. I didn't think we got silencers here. She give the uni's any trouble at the scene?"

"Ah, yeah, you might say that. Spun around on the arresting officer so quickly, all he knew was that his firearm was no longer in his hands. She had disarmed him and pointed it at his face. Then he said she disassembled the weapon so fast he couldn't see anything but gun parts dropping all over the ground. After that she gave them no trouble. Scared the shit out of the guy though."

"I bet."

"The victim is another story. Even thoughhis face is bashed in pretty good, the arresting officer was able to recognize him. Got a record a mile long. Several outstanding felony warrants."

The lieutenant looked at him. "So let me see if I've got this straight. The vic is a perp we've been looking for. He's broken to pieces in an alley, two GSWs, then we find her near the scene? Is that and the gun the only thing that ties her to the vic?"

"The weapon was still warm. And her knuckles have fresh blood on them. His, not hers."

The lieutenant crossed his arms. "Shit, look at her. She can't weigh more than hundred and twenty pounds, wet," he said as he glared into the room where she lay. "Then again, look at the musculature. She looks like that actress from that second *Terminator* movie. You know, when she got in shape? What was her name?"

"Linda Hamilton."

"Yeah, a blond-haired Linda Hamilton. And she won't tell us her name? You run her prints? Anything come back?"

"Sort of."

"The computer couldn't find a match?"

"Not exactly. Weirdest thing I've ever seen. The computer found a match, but the results were *redacted*."

"What do you mean, redacted?"

"Just like I said, redacted. They were blacked out on the computer monitor."

"You've got to be kidding me."

"I printed it out so you could see." The detective held out a piece of paper.

As Lieutenant Pence studied the printout, he shook his head. "What the hell?" Everything that would normally identity the matching fingerprints was blacked out. "Is she CIA or something?"

"No idea, but she's highly trained, that's for sure."

"You try to talk to her?"

"Yup, twice. Doesn't even look you in the eye."

"This is bullshit," the lieutenant said. He took a deep breath, opened the door, and walked into the hospital room. He placed his hand on an empty chair near the bed ."Mind if I have a seat?" he said, but didn't bother waiting for a reply. As he pulled the chair closer to the bedside, he said, "So? How are things going with you?"

Her eyes flared. His attempt at levity had gone nowhere.

He glanced at her deep-bronze skin and sun-bleached hair and knew she was likely a local. "Tourist season has been good this year. It's great for the island economy, don't you think?" He craned his neck to make eye contact but the effort proved futile. "Look, I'm just trying to make small talk. You seem like a person in need of a friend right now."

Without looking over, Jana said, "Some women would take offense to what you just said."

"Really? Why is that?"

"A lot of guys walk up to you in bars and say things like that. 'Hey, babe, looking for a friend?' But it's not your friendship they're interested in."

"My name is Jack. I'm not trying to make a pass at you. I'm a detective. You know, this conversation would go much better if I knew what to call you."

Jana said nothing.

The lieutenant continued. "You busted that guy up pretty good. He's in surgery, in case you were wondering. Where'd you learn to do that?"

She shifted in her bed and looked at the restraints on her wrists.

"It doesn't look good, you know?" Pence continued. "You not talking to me. We've got a man broken to pieces and, unless you

13

can tell me what happened, the district attorney is going to push for attempted murder." He paused a moment to let the statement sink in.

"The prick didn't try to kill me."

"The charge of attempted murder wouldn't be filed against him, it would be filed against you." He watched her facial expression. "I take it you disagree? The charges are real, miss. I tell you what, why don't we share information? I tell you something, you tell me something. Is that fair? And since I don't know your name, I'm going to call you Jane, Jane Doe. That's what we do in an investigation where we don't know the name of the subject. So, Jane, I'll start. What interests me about the victim's injuries are the gunshot wounds. One to the kneecap, one to the groin. Those kind of makes a statement, don't they? Did you find yourself in a bad position, and this, perhaps, was self-defense?" But when she made no response, the lieutenant got up to leave. "Listen, Jane. If you aren't going to talk, you don't give me any choice. Once the headshrinker clears you, you'll be taken back to police headquarters. And you might as well make yourself at home. You might be there quite a while."

5

Off the Reservation

Sometime the next morning Jana awoke at the police precinct to the sound of metallic keys throwing a heavy bolt. A uniformed officer stared down at her. "Jane Doe, number zero six six seven three? Right this way, you have a visitor."

"A visitor?" she said. She rubbed sleep from her eyes and sat up then looked at the officer. "Get a good look? You like watching women while they sleep?"

The officer rolled his eyes.

Jana stood. "How can I have a visitor? There isn't even anyone on this island that knows I'm here."

"This way."

He held her by the arm and escorted her down the cinder-block hallway toward the interrogation room. The officer opened the door and motioned to an open chair. Seated at the table were Lieutenant Pence and a man whose back was to her. When he turned around, she immediately recognized him. He was a man from her past, a man named Cade Williams.

The lieutenant looked at Cade and said, "Alright, Mr. Williams, she's here." He glanced at the uniformed officer standing by the door. "You don't need to stay. But make sure no one is in the observation room," he said as he pointed to the mirrored wall of glass. He looked back at Cade. "Now, can you tell me what the hell is going on? Why is the National Security Agency on my island?"

Cade looked at her. "Jana, sit down for God's sake. You want to tell him, or should I?"

Her eyes were locked on his as she approached the table. She leaned her knuckles onto it and spoke through gritted teeth. "I was doing just fine on my own. I don't need your help."

"That's not the way I see it," Cade replied. "Let's see if I can recap the last many months of your life for you. Then we'll see whether or not you need my help. First, you leave us without a trace. You don't tell anyone where you're going. It was as though you disappeared off the face of the earth. You go off the grid and assume a new identity. And from what the lieutenant tells me, and from the looks of you, you've apparently acquired a bit of field training during that time. A new-found penchant for snapping femur bones as if they were twigs, then shooting men in the balls? Should I continue, or do you want to take over from here?"

Jana yanked the metal chair back. It scraped against the cement floor, and she sat.

Cade shook his head. "I don't even know you anymore."

"Wait a minute," the lieutenant said. "This is not exactly the type of cooperation I was hoping for. If there's history between the two of you, and from the looks of it, bad history, why didn't you send someone else?" He leveled a finger at Jana. "I want to know who she is She's charged with aggravated assault and attempted murder. This is not the United States. The isle of Antigua is a sovereign country, sir. And you are withholding state's evidence."

"Relax, Lieutenant," Cade said as he leaned back in his chair.

"I just wanted to give Jana a chance to speak for herself. She doesn't appreciate it when people speak for her. At least she didn't back when I knew her." Cade shook his head. "Lieutenant, meet Special Agent Jana Baker, formerly of the FBI."

The lieutenant traced his thoughts. "You're telling me this is *Agent* Baker? The one that stopped those two bombings?"

"And I can tell you she certainly did not commit assault or attempted murder on your island."

The lieutenant stood to emphasize his point. "*Agent* Baker, is it? I suggest you start talking so we can straighten this thing out. And your story better be pretty good. Mr. Williams is not apprised of all the evidence against you, but I am. And the DA is more than a little agitated. He wants to throw you under the prison."

A tense silence ensued, then Cade said, "I've seen all the evidence against her."

The lieutenant glared at him. "You couldn't have seen the evidence."

Cade saw no point in explaining that NSA had accessed the police computer during the night and downloaded everything. "Jana," he said, "this thing could get ugly. The assistant US attorney is on a plane right now. He'll be here in an hour. And if you don't start cooperating with Antiguan authorities, he's going to be pissed."

Jana almost yelled. "I don't work for him anymore, do I?"

"That may be, but Uncle Bill pulled a lot of strings to get him sent down here. He's coming to help you, you understand that?"

She spoke as though her jaw would not open. "He shouldn't have put his hands on me."

The lieutenant turned to listen closer. "Who? Who shouldn't have put his hands on you? Are you saying you were assaulted?"

17

"He would have liked to assault me. He would have liked that very much. So, I defended myself."

The lieutenant crossed his arms. "You're telling me you acted in self-defense? I've got a man lying in intensive care with multiple compound fractures *and* gunshot wounds. The surgeons spent most of the night rebuilding the bones in his face. Is that what you call self-defense?"

Jana slammed a fist into the table. "Got what he deserved!"

"Oh boy, here we go," Cade said.

"I told the prick to keep his paws off of me, and I meant it."

The lieutenant paced the room. "Apparently so. And after that gunshot to the groin, I suppose he'll think twice before trying that on another woman, is that it?"

"Lieutenant," Cade said, "it's obvious this was an attempted sexual assault. The victim defended herself. Case closed."

"Case closed, my ass," Lieutenant Pence said. "The district attorney will decide that, the *local* district attorney. We are holding her until the investigation is complete."

"That won't be necessary," Cade said.

"Oh really?"

Cade cocked his head. "Lieutenant, let me ask you a question. When were you going to disclose the perpetrator's criminal record to Agent Baker here?"

The lieutenant's arms dropped. "How do you know about that?"

"We are the National Security Agency, we know what we know. And what we don't know, we find out. Take you for example. An American, born in Brooklyn. Seventeen years with the NYPD. Got hired by the island recently to head up the police forces. Very impressive, Lieutenant, really. But let me help you." Cade pulled a piece of paper from his jacket pocket. "Montes Lima

Perez, attempted burglary, 1992, investigated for arson, 1994, looks like he started running drugs in '95. Three counts of possession in that year. Not a bad start, is it? Now we're on to 2002 when he resurfaced after doing six hard. Didn't take him long to catch up with his old friends though. Three counts of attempted rape, did another year hard. Then he hits the big time. 2005, busted with sixteen kilos of cocaine. Now suspected of having ties to the Oficina de Envigado Cartel. Goes inside one more time for *ten* long. Then shows up here a month ago. So I'll ask you again, when were you going to mention the fact that her attacker had a criminal record as long as my Johnson?"

The lieutenant never broke eye contact. "So it's your decided opinion, in all your years investigating homicides, sexual assaults, and the like, that I am out of line here? I worked homicide for twelve years."

The sarcasm stabbed Cade in the gut but he did not flinch. He knew as well as the lieutenant that the NSA didn't investigate crimes of that nature, unless they intersected with a matter of national security.

"Is that what the NSA teaches you? Homicide investigation?" the lieutenant said.

"Don't hand me that crap," Cade said. "I may not be a homicide detective, but as a top-level analyst at NSA, I see some pretty awful shit."

"And if it were up to you," the lieutenant continued, "I suppose you would let *Miss Congeniality* here go? No questions asked? National hero to the United States and all?"

"You're an American," Cade said.

"And I've got a duty to my employer, the government of Antigua, and I say her story stinks."

Jana glared at the lieutenant through the slits of her eyes.

Cade said, "Lieutenant, I suggest you give me an answer, and give it to me right now. If the US attorney gets here and finds you not cooperating, he's going to rip your Adam's apple out and hand it back to you."

"I may be an American, but the Antiguan government does not respond to idle threats of the United States!"

"No?" Cade jabbed. "Since you're new here, maybe you weren't aware that Antiqua receives a lot of aid from the US. When a senior member of the US administration shows up at your doorstep and makes a request, you jump or have your ass handed to you."

"So here's my problem, Mr. Williams. I started out investigating a case that looks suspiciously like attempted murder. It turns out, allegedly, it was simply a woman defending herself against an attacker. Where I get a little hazy is when I come across the fact that we have a highly trained special agent here. In a court room, whether on the isle of Antigua or in the United States, the law divides us into two simple categories: those that are untrained and have little control over their actions during a crisis situation, and people like her," he pointed to Jana, "those *with* training. Extensive training. People like that are the ones expected to use restraint. After she hyperextended the perp's elbow so far that it snapped backwards, he was down and would not have been able to continue the assault. But she didn't stop there." He squared off in front of Jana. "Did you? No. You proceeded to snap his leg nearly in half. And when did the face beating commence? After he was flailing on the ground in pain? Huh? How about the gunshot wounds? They look suspiciously like the type of GSWs we see in execution-style killings. Did you kneecap him first, or was that after you blew his dick off?"

Cade stood and placed a pointed finger in the man's face. "Hey, she defended her life. It's as simple as that."

"Is it?" the lieutenant said as he again looked at Jana. "And what about the silencer? I want an answer, Agent Baker. Nothing? Once my forensic team does an analysis of the crime scene, are they going to tell me that I'm right? He was lying on the ground when you shot him, twice?"

Jana's hands formed into fists and her jaw clenched. "Got what he deserved," she said again.

The lieutenant walked back to Cade. "Your," he searched for the right word, "*asset* is out of control. When I was in Desert Storm, we called it *going off the reservation.*"

"Are you going to formally charge her?" Cade pressed.

The lieutenant started to leave but paused. "No, not just yet. But she is not to leave this island."

Cade pulled Jana up and said, "This interview is over."

6

The Pop of the Mind

4:00 a.m.

Jana lay in bed with a sheet draped over her body. Her pupils darted from side to side as she entered the deepest stage of sleep, stage five, rapid eye movement. Her right hand trembled and goosebumps formed on her arms. She had descended into a dream and began to hear frightening voices, although she couldn't tell where they were coming from. Her body was cold and all she could see was darkness. Fear built in the pit of her stomach, yet no matter how hard she tried, she could not pry her eyes open. It was as if they were draped in heavy sheets of lead.

Jana's heart began to pound as the voices became clearer, and the clearer they became, the harder her heart pounded. She recognized them, yet there was something different this time, something that sounded close and unholy, like the sound of a trio of beasts consorting against her. She'd never heard them with such vividness, and panic filled her soul.

There were three voices in total, each with its own distinct tone.

The first whispered to the others, "We should kill her."

Jana struggled to open her eyes and wake from the nightmare.

She had become locked into the dream, a dream from which there was no escape.

She'd previously fled the life of a federal agent and retreated to Antigua, a place of tranquil waters and calm ocean breezes, in the hopes that her nightmares would subside. But now in the dead space of night, she knew they might never end.

Then another replied, "We *will* kill her. The jihad will not be complete until she is dead."

The more the voices spoke, the colder Jana's skin became. She had entered a place of terror where past events tore at her psyche. She found herself tumbling down what looked like a long, dark tube that led into the pit of the nightmare. She backpedaled with her feet, but could not stop the downward fall.

Each time one of the voices spoke, Jana felt a burning sensation across the upper part of her torso. And since her skin had become cold and clammy, the pain was intensified.

"Retribution will be ours," another voice said. "She is so much like her father before her, a traitor to his own country, his own blood. Yet she does not see it," the voice laughed, "but she is a criminal to the core, just like he was."

No, Jana thought, *I'm not like my father. I can't be. I can't—*a shiver rode the length of her body and the tremor in her right hand intensified.

"How will we kill her?"

"She will do it herself," the centermost voice said through a laugh that curdled Jana's stomach.

"But how?"

"It will be simple. We will show her," the laughing voice said. "We will show her again and again." The voice lowered to a whisper, "Show her now."

Suddenly, and as though someone had flipped the power

switch on an old movie projector, what looked like home movies appeared in front of her. Light popped and flickered and Jana squinted into the brightness. Her heart beat faster and she struggled to focus on the images. She could see herself, it was like watching one's life from a distance. These weren't old home movies from her childhood, these were her worst terrors. It was the nightmare, the same nightmare she had relived over the past year, only this time it was worse.

As the movie rolled on, she saw herself again seated in a wooden chair in the center room of a remote cabin, her hands and feet bound. She had been stripped down to her undergarments. This was the same cabin she had awakened in after having been abducted during the throes of a horrific terrorism investigation the previous year. The scene was so vivid, yet against the backdrop of her present life here on Antigua, it represented a complete and total paradox; one she could not reconcile.

And there the vision was. A Middle Eastern man towered over her and glared with coal-black eyes; the smile of a madman painted on his face. His thick, black hair, broken by a single shock of white, was wild and unkempt. It was Waseem Jarrah, the most wanted terrorist in the world.

Jana had hunted Jarrah for three years, yet she had left that life behind with the specific intent of starting fresh, living a simple existence. She sought to surround herself with the beauty of nature, and the anonymity of self that she could not find back in the dark hallways and dangers of the FBI.

Back then she believed killing Waseem Jarrah would cause her post-traumatic stress episodes and nightmares to subside. After all, he was the person that had orchestrated the nightmares in the first place. She believed Antigua's breathtaking blue waters would wash away her terrors and carry them out with the tide, the waters returning the next day, clean and new. But now, although she did not know why, she began to understand that her fears would never leave her.

As Jarrah spoke to her in the vision, the center-most scar on her upper torso burned and she winced in her bed. The trio of gunshot wounds along her chest had been left there by one of Waseem Jarrah's disciples two years prior—terrible calling cards that would never let her forget.

"Perhaps it is time for you to learn the truth, Agent Baker," Jarrah said as he pulled a piece of paper from a backpack on the table.

His voice felt like a cigarette singeing her skin at the site of the scar. And she was sure this time; the scar was moving, as though it were the mouth of Jarrah himself. On the bed, Jana's heart rate exploded and the vibration in her hand increased into a thrash.

The nightmare played forth and Jarrah held the paper in front of her. Jana pulled against the bindings on her hands and feet but could not free herself. Then Jarrah withdrew a knife from the backpack, an ancient blade, razor sharp, and walked behind her. He held the edge against her throat, the effect forcing her to hold her head upright.

Jarrah again raised the paper in front of her. "Read it," he said with grit in his voice.

"I can't! I can't!" Jana screamed. The blade touched her throat and blood leaked onto the cold steel. He let the paper drop to his side.

"Tell me, Agent Baker, did you search for more information about your parents?"

Jana's sobbing was low and silent. She struggled to keep her neck high enough to avoid another stinging cut.

"Answer me, Miss Baker, or things will not go so well for you." Jarrah's tone had deepened.

"Yes," she whispered over the building lump in her throat.

"And how much did you learn? Were you able to uncover the truth about them?"

She started to speak, but the blade touched her in the same spot and she winced.

"Oh, are you not able to speak freely? Such a pity," Jarrah said, now laughing. "Perhaps you see the way a woman should be, submissive." He removed the knife and laid it on her lap. "Now, please continue."

"Did I learn the truth about them? Yes, but I've always known the truth about my parents. Having a father who died of cancer and a mother of a car accident is nothing to be ashamed of."

"The information-gathering capabilities of the FBI, NSA, and CIA at your fingertips, and that's the best you can do?"

"It's the truth."

"Is it?" he said, a smile oozing onto the edges of his lips.

He held the sheet of paper in front of her again. At the top, the paper read:

State of North Carolina, Certificate of Live Birth.
"Read the name and date of birth aloud, Miss Baker."

Jana squeezed her eyelids shut to push free her tears.

"Jana Michelle *Ames.* Born October 19, 1986. But, but . . . this isn't me. My name is Baker."

"Is it? Read the names of the birth parents listed here, please."

"Father, Richard William *Ames,* born December 16, 1959. Mother Lillian Baker *Ames,* born February 9, 1960."

"Fascinating, Miss Baker, isn't it? It is true, you do not

recognize the surname *Ames*, but your father's name was Richard William, was it not? He was born on December 16, 1959, correct? And your mother, Lillian Baker, was, in fact, born on February 9, 1960. And let's examine this date, October 19, 1986. This is *your* birthdate, correct?"

Jana's mouth hung open.

Jarrah continued. "And your mother's maiden name was, in fact, Baker, was it not? Baker, the same surname of your grandfather. How very interesting. I can tell by that stupid expression on your face that you have never known the truth."

Jana shook her head and more tears streamed down her face. "No. No, this can't be. You falsified these documents! This is not my birth certificate!"

"Is it not? Yes, it would be a most disturbing revelation indeed. A federal agent just now discovering her entire life to be a lie."

"My life is not a lie!"

"Tell me. How is it that you were not aware of your own surname?"

"My last name is not Ames, it's *Baker*. It's always been Baker. My parents were never married. Are you happy now? They never married. When my father died, I was two years old. That's why my last name is the same as my mother's."

"Is that what your grandfather told you? Hmmm, I see. And what then was said to be your father's name?"

"His name was Richard William."

"Richard William? It is true, the name of William is used in the Western world as a surname, but more commonly as a first or middle name, no? The surname of *Williams*, with an *s* on the end, is much more common. And this birth certificate says Richard William *Ames*. It is quite a coincidence that all the first names, middle names, and birthdates match up to you, your

27

mother, and your father. Well then, let's read further, shall we? These documents are so fascinating." Jarrah was enjoying Jana's anguish.

He held up another document. At the top, it read:

FEDERAL BUREAU OF INVESTIGATION
UNITED STATES DEPARTMENT OF JUSTICE
WASHINGTON, DC
CURRENT ARREST OR RECEIPT

Further down on the paper was a mugshot and other details. A droplet of blood rolled down Jana's throat and landed in her lap. Her eyes locked onto the mugshot.

"You look white as a sheet, Agent Baker. The face looks familiar, no? A striking resemblance to your father, is it not? Now, read for me this part here," Jarrah said as he pointed.

Jana's voice became monotone as she read the words. "Date arrested or received, 10/29/1988. Charge or offense," Jana's body shook. "18 U.S.C. 793 : US Code - Section 793: Gathering, transmitting, or losing defense information." Her body rattled into the overwhelming emotions. "No. No, this isn't my father. It isn't true!"

"But it is true, Miss Baker. The evidence is right in front of you. And having been at the top of your graduating class at Quantico, I assume this is a federal code section you are familiar with. And this *is* a federal arrest warrant, isn't it? Tell me, what does code section 793 pertain to?"

"Espionage," she whispered.

"Correct, Miss Baker, espionage. Spying. And how interesting the date on this document is. October 29, 1988. You would have been two years old at the time." He put his face against hers and she tried to recoil from his nauseating breath. "That particular date is etched into your memory. Don't lie to me, Miss Baker."

"Yes," she said as a tear rolled down her face.

"And what does October 29, 1988 mean to you?"

"It's the date my father died." The enormity of the revelation lay upon Jana's psyche like a thousand-pound weight.

"Your honesty is refreshing. *October 29, 1988.* The date your father died. Now, perhaps, you are starting to believe. Your father didn't die on that date. It's the date he was arrested, arrested for espionage against the United States."

"No!" she screamed.

"You don't know how much like your father you actually are."

"No!" she screamed once more, this time the effect causing her to awaken from the nightmare.

***

Jana sat upright in her bed, and tears burst forth, unabated. She wrapped her arms around her herself, but then loosened and her fingers found their way to the three bullet-hole scars on her upper torso. The burning sensation on the center one was visceral. Now that she was awake, Jana sensed the vibrations in her right hand and knew that a PTSD episode was moments from overtaking her. *I can't be like my father. I can't be,* she thought. She tried to rid her mind of the awful images, but the realization that the centermost scar now represented Waseem Jarrah caused a wave of intense nausea to roll her system.

She struggled to control the images still flashing in her mind. But this time other images mixed in as well: memories from her childhood—a photo of her and her father sitting together on a sled, the smell of his aftershave, her as a toddler on the couch with her father outside throwing snowballs at the window to make her laugh. But the thought of him having committed treason was the most intense. As much as she tried to convince herself that she could not possibly be like him, the vivid memory of how she left the FBI, and the things she'd been accused of, gushed forth. The popping and flashing was as bright as a strobe, and the room began to spin.

"No, no, no," she said to herself with determination in her words. "You can stop it from happening. I know you can. Come on, Jana, get a grip." Each word vibrated out as it crossed her tightened vocal cords. She rocked back and forth on the bed and began a series of deep inhalations. "Find it, Jana. Find it," she said as she closed her eyes. "Come on, think back."

Before she had begun her career with the FBI, she hadn't known terror could be this big. She'd never considered the enormity of the costs, larger than anything in her experience.

Waking from the nightmare was the first step toward thwarting the PTSD episode, but this one set her into a tailspin she couldn't recover from. The episode began like many of the others, as though a lion was punching its head through a taught net. Then came the gut-wrenching feeling that her heart would burst from her chest. Jana struggled to vacuum up enough oxygen as the tears streamed down her face. This time she was seeing the nightmare even though she was awake.

With all her strength, she thought back to the safest place she knew in her childhood. It had been a simpler time, when she would flee to the safety of a favorite hiding spot. She pictured her then seven-year-old self at her grandfather's rural farmhouse in the rolling hills of Tennessee. She watched herself descend from the front porch, run down the creaking steps and across the hayfield. Once at the wood line, she ran through the opening in the muscadine vines, a tangle of leafy green ropes that twisted and snaked through tree trunks and other foliage. She ran down the path and up the next hill. "The path used to be an old game trail," Grandpa had told her, "streaming with whitetail deer," a species he'd hunted in his younger years.

Once she crested the top of the hill, she could see it. *The fort*, as she had called it, was nothing more than heavy branches leaning against a sheer piece of granite outcropping. The rock stood about four feet tall and formed the fort's wall on one side. The branches joined together to create a roof which was covered in a heavy layer of leaves. The door was made from a bramble of vines which Jana could shift aside. When pulled closed, the vines served to camouflage the entrance from prying eyes.

It was her fort, her hiding place, and after the deaths of both her parents, represented the only place where little Jana had felt safe. There were times in those days when she felt like she couldn't breathe. But here in her fort, everything became calm. It was quiet and no one, not even her grandfather, knew where she was.

Now, in the tiny bedroom of her bungalow, Jana wondered why images of her father had become interspersed with those of the terrifying ordeal with Waseem Jarrah. She'd gotten good at mentally running to her fort just before PTSD episodes started, and most times, the effect thwarted their advance. But this time, the harder she tried, the more fiercely the PTSD grabbed her. She felt as though her lungs couldn't draw another breath. The fort blurred in her vision and she lost grip on the memory. Jana's body convulsed as her pupils rolled into their sockets. The last thing she remembered was seeing the mugshot of her father on his arrest record. She blacked out and would not regain consciousness for several hours.

7

A Vile Gift

Diego Rojas gripped the stair rail, and his jaw clenched. His agitation had increased upon learning his personal bodyguards would not be permitted at the meeting. He'd been to many such meetings, but, in his home country of Colombia, he always had the upper hand. Here on Antigua, as Rojas descended the wooden staircase, a single word entered his mind. *Vulnerable.* The basement was dark and boards creaked under each step. He saw nothing in the darkness below until a man seated in the far corner flicked a lighter at the tip of a cigar. As the man drew against the smoldering tobacco, an amber glow alighted black hair, a thick beard, and eyes like dead glass. The man said nothing.

To Rojas, he appeared quiet, reserved. Yet Diego Rojas sensed something about the man that troubled him. It was like looking at a boiler that held too much pressure.

The meeting had been arranged months in advance. Rojas was accustomed to danger, but the heightened sense of it tasted like sulfur in his mouth. He had been weaned on danger from birth. But these people were different. It was one thing to know you had the power of an entire drug cartel behind you. It was another to be engaged in business with an organization of this sort.

The man motioned to a chair. Rojas turned and looked up the staircase at an oversized man of Middle Eastern decent blocking the top of the stairs. The man shut the door. The sound of a bolt throwing home reverberated. There was nothing left to do. Rojas walked toward the chair.

Raised in the Hindu Kush region of Afghanistan near the borders of China and Pakistan, the man spoke, his accent a muddle of the three cultures. "Our paths have crossed and now our destinies become intertwined."

Rojas waited.

"You are aware of our arrangement, are you not?" the man said.

Rojas nodded. With people such as these, it was better to speak less.

"And do you foresee any difficulty in delivering what has been discussed?"

"I do not."

"Then we will double our volume, beginning immediately."

"Double? But—" Rojas said.

"I am not asking," the man said. He drew from the cigar and squinted into the smoke. "We intend to hold up our end of the bargain. Your little problem in Colombia will be taken care of. And all the loose ends will disappear."

Rojas stuttered. "We are not prepared to move that much. It will draw attention."

The man's eyes focused on the amber tip of the cigar. "Or perhaps our people there will deviate from that plan, and the bomb will detonate elsewhere? Then another might find its way to a coca farm here, a processing laboratory there. . . . As for our new arrangement, you have no choice."

Rojas's voice fluttered. "We will handle what must be handled." The man stood and extended his hand. He was taller than Rojas had envisioned. "Delivery will occur at your estate."

"That was never discussed! We cannot take delivery of your shipment at my estate."

"And I will be there personally to oversee so that we have no mistakes."

Before Rojas could respond, the man walked through the darkness and opened a door.

Rojas thought, *This deal is getting worse at every turn.*

The man stopped and said, "But to celebrate our little partnership, I have brought you a gift from my homeland." From out of a blackened corner of the room Rojas heard feet shuffling against the cement floor and the sound of a woman struggling. A man standing behind her pushed her forward into the dim light. Her hands were bound behind her back and there was duct tape over her mouth.

"She is young and fresh," the man in the doorway said. "We have saved her for you."

The woman yanked against her oppressor, a greasy man who held a knife to her throat.

Rojas allowed himself to gaze upon her trim body.

The man continued. "It is true, she is culturally different from you, but Middle Eastern women, Mr. Rojas, oh, they can be so enjoyable. This one, I'm afraid, may need to be taught manners."

Rojas smirked, then walked to her. He placed unwanted hands on her body and said, "Your gift is most generous," and speaking of their business arrangement said, "We will redouble our efforts."

The man smiled. "I know you will," he said before disappearing. The door slammed closed. He was gone.

"Now, my dear," Rojas said to the girl as he towered over her and looked down her blouse. "You and I shall become well acquainted."

She kicked at him and he cracked the back of his hand across her face. The man behind her held tight.

"Take her to my car. I will have to begin by teaching her respect."

8

Right in the Middle

As they exited police headquarters, Cade squinted into the stark morning sunlight and donned a set of Ray Bans.

Jana turned to him. "I don't go by that name anymore."

"What name?"

The pair walked into the parking lot. "*Agent* Baker. I'm not a federal agent anymore and you know it."

"Come on, Jana. I know you wanted to drop out of circulation for a while, but it's time to come back to reality."

"Reality? This is my reality. I haven't gone by the name of Agent Baker in over a year. And I'm never coming back. I'm not going back to the Bureau."

"When you disappeared last year, you not only left the Bureau, you left me. Did you ever think of that? What about us, Jana?"

"There is no more us."

"Why don't you just stab me in the heart with a knife? It would be less painful than to hear you say that."

"I'm not who you think I am, Cade. I'm not the girl you fell in love with. She's gone. That girl is dead."

"Oh yeah? Well that's bullshit!" Cade belted. "That's you running away from our relationship."

Jana continued walking across the parking lot as the stinging truth of his statement hit home.

Cade said, "There is something different about you, I'll give you that. And I'm not talking about the bronze tan or new musculature in your shoulders."

"What, then?" she said as she turned and squared off in front of him.

"It's those," he said, pointing to her eyes. "They're different. It's like you're made of stone. Do you realize you haven't smiled a single time since I've been here?"

She started to turn but he grabbed her arm.

With the reflexes of a cat, she jammed her opposing hand on top of his wrist and spun toward him and applied a painful wrist lock. "Ow, shit!" he said, as he bent his chest forward in an effort to lessen the pain rocketing up his wrist and arm.

Jana released her grip.

Cade stood and rubbed his wrist. "Jesus, Jana."

"I'm not going back. I'm never going back to the FBI. If you came here for that, you can forget it. Tell them you couldn't find me. Tell them I am dead." She turned and began speed-walking across the parking lot but yelled back to him, "They made it pretty clear they didn't want me anymore, and for once, I agree with them."

When she reached the road, Cade finally called out, "Kyle is missing."

Jana stopped in her tracks but did not turn.

A long silence ensued.

She turned her head halfway toward him. "What do you mean *Kyle is missing?*"

Cade walked toward her. "He was on an op. He went dark four days ago. No one has heard from him since."

Jana faced him but kept the distance. "Why didn't you tell me?"

Cade exhaled. "You're not a federal agent anymore, remember? Me telling you this is a violation of national security."

Jana walked to him and jabbed a sharp finger into his shoulder. "You son of a bitch. I can't believe you just said that. Kyle is one of my only friends in the world. I'd trade my life for his. And you know as well as I do that I was forced out of the Bureau under bullshit circumstances." She paused and the silence was punctuated by the lonely call of a distant seagull. "In case you don't remember, there was no one to help me on the canyon rim that day when that terrorist prick Waseem Jarrah tried to kill me and detonate a nuclear weapon. When I killed him, I stopped what would have been the worst attack against the United States in its history. And they threw me out because I killed his accomplice, Rafael? The one that was about to rape then murder me? Excessive use of force? What a bunch of bullshit! I did what I did and I would do it again. It was clear to me then just like it's clear to me now. They both got what they deserved."

"There's that temper of yours again. Jana, they pulled your badge and credentials because Rafael was unarmed when you pumped twelve rounds into his chest and balls. He was lying on the ground with gunshot wounds already. You killed him in cold blood."

"That son of a bitch was about to rape me. And after he was done having his fun, his instructions weren't just to kill me. He was to skin me alive. I don't give a shit whether he was unarmed or not. He got what he deserved."

"You know, I told Uncle Bill that me coming down here was a mistake. I told him you would react this way."

"Well I guess you were right."

"Uncle Bill misses you, Jana. He talks about you all the time.

It's like listening to a grandfather talk about a grandchild."

"Well I miss him too. As much stress as it was to be at NSA headquarters working on those terrorism cases, he was the best part." Tension eased from her shoulders. "Is he still eating those bright-orange snack crackers?" Jana allowed a slight smile to emerge.

"It's getting tough on him. He's getting old and can't keep this up forever. Knuckles told me there was a pretty good chance Uncle Bill would be retiring soon. But when Kyle disappeared, that idea went right out the window. We've got to find Kyle, Jana. I didn't come down here to bail you out. I came down here to get your help."

"Where was he working?"

"Last known location was here, on the isle of Antigua."

"What? He was *here*? What the hell was he doing on Antigua? Hardly a hotbed of criminal activity. What kind of op did CIA have him on?"

"You know I don't have access to that information. But it had something to do with drugs."

"Drugs? What's the CIA got to do with—" She stopped midsentence. "Tell me the truth. Is Kyle the only reason you're here?"

"Does it matter?"

Jana's hands went to her hips.

Cade said, "Alright, I came here for Kyle, mostly. But there is more at play here than you realize."

"What is that supposed to mean?"

Cade exhaled. "Kyle knew you were here, Jana. He wouldn't tell me, but he was keeping tabs on you. He's always felt that you are in danger."

"I'm not in any danger. How could I be in danger here? I work at a tiki bar on the beach serving drinks with little umbrellas in them to overweight tourists. No one even knows who I am."

"Oh no? Last year, before you vanished off the face of the earth, you killed the leader of the most dangerous terror organization in the world and your face was splashed all over the papers. Not to mention all those pictures from when the president came and decorated you lying in a bed at BethesdaMedicalCenter. You're recognizable. You're in danger and you always will be."

"I don't want to hear it. Get to the point. What do we know about Kyle?"

"Both the Los Rastrojos and Oficina de Envigado cartels have quietly set up camp here on Antigua. They are the largest cartels in Colombia now. They're pushing drugs through to the US on a new route. Los Rastrojos has been here for over a year, but Oficina de Envigado is trying to muscle in. Both cartels are trying to keep the violence to an absolute minimum to avoid attracting attention. And as it turns out, the perp that you put in the hospital last night happens to be the Oficina de Envigado cartel's number two on the island. Late last night we intercepted a cell phone conversation between members of the Los Rastrojos cartel. They've taken notice of your handiwork, Jana, and are most impressed. You are right in the middle of this thing now."

9

Into the Light

"Let's start from the beginning. Are we sure Kyle is missing?" Jana said.

"You know him, Jana. He's like a machine the way he works. Kyle communicated on a daily schedule. It's been four days. He's gone dark. We don't have anything other than that."

"Same time every day?"

"No, he uses a cypher to calculate the appropriate time to communicate each day. It was always different."

"And how long has he been down here?" Jana said.

"Six months."

"He's been down here six months? Christ. And he's been checking up on me that whole time?"

"I told you," Cade said. "He's worried about you."

"And he didn't stop once to say hello?"

"He knew you needed your space. And remember, officially he's down here for work, not to check up on you. But, he had influence on being assigned here."

"Oh, come on. He's a puppy dog. Influence?"

"Jana, you've been out of circulation longer than you think. In the war on terror, things move fast. A lot has changed since you left. In fact, when you stopped that last nuclear attack, the

41

gloves came off. Kyle is a part of that now."

"It's me, Cade. Stop talking in riddles," Jana said. "You're telling me CIA allows Kyle to decide where he goes and who he investigates? And what's this got to do with drug trafficking? Isn't that the DEA's responsibility?"

Cade stopped in front of her but shook off the question. "Kyle took a lot of shit for sticking up for you, after you wasted Rafael, that is. You had resigned. Threw your badge and credentials at the director of the FBI as I recall. But Kyle defended you at his own peril. You have no idea how far he went for you."

"Wait a minute. You're telling me there are elements in the Justice Department that wanted me prosecuted, aren't you?" She shook her head. "Why am I just now hearing about this? Those pricks want their bureaucracy? They can have it. I want no part of it."

"Jana, when you shot and killed Rafael, an unarmed suspect, it was tantamount to murder. You and I were there. And we both know that's bullshit, but that's the law. Besides, after you resigned, you disappeared. Hell, none of us could have found you to tell you anyway."

Jana knew he was right. She looked across the parking lot and into the turquoise waters of SideHillBay. Her mind drifted back to that terrifying day on the remote canyon rim one year prior, and her eyes became glassy. She had narrowly averted death, and now the horrors came flooding back.

She looked at Cade. "*Kyle* found me," she said.

Cade glanced down and noticed Jana's hand had begun to tremble. He knew it was a precursor to a post-traumatic stress episode. PTSD had plagued Jana's existence and it apparently had not abated. He said, "Kyle testified before congress in closed session. It even took Uncle Bill, with his sky-high security clearance, a while to get a copy of the transcripts. I won't lie to you, Jana, it wasn't pretty. Kyle faced seven hours of questioning by senators."

The shaking in Jana's hand increased.

Cade placed a hand on her shoulder and spoke just above the volume of the gentle island breeze. "But in the end everything turned out okay. It took a long time, but he was so focused on getting your record cleared, they couldn't shake him. He was like a rock. He reminded them over and over the ordeal you'd been through, and that without you, much of the United States would be buried in ash right now."

Jana's hand shook harder and she leaned down and placed her hands on her knees. From Cade's view, it looked as though she might be sick. But before he could say anything, she closed her eyes and began a series of long exhales. A minute later she stood and stared again into the distant ocean horizon. "We might as well get started."

"You're going to help us?"

She looked at him from the side of her eye as the statement processed, then she launched at him. "I will never, ever leave Kyle behind! I can't, I can't, I can't," she yelled. Cade's mouth opened but before he could say anything, she continued "Don't you ever question my loyalty like that. And let's get one thing straight. I've spent a long time trying to forget the past, and I'm not going back to that life. You got it?"

As they walked toward a parked car, he said, "You don't have to bite my head off. And, hey, Kyle and I go back a long way too, so don't think you're the only one that will do whatever it takes."

"Just take me to wherever we're going," she said. "And tell me everything. Don't leave anything out."

10

Kyle Interrogated

Kyle didn't so much wake up as come to. He was disoriented and felt awful. Something akin to a hangover with an elephant sitting atop your body. His joints hurt, his head spun, and the nausea was so intense he felt he might be sick.

It was only then he realized a man had been standing behind him this whole time. The man yanked his hair back and pried open one of his eyes, then flicked on a penlight to examine the pupils.

Kyle was exhausted and had a deep, ingrained feeling of panic, as if needles were jabbing into his heart and lungs. He had somehow descended into what could only be described as severe depression. It was deep and dark and carried with it a feeling like he'd never pull out. But mixed into the depression was anxiety stronger than he'd ever felt, and he gasped at the air.

The long-haired Latin man pulled open the steel door, which again scraped across the cement, sand and grit crunching underneath. Kyle had no sense of time. He couldn't tell whether Diego Rojas reentered the room a moment later or hours later.

Rojas checked Kyle's pupils himself and a deep smile formed on his face. "Muy bien," he said. "I believe now you are ready to talk? But before we get to that, Agent MacKerron—"

"I'm not an agent," Kyle murmured back, but his words were barely intelligible.

"Of course you are," Rojas said through a grin. He held out a syringe for Kyle to see. It was filled with a clear, dark liquid. "One of my specialties. I studied chemistry during my undergraduate work at Universidad Nacional de Colombia, but it wasn't until I did my masters at UC Berkeley that I really came into my own." He walked a slow circle around Kyle. "My chosen field of study was chemical and biomolecular engineering, and I was very good. What we've been injecting you with is a cocktail of my design. As a DEA agent, I am sure you are aware that Colombian cartels no longer focus solely on cocaine. We have a far more diversified portfolio than ever before. Everything from extortion, illegal gold mining, gambling, and this," he held the syringe to the light, "synthetic drug cocktails."

Kyle mumbled something unintelligible.

Rojas listened, then shook his head. He looked at the other man. "Bring me my bag." When the man returned, Rojas removed a vial and inserted a new syringe into it and drew a dose of clear liquid. He stuck the needle into Kyle's shoulder and squeezed. "Epinephrine," he said. "Adrenaline." He waited a few moments until Kyle's eyes brightened. "There we are. Now where was I? Ah, yes, what we've been injecting you with is a combination of four ingredients. Synthetic, liquefied crack cocaine, heroin, and two of my new favorites, scopolamine and 3-quinuclidinyl benzilate, truth serums." He smiled and continued walking a circle around Kyle. "We've been experimenting for the last few years and honed it to perfection. You are both addicted to the narcotics and willing to tell me anything I ask."

Kyle's chest heaved up and down with morbid pain flooding his body.

"The misery you are suffering right now can be stopped, all with this needle." He inserted the needle into a vein in Kyle's arm. "In this dose, I've decreased the heroin and cocaine. You are getting a strong bolus of my truth serum cocktail. Why don't we begin? But first, let me tell you why you are here. I want to know everything you know in your investigations of my competitors, the Oficina de Envigado cartel."

A mild euphoria permeated Kyle's chest and he felt like a million pounds had been lifted off him. The nausea and extreme joint pain also subsided, as did the other symptoms. And in all of this, he felt free, like he was floating.

Kyle struggled, but the power of the drugs overwhelmed him and there was no point fighting the inevitable. The truth began to pour out. "I'm CIA," he laughed, though Diego Rojas's intelligence information said otherwise.

"The drugs are almost at full effect," Rojas said, not realizing Kyle was telling the truth.

Warmth and unadulterated joy washed through Kyle's body. "I came down here to penetrate the Oficina de Envigado, and it's been a blast," he said through drooping eyelids and a smile.

Gustavo Moreno, Rojas's intelligence officer, walked into the room and leaned against a wall.

"And how many other DEA agents are on the island?" Rojas said.

"Why do you keep asking about DEA? I told you, I'm—"

"How many others on the island?" Rojas smiled to play into Kyle's drugged euphoria.

"Others? There aren't any others, man. It's just me. Hey, can we go to the beach?"

Rojas glanced at Moreno and shook his head. His agitation was building. "And how about our friends in the United States?"

"Oh, yeah, got lots of friends back home."

Rojas started to raise up but caught himself. "No, I mean communications monitoring, signals intelligence. Eavesdropping, Agent MacKerron. To what extent is the NSA or others at FortHuachuca in Arizona listening in on the operations of my friends at Oficina de Envigado?" Rojas knew the truth. If his competitors in the Envigado cartel were under the watchful eye of the United States through secret monitoring, then his own cartel, Los Rastrojos, had either been compromised or wasn't far behind.

"Oh, those guys at NSA are great," Kyle said. His eyes glazed. "Them? Nah, if I had found more, they would have joined the party, but not until then. You think NSA doesn't have enough to do sniffing out terrorists? They don't have time for this drug business." Kyle laughed and slumped over. The guard pulled him upright. "And what else did you say? Oh yeah, FortHuachuca. Yeah, no, those boys don't ask me for permission before snooping."

"Is that so?"

"Yeah, they got a lot of stuff pointed this way though. Always looking for drug runners trying to sneak their plane or cigarette boat under the radar. Always trying to intercept cellphone calls between members of a cartel. You know, crap like that."

Gustavo Moreno handed Rojas a manila file folder and Rojas opened it. Moreno said, "FortHuachuca, Cochise County, Arizona, Patron."

"Hey," Kyle interrupted. "Didn't they call Pablo Escobar, El Patron? *The boss?*"

Moreno said, "That's about fifteen miles north of the Mexican border."

Rojas spoke as he read, "Over eighteen thousand people are

employed at the military base. Home of the 111th Military Intelligence Brigade. And I do love the US military's use of acronyms, don't you? United States Army Network Enterprise Technology Command, NETCOM. Army Military Auxiliary Radio System, MARS."

"Hey, man. MARS, like outer space," Kyle said. "What's in that needle you gave me? I feel awesome!"

Rojas did not look up from the intelligence report. "Yes, I'm sure you do. But the effects won't last long. The Information Systems Engineering Command, ISEC. The United StatesArmyIntelligenceCenter. What? No acronym? How disappointing. And, I've saved the best for last. FortHuachuca has," he looked at the report, "a radar-equipped *aerostat*, one of a series maintained for the Drug Enforcement Administration. How very fascinating." He looked at Moreno.

Moreno said, "An aerostat is a type of helium balloon that is lofted to elevate radar and other surveillance monitoring systems, Patron."

"Yeah," Kyle said. "They've got some pretty cool shit."

"The intelligence community and the DEA seem to be very well aligned, do they not? A series of radar and listening devices maintained for the DEA. I'll ask you again, Agent MacKerron. To what extent are the intelligence-gathering capabilities of the United States eavesdropping onto my island?"

"Oh, man, I don't know. Like I said, those military boys don't ask for permiss—"

"I don't care whether they ask your permission or not!" Rojas screamed.

"Dude, so hostile. I don't work with those guys. I don't know what they're up to." Kyle's chin lowered to a rest on his chest. Then he popped up. "And besides, don't you cartels just change up your routes whenever Uncle Sam is getting close? What's the big deal, man?"

Rojas shook his head and said to Moreno, "We have to assume we've been compromised. The timing could not be worse." He turned on Kyle. "What's the big deal, you ask? Changing routes is not a problem, Agent MacKerron. But this is a much bigger issue. I'm afraid you've gotten in way over your head and have no idea what is at stake. Now, tell me about the operations of the other cartel, Oficina de Envigado. How many people have they moved onto my island?"

"Best I can tell, about sixty. But you know," Kyle said as he looked through the haze of his stupor, "sometimes I lose count. Don't take this the wrong way, but some of those guys look alike. Kind of hard to tell them apart," he laughed.

"Sixty?" Rojas said as he glanced at Moreno. "Were you aware of their numbers?"

Moreno looked at the tops of his polished dress shoes.

"And who have they moved into position to run the organization here?"

"Well," Kyle laughed. "It's sure not a guy named Montes Lima Perez. Got his ass shot off and kicked all to pieces by a girl. Yeah, this girl—"

"It just happened, Moreno said. "An informant at the Royal Police Force said he's in the intensive care unit. Montes Lima Perez was number two on the island, their top security man."

"Someone is making a play?" Rojas said. "Trying to muscle in on their organization? Are you telling me we've got a third player on the island? Now, at a time like this? We can tolerate no disruptions to our plans. Everything is riding on our ability to keep things quiet."

"It's too early to tell," Moreno said with his palms raised toward

Rojas. "We will have information about the girl within the hour. I've got a friend at Caricom's Joint Regional Communications Centre."

"Hey," Kyle said, "You like acronyms, right?" He turned to Moreno. "Tell him about the CIP and the JRCC," the last syllable rolling off his tongue like a song.

Moreno, whose expression never changed, said, "Caribbean Citizenship by Investment Programmes, or CIPs. JRCC is one of Caricom's intelligence agencies. They monitor the movements of persons of interest, including those who may be a high security threat to the safety and security of the region. They'll be aware of the girl and who she's working for."

"Wonderful," Rojas said, though his voice was showing telltale signs of a growing impatience. "I want to know who she is. I can't afford to have a drug war in the streets, not now. We've got to keep everything quiet, or else . . ."

11

Flow of Drugs

"I still don't know how this isn't in the hands of DEA. How did the US become alerted to the new flow of drugs?" Jana said.

"Wow, when you make a decision, you really make it, don't you?"

As they got into the car, Jana's eyes traced the horizon of the ocean in the distance.

Cade started the engine and pulled out of the police station parking lot.

"Where are we going, by the way?"

"Safe house," Cade said.

"Safe house? What safe house? You're an analyst at NSA, not field personnel. What the hell would you know about a safe house?"

Cade ignored her.

"Since Antigua is in play, Kyle has been down here," Cade said, "recruiting people on the inside to gather intel against the Oficina de Envigado cartel. What we're afraid of is that he got too close and his identity was compromised."

As the vehicle wove its way up into the Antiguan hills, Jana said, "You know I love Kyle like a brother, right? He's always looked out for me. Saved my skin more than once."

"Hey!" Cade belted. "It wasn't just Kyle who saved you last time. And now that we're on that subject, you're right, I'm not field personnel. I understand that. But I took a bullet for you last year, and to hear you tell it, I wasn't even there. You may want to forget the past like it never happened, but it did happen, Jana. We happened. And you're not going to pretend there was nothing. Dammit, I was in love with you. And I know you felt the same way."

"I don't owe you anything, Cade."

"Owe me?" he almost yelled. "You don't owe me? That's bullshit. I'll tell you what you owe me. You owe me an explanation."

"An explanation for what?"

"We were in a relationship that was going somewhere, remember? Jesus. Who are you? I want to know why you left me."

"I told you, we're over," Jana said. "I'm no longer the girl you fell in love with. That girl is dead. She's gone."

"That may be, but I want to know why you left me."

"Why I left you? I just finished saying—"

"No, not why you ripped my heart out and stomped on it. Why you left me to bleed out after I got shot in that cabin last year."

Jana's memory raced back to the scene that day, to the remote cabin deep within Wyoming's YellowstoneNational Park. After she had been abducted by Rafael, Cade and Kyle had kicked down the cabin's door. In the ensuing melee, Cade, Kyle, and the suspect had been shot. Once freed from her bindings, Jana had shot Rafael to death as he lay helpless on the floor.

Cade continued. "If it hadn't been for that park ranger, I'd be gone. When you went after Waseem Jarrah, you bolted out of that cabin without a thought in the world about whether I lived or died. It was then I knew. I knew you had left me."

Her hand trembled and the edges of her vision began to darken—the PTSD episode was renewing its fight. "I did what I did so I could stop Jarrah from detonating, and you know it. If I hadn't bolted out of that cabin, he would have set off the nuke."

"I know that. But you didn't so much as glance back at me, or consider the possibility that even if you were to stop Jarrah, that I might be dead when you got back."

"I'm not going to apologize for stopping the largest attack ever attempted against the United States."

"No one is asking you to. But after all we'd been through . . ." Cade allowed the thought to trail off.

Jana looked out at the tropical foliage lining the roadside in an attempt to distract herself from the memories that had haunted her since that day. She switched the topic. "If Kyle's been compromised, you know as well as I do that he may have been tortured."

"You're right. You're not the girl I fell in love with."

Silence permeated the air. It was Cade who finally broke it. "I might know what happened to Kyle. We've got to find him."

"You think I don't know that?" Jana looked at Cade through the corner of her eye as the car banked up another curve. "Wait a minute. You didn't just come here to find Kyle, did you? Kyle believed I was in danger. You came here because you already knew he may have been tortured, and that puts me in direct danger. If he knew where I was, the drug cartel may find that out. You came down here for me. You came here to pull me out."

"Something like that," Cade said. "But it's not that simple. I didn't come here to pull you out."

"Hold on," Jana said as her thoughts played forward. "I know exactly why you're here. You're not here to pull me out, are you? You want to use me as bait!" Her jawline clenched.

The rainforest surrounding the roads began to form a tunnel over the roadway the higher the car climbed.

When Cade did not reply, Jana continued. "In fact, you're not here for me or Kyle."

This time Cade jammed on the brake and the car screeched to a halt on the quiet road.

"I can't believe you just said that. After everything the three of us have been through. You and Kyle knew each other from the Bureau, but Kyle and I go all the way back to undergrad at Georgia Southern. I trust him more than anyone in the world. And you? You and I were practically living together. I was in love with you, and now you think I've come down here to further my career? To say the words 'that hurts' wouldn't do it justice. Kyle's life is on the line, your life is on the line. But there's a lot of other things at play here. It's bigger than any two lives."

"And there it is. You've come down here to use me as bait." Jana's hand shook harder as she began to realize she was no longer safe on the island, a place she had come to know as a bastion of anonymity, a place to hide. And the very people she trusted now saw her as nothing more than a bartering chip. Her body shivered.

Cade began driving again. "Does the United States government want me to convince you to be used as bait in an investigation? The answer is yes. It's the only way to draw the players out into the open. But as far as my career goes, I got in deep shit arguing against this plan. But in the end, I had to agree with them. There's no other way."

"How very noble of you."

It was a stab in the gut and Cade gave up all hope of resurrecting their relationship.

"When I said there's a lot more on the line than you realize, I

54

meant it," Cade said. "Heroin flowing through Antigua is making its way all across the US. And this isn't just typical heroin. It's heroin laced with . . ." Cade stopped.

"Go on," she said.

"It's laced with fentanyl."

Jana thought back to the night Rafael had abducted her. He had drugged her with an aerosolized form of fentanyl in order to render her unconscious and kidnap her.

"And the more that sells, the more kids die. Overdoses are at an all-time high. Then there's the isle of Antigua itself," he said as he waved a hand at their surroundings. "Like I said earlier, the cartels have been keeping violence to a minimum to avoid attracting attention, but if they get a foothold, the government here could lose stability. Then there's DEA."

"What about them?"

Kyle leveled a stern gaze at her. "Drug Enforcement is in this up to its ears. Even though Kyle was CIA, he was working hand in hand with DEA down here. And you know how Kyle is. He never met a stranger. He has a way of building trust in everyone around him. Apparently, DEA now practically consider him one of their own, on the same team."

Jana's thoughts pinged from one side of her head to the other. *I'm not just going to help find Kyle, I'm going to have to go undercover. I'm going to have to go deep, and there won't be anyone to protect me.* "Go on," she said, though her breathing became erratic.

"There's more than just a little anger brewing. Over the last four days, every time I talk to DEA about Kyle, they bring up the name Kiki Camarena."

"Kiki Camarena?" Jana said as her eyes closed tight.

"He was before our time, back in the early '80s," Cade said. "Kiki Camarena was a DEA agent working deep cover in Mexico.

He disappeared. He had gotten way too far in. When he couldn't be located, news of his disappearance made it all the way into the Oval Office. Reagan was so pissed off that he called the president of Mexico and threatened that if Camarena did not resurface, immediately, he would instruct the US State Department to issue a code-red alert for Americans traveling to Mexico. It would have dried up the Mexican tourism business within days. Not long thereafter, the body of Agent Camarena came forward. He had been tortured to death. It was the beginning of the United States' drug wars into Mexico and Colombia. The gloves came off. Special-ops teams were inserted all over the place. They carried out a lot of raids, burned crop fields, and took no prisoners, and I think you know what I mean. When anyone in DEA so much as mentions the name of Kiki Camarena, it's a precursor. They're angry, they're impatient, and time is running out."

12

The Safe House

The car pulled further up the hillside of Gray's Farm Main Road, past the Old Sugar Windmill up to a small house overlooking HawksbillBay, a beautiful stretch of pinkish sand and turquoise water. The house was shrouded in tropical vegetation and trees that overhung from every angle. As the tires crunched across the gravel-like driveway of crushed seashells, Jana said, "This is your safe house? Well, you certainly know how to treat the ladies."

"It's not that bad."

"Not that bad? Look at this dump. Christ, the little hut I live in is nicer than this. And that's on a bartender's salary."

"But it's nice inside."

"Your plane touched down at the airport an hour ago. You went straight to the police station to argue with the cops until they let me out. You haven't even been here yet."

"You never let a guy get the edge, do you?"

"Montes Lima Perez found that out the hard way."

"That's just cold," Cade replied. They got out of the rental car and Cade looked across the roof at her. "Want to tell me what really happened? Perez didn't attack you, did he?"

Jana spoke through gritted teeth. "If I want a man to put his hands on me, I'll let him know."

"Let him know? Two compound fractures and two GSWs? That's what you call letting him know? I'll ask again, and I want the truth this time. He didn't attack you, did he? Tell me what happened."

"Or what?"

"Or I'll go back and tell the lieutenant to arrest you."

"Like I give a shit," she said, though they both knew that was a lie. Jana exhaled. "Fine. It was a Monday night. I had the night off and went to a local club. He wasn't a bad-looking guy. He asked me to dance, we danced. He bought me a drink, we drank."

"I didn't know you had a thing for Latin guys."

Jana ignored the statement. "I told him I had to go, but he followed me outside. Said he wanted to make sure I got home safely."

"And you believed that crap?"

"Of course I didn't. I'm not an idiot, and I knew that look in his eye. I knew what he wanted. I just didn't want the same thing."

"You're walking alone at night with a guy you don't want to spend the night with, and you just happen to turn down a dark alley?"

Jana went silent.

Cade continued. "See, this is where your story gets a little hazy to me. How did you happen to walk down that alley when you knew full well this guy might try something?"

"Cade, I didn't know he had a criminal record. Certainly not one that included sexual assault."

"Go on."

"About halfway down the alley he pulls me close to him and starts to kiss my neck."

"Did you tell him to stop?"

"God. It's like I'm being interrogated. No, I didn't. You happy now? But when I finally did, that's when his hands started crawling all over me. And then I—"

"You can stop right there. You *lured* him, didn't you? You lured him down that alley."

"I did no such thing."

Cade couldn't help but notice she had broken eye contact. He walked around the car and squared off in front of her. "I checked, Jana. The cops may not have picked up on it yet, but the walk from the club back to your place does not include that alley. You went out of your way to bring him to a dark, secluded place, didn't you?" He paused a moment, waiting for an answer. When one did not come, he continued. "You know what I think? I think you can't get past your ordeal with Rafael. You had a gut feeling that this guy Perez was bad news and you figured you'd teach him a lesson, like the one you taught Rafael," he blurted as he leaned over her. "You went off on him, didn't you?"

"What the hell would you know about my ordeal with Rafael?" she replied, almost yelling. "You didn't show up until the last minute. And you don't know me!" she said as she shoved him backward. "You don't know what's going on inside my head."

"What I know is that you're not the girl I fell in love with. That much is perfectly clear. What I suspect though, is that you decided a long time ago that you would never again be a victim, so you found yourself some training. Christ, look at your shoulders and arms. Look at how you broke Perez into pieces. The guy must have seventy pounds on you."

Jana looked away.

"And at that nightclub, once you got a bad feeling about Perez, you decided you'd test him on it."

Her head snapped back. "Yeah, I decided to test him," she said with a steely look in her eyes. "And my gut was right on point. He was a thug dressed in a nice package, and I taught him a lesson. He won't be forcing himself on another woman ever again, that's for sure."

"Not now that you shot his balls off." Cade shook his head. "Tell the truth. The broken bones came first, didn't they? And then the smashed face? And while he writhed on the ground, you shot him, twice." Cade crossed his arms. "Not so different from what you did to Rafael back at the cabin. So what do you have to say now? What am I supposed to think? That you're *not* a loose cannon?"

"What I do has nothing to do with you," she said.

"It does now. The only thing we have in common is a past. A past and Kyle. Kyle needs our help, and I have to know you're not going to lose your shit again if things go sideways."

She poked a sharp finger into his solar plexus with just enough force to get his attention. "I am in complete control."

"Then why is your hand shaking?"

Her mouth dropped open and she looked at the hand.

"I was right," Cade continued. "Your hand starts shaking right before you have a post-traumatic stress episode. Using you is a bad idea."

Cade continued his line of questioning. "So what about it? It was a PTSD event that sent you to the hospital last night, wasn't it?"

She turned her back. "I've got control of it," she said as she crossed her arms. "I left the Bureau to get away from it. All the stress, the male-dominated culture, the damned terrorists. PTSD had taken over my life. I came down here to start again, to not have to face down another terrorist, about to be killed at any moment. I'm not saying I'm happy, but I'm happier here than I've been in a long time. I had no idea how bad it had gotten until I got here. It was then I realized it. In my life at the Bureau I had forgotten."

"Forgotten what?" Cade said.

"Forgotten who I was. Forgotten how to relax. I couldn't even recognize myself."

"And now?"

Her eyes became glassy again as she stared out into the blue waters. "I don't know. Maybe I never really knew who I was in the first place." She shook her head abruptly. "But I don't have time for that right now. Am I stable, you ask? I don't give a shit about that. If Kyle is in trouble, I'm going to help him, and there's nothing you or anyone else can do to stop me."

13

Whereabouts

"I'll ask again." Rojas looked at Kyle. "Hey, wake up." He slapped Kyle. "We're talking about the Oficina de Envigado cartel. Who is in charge of their operations on the island?"

"Gaviria," Kyle sang. "Don't you just love saying that name?" His glazed eyes and thin smile spoke volumes to the euphoria he felt inside.

Rojas whispered, "Carlos Ochoa Gaviria." There was shock in his tone. "I knew his father." For this part, Rojas did not need Gustavo Moreno to hand him an intelligence report. "A former member of Muerte a Secuestradores." Rojas began to pace the room. "Gaviria's father ran the MAS, a paramilitary arm of the original Medellín Cartel. It was huge. It had the backing of the Colombian military, the Colombian legislature, small industrialists, wealthy cattle ranchers, it ran the gamut. And just to keep trade normalized, even Texas Petroleum, a US-based corporation with a huge investment in the region, was a contributor. Carlos Gaviria would have gone with his father and been raised in that environment. Carlos Gaviria would have gone with his father and been raised in that environment. Enforcement, murders, kidnapping, torture. He would have seen it all."

Moreno said, "Patron? Perhaps Gaviria has not yet worked his way up within the new cartel."

"No," Rojas said as the thoughts percolated. "No, this is something else. Gaviria would be high up in their organization. Very high up. This means that Oficina de Envigado, the very successors to the Medellín Cartel, are making a much bigger play of Antigua than we thought. This raises the stakes."

"Would you like me to gather more intelligence on Senior Gaviria, Patron?"

"Of course, you fool!" Rojas screamed. "I want to know his whereabouts. I want to know what he had for breakfast this morning. I want to know everything. The timing could not be worse. We're going to have to do something."

"Yes, Patron," Moreno said.

"No, Agent MacKerron, changing a drug route is not the issue. What we're involved with is much, much bigger than drugs." He turned to Moreno before leaving. "Keep him alive. No one touches him. We may need him later."

14

Training

Once they were inside, they looked at the dust-covered sheets draping the furniture.

"We're not going to talk about us anymore, got it?" Jana said. "I'm only doing this because of Kyle. What assets do we have at our disposal? And don't try to tell me you can't disclose that because of national security. I'm in on everything you know."

"We don't know if the electricity works in here or if there's running water, but you want to talk about assets?" Cade exhaled. "Let me get my stuff. I need to get the comms equipment set up. Then we'll talk."

Cade went back out and opened the trunk. He removed two large cases and a rolling suitcase and brought them inside. He placed one on an old wooden table and keyed in a passcode on top of the case. From it he withdrew an armored laptop and an IsatHub Wi-Fi satellite collapsible hotspot.

"Hardly anyone on the island knows we're here," Cade said. "I'll be set up in a few minutes. We'll have a direct uplink to NSA." He looked at his watch then shook his head. "Uncle Bill is going to be pissed. I'm already late. Here, plug that in," he said, handing Jana a power cord.

"Is this all the equipment you have? What about weapons?

What local assets are at our disposal?"

"We have DEA."

"That's it? How many agents?"

"One," he replied.

"What? They're only giving us one agent? What about all that talk about the murder of Agent Camarena? From the sound of it, I thought there were thirty hardened operators suiting up for a raid."

"Thirty?" Cade said. "This is Antigua. It's a pretty quiet place as far as drugs go, until recently, that is. This discovery of the cartels investment here is new. The DEA agents I was speaking of are in the Bahamas and the USVirgin Islands. They're listening to their contact here. And besides, Kyle's disappearance is a theory."

"A theory? I thought you said—"

"Remember, all we know is that he's gone dark. CIA isn't so convinced. They're accustomed to assets that go dark for months at a time. But it's Kyle we're talking about. He is relentless in his patterns. He doesn't go dark, but no one seems to believe me."

"But Uncle Bill is on board, right? He and Knuckles?"

"Uncle Bill doesn't believe Kyle is missing. But once we convince him, he can put the full weight of the NSA behind this if need be. You've got to understand. It's the war on terror, our assets are stretched thin. He can't commit resources until we are sure."

"Oh, great," Jana said. "A bunch of guys with satellites, listening devices, computer hacking? Not exactly the collection of Jack Reacher superagents I was hoping for."

Cade's mouth dropped open. "Hey, *I* work at NSA."

"My point exactly," Jana said through a smile. "Satellites,

listening devices, computer hackers. A bunch of geeks. You said DEA has a contact here?"

Cade Cade booted up the laptop and positioned the satellite uplink in front of a bay window, then initiated the secure connection. "I'll tell you about the DEA guy if you tell me about your guy."

"My guy?" Jana said as she looked at him.

"Yes, yours."

"I'm not following you."

"Sure you are. I'm talking about your *guy*. The one you've apparently been spending so much time with. The one who trained you? Surely you remember him."

Her face washed free of expression. "What makes you think there's someone?"

"That's what we call a nondenial. The FBI trained you, Jana. But they didn't train you anywhere near to the extent that you are apparently trained now. There's someone here, someone you've been spending a lot of time with. Someone who's trained you in what? Spec ops? Close-quarters combat? What else? Interrogation techniques, how to defeat a polygraph, demolitions? Come on, out with it."

"Fine. I met someone. He never talks about what he did in his past or what he does now, but it's obvious he was an operator of some kind. I've been training with him for months. He taught me more than I ever knew. Like you said, the Bureau trained me, but where their training left off, his picked up."

"What else did he teach you?" he asked.

"Hey!" she yelled. "Back off. I'm not talking about my personal life with you."

"And there you have it," Cade said. "The nondenial. He wasn't just some guy who trained you in weapons and tactics. You were seeing him socially."

An awkward silence ensued between them and Cade turned his attention to the laptop.

Finally, Jana said, "Anyway, that's over now. We went our separate ways."

"Jana, I get it. You and I were over. You found someone. You moved on. But why the training? What possessed you to go so hardcore?"

"I'm not hardcore."

"What a load of crap. This boyfriend of yours didn't just train you because he was bored. You asked him to."

"I'm done talking about him. I've come clean with my piece. Now tell me about the DEA asset."

"He's a contractor."

"He's not real DEA? My God, how are we going to find Kyle and pull him out with no help?"

"DEA puts a lot of faith in him. He's been down here a long time and apparently he's well connected. He's got their ear, that's for sure. He's the one telling DEA they need to send a crew down here and tear this place apart until they find Kyle."

Jana closed her eyes. "So, it sounds like Kyle must have been in touch with this asset. Otherwise, how would he have known Kyle was missing?"

"That would be the assumption," Cade said as he banged away on the keyboard. "Well, we'll find out soon enough. The asset will be here any minute."

"He's coming here? I thought you said no one the island knew about this place."

"Jana, the DEA has trusted this guy for years. And we need his help." Cade pointed at the laptop. "See? Here's his ping on the monitor. He's just up the road."

"Wonderful. Can't wait to meet him," Jana said, though her sarcasm was obvious. "He'd better be good. If he's the only asset we have, that is."

"Don't forget, we've got whatever we need from Uncle Bill, if we can just convince him. Perhaps you forget how effective NSA can be at this."

"It's going to take more than code breaking to find Kyle."

"Look, I need more information. We don't have much time and you know it. I can't be down here blind. Your personal history might be your business, but there's more at stake than that. I want to know about this boyfriend of yours. I don't want to be blindsided by some rogue. Did you ever stop to think that the guy you've been shacked up with is not who you think he is?"

"What's that supposed to mean? Are you saying he's involved somehow? You don't even know him. Besides, he stopped showing up. We're not exactly seeing each other anymore."

"Did you bore him to death?"

"That coming from the self-proclaimed dork," Jana said with a smirk.

"Fair enough. So he didn't tell you about what he used to do for a living? What type of training did he give you?"

"Weapons, close combat. A form of Brazilian jiu-jitsu. Arm bars, wrist locks, joint protrusions."

"Joint protrusions? You mean you hyperextend the joint until it snaps back the other way? Hmmm, sounds similar to injuries suffered by a certain perp whose medical records I examined last night. He taught you how to do that?"

"He can teach how to kill in dozens of different ways, and I wanted to learn all of them. Strange thing is, he can be so gentle."

"I don't think I want to hear how tender he can be when both your heads are on the pillow."

Jana threw her arms in the air. "Did you think after I left you I was going to be celibate for the rest of my life? I met him right after I got down here. I was struggling with all those emotions, and a lot of physical pain from my back injury. He struck up a conversation with me at the bar."

"Bar? You mean that little tiki hut you work in."

"He could see I was in pain so he offered to massage my back."

"Yeah, I bet he did."

"No, it wasn't like that," Jana said as she thought back to the encounter.

"Girls always think the guy just wants to be friends," Cade said as he shook his head.

Jana ignored him. "He recognized me from my face being splashed all across the media after the attempted bombing. It kind of frightened me at first. I mean, I didn't want anyone to know who I was. I wanted to disappear and start with a fresh slate. But being one of the few Caucasians that live here, and being from the States, he knew."

"What's his name?" Cade said while his fingers waited on the keyboard.

"You're going to pull his background?"

"Of course I am. I'm tapped into the NSA database. Like I said, if things go bad, I need to know who's down here."

"You're paranoid."

"Name," Cade said.

"He's *not* a threat."

"You're not going to tell me his name, are you? Fine. At least give me his description. Caucasian?"

"Six feet, one hundred and eighty-five pounds. Long, curly blond hair." Jana smiled at the thought. "Lean, very lean."

"Lean? Uh huh." Cade typed the description as if taking dictation. In his typewritten notes, he substituted the word "lean" with "muscular."

Jana sat and propped her feet on a covered coffee table and Cade glanced out at the driveway as a vehicle pulled up. "Six feet, one hundred and eighty-five pounds you say? Would you say the hair is true blond or more sandy?"

"Sandy. What does that matter?"

"Dark tan? Likes the unshaven look? Wears one of those woven cotton rope bracelets on his wrist like the locals?"

"Wait, what?"

"Did he tell you his full name?"

Jana thought about the question for a moment. "Come to think of it, no. Just his first name. I assumed he liked his anonymity. It wasn't important to me, so I didn't press it."

Cade cocked his head at her. "You slept with a man and you only knew his first name? Did he give you his real first name, or did you just call him *Johnny*?"

Jana sat straight up. "Now how the hell do you know that? Wait a minute," she said as the thought played forward. "You've been spying on me. You son of a bitch! Eavesdropping from your little cubical at NSA."

Cade held both hands up. "Didn't even know where you were until yesterday."

"Then how do you know—"

"Because he's here," he said.

Jana spun toward the front of the house and looked out the bay window. Her mouth dropped open.

"Congrats, Jana," Cade said. "You've been dating John Stone, private contractor to the DEA."

15

Enter the Stone

Stone walked in and propped his shades on the top of his head, pulling his long sandy-blond hair from his face. His skin was bronzed, and he carried the relaxed air of a local.

Jana's mouth hung open.

Stone's hands found their way into the pockets of his tattered shorts, but even in his nervousness, he could not stop looking at Jana. His blue eyes were calm, almost tranquil. He looked like a person just waking from a restful sleep. "Hey, Baker," he said.

Jana began to speak but no sounds emerged.

"Oh. My. God," Cade said. "Well, this is awkward, isn't it?" He looked at Jana, whose facial expression displayed something between shock and anger. But he could see something else in her eyes, something she was trying to hide—exhilaration.

"You," she blurted. "What are you doing here?"

His voice was soft, disarming. "I know you're mad," he said. "And I'm not here to hand you any excuses. I disappeared on you, babe, and it's my fault."

"Your damn right it's your fault," she said. "You don't do that. You don't just up and vanish when you're in the middle of something."

Cade watched the two of them and bit his lower lip. He was

witnessing something he had hoped he would not.

"I know. You're right," Stone said.

"Well I don't want to hear it," Jana said.

Stone went silent and waited. He was giving her time.

"So spit it out," Jana said. "Why did you leave me? You meet someone else? I hope she was worth it."

Cade wanted to melt into the aging floorboards.

"Baker, there's no one—"

"Yeah, right," she interrupted.

Stone walked toward her and put his hands on her shoulders. "Look at me. I mean it. There was no one."

"You haven't called me in a month," she said with anger lacing her words.

"I was on an op," Stone said. "Look, I knew you were Bureau, back before you came down here, and you knew I was . . . well, you knew I worked in a similar field. I was on an op and I couldn't share anything with you."

"An op? You up and disappear for a month? What kind of op? Now I learn that you're supposed to be some contractor for the DEA? What else do I not know about you?"

"Didn't you ever wonder where I learned it all? All the training I gave you? The weapons and tactics. The hand-to-hand. Demolitions, all that?"

"Yes, I wondered. But I assumed you had been in the military and didn't want to talk about it. But that doesn't give you the right to disappear."

"I couldn't talk about my work, Baker. Not until now, that is. Now that you're back in the fold."

"I'm not *back in the fold*," she said. "I'm not Bureau. I'm never going back there. They don't run me. *I* run me."

Cade broke in. "Okay, okay. Can we interrupt this brush with the past? We've got a man missing."

Jana did not acknowledge Cade. "You never even told me your last name. Not that I was asking, mind you. So is John your real name?"

"Of course it is. I never lied to you. And yes, I was military. But you're right, I didn't want to talk about it. There's a lot of stuff I never want to talk about again. I'm just sorry it hurt you. I didn't tell you about myself because I didn't want to get burned when it ended."

"You assumed it *would* end," Jana said.

Cade again wished he could be anywhere but here, listening to his ex-girlfriend talk with a person she obviously had feelings for.

"Didn't you?" Stone said.

Jana looked him in the eye and then her mouth opened.

To Cade, the expression was akin to someone who had just located[KM1] the missing piece to a puzzle.

Her hand found her mouth and covered it and she took two steps backward. "Oh my God," she said. She pointed at Stone. "Your last name is *Stone*? It can't be. It can't be."

"What?" Stone said.

"Your eyes. That's why there was always something so familiar about you."

It was Cade this time. "What are you talking about?"

"Eight years ago," Jana said shaking her head. "I was just out of college."

Cade said, "You two met eight years ago?"

"No. My first job, before the Bureau. I went to work at a software conglomerate. I did investments for them. It turned out my bosses were up to no good. I ended up being a material witness for the FBI. I just happened to be in the wrong place at the wrong time, and he approached me. My involvement in that case is what made me reconsider my entire career path. It's what made me think about being an FBI agent in the first place."

Stone scowled. "Who? Who approached you?"

"I didn't put two and two together until just now when I heard your last name. But you have his eyes. Oh my God. How could I have missed that? You have his eyes. Agent Stone, that's who."

Stone replied, "I'm a contractor now, Baker. And besides, in the military we were known as *operators*, not agents. I never went by the name Agent Stone."

"Not you," Jana said, "your father. Your father is Special Agent Chuck Stone, isn't it?"

This time it was Stone whose mouth dropped open. "You know my father?"

"Do I know him? He saved my life. Yes I know him."

Silence permeated the space the way smoke fills a room.

Cade said, "Great. My ex-girlfriend has not only moved on, but apparently worked herself up a whole new family in the process." Humor was his only defense. "You'd think that since I work for the NSA, I'd have known all this already." He gave a little laugh, but it went nowhere.

Jana shook her head and her face hardened. "You should have told me more," she said. "But we don't have time for this. We need to get down to business." She crossed her arms and looked at Stone. "What do you know about the disappearance of Agent Kyle MacKerron?"

16

Last Sighting

"Wait," Stone said, "Baker, hold on. You knew my father?"

Jana waited a moment but finally said. "Yes. This was back in the Petrolsoft case."

Stone's mouth opened as if to speak but all he could do was exhale.

"Petrolsoft?" Stone finally said. He looked at the floor. "I think I need to sit down," he said as he leaned on an ottoman then sank into the cushions. "Dad nearly died on that case. He was shot in the chest. The only reason he didn't die was because—" He looked at Jana.

Jana interrupted. "They got a helicopter evac. I know, I was there. His blood was all over me."

"I can't believe that was you," Stone said. "He was in intensive care for days. We didn't think he was going to make it. It wasn't until a few months later—I had just gotten selected by First Special Forces Operational Detachment and was about to deploy—when dad finally told me about the case. "

"First SFOD-D?" Cade said. "So you were Delta Force."

"Yeah. We did a lot of stuff. All under the control of JSOC."

"JSOC?" Jana said.

Cade answered. "Joint Special Operations Command. Whenever we recommend an incursion into another country, we call JSOC. If approved, they assign either a team from Delta or one of the eight SEAL teams."

"Anyway," Stone continued, "Dad had been medically retired and figured since I had gotten my security clearance, it would be okay to share the details with me."

"He'd been at the Bureau twenty-three years," Jana said. "He was already qualified for retirement, but didn't want to."

"Yeah," Stone said. "The things he told me about that case. He talked about a girl he'd recruited to work undercover. He said she was the gutsiest thing he'd ever seen." He continued staring at her. "I can't believe that was you. You risked your life. And not only that, the other agents said it was you that stopped the bleeding. It was you that saved my dad."

Cade glanced between them. He watched as tension eased from Jana's face and shoulders. It appeared as though her earlier anger had melted.

"He saved mine," Jana said with a sweet quality to her voice. "He was the real hero that day. If he hadn't burst into that apartment, I'd be dead right now. He's the reason I went to work as an agent."

A long silence ensued and Cade shifted back and forth. It was as if the other two had forgotten he was there. He said, "I hate to interrupt this lovely story, but can we get back to business?"

"Kyle approached me a while back," Stone said. "He was new on the island and I was still trying to figure out who he was."

"What initiated him approaching you?" Cade said.

"How do I say this?" Stone replied. "I've got a particular *reputation* down here."

"What reputation?" Jana questioned.

"I'm known as a guy who can get things done," Stone said.

"Get things done?" Jana said to Stone. "You couldn't even find your shirt in the morning." The young couple laughed at the inference, but Cade shut his eyes.

"Like what kind of things?"

Stone removed the sunglasses from the top of his head and dropped them into a loose shirt pocket. "To the cartels, I'm known as a mule. I move drugs from point A to point B. It puts me in the perfect position to know what cartels are moving what product, and where it's going. Then I tell the DEA about it. Well, not all the time, but some of the time."

Jana cocked her head. "You don't disclose all the shipments? You work as a contractor for them, right? Isn't that withholding evidence?"

Stone said, "It's not that simple. To survive down here as long as I have, you've got to be damned careful. If I told DEA about every shipment, they'd go and intercept it. How long do you think I'd stay alive? Besides, there are times when one cartel or another wants to test me. They've had shipments get seized, so what they do is, they set me up on a milk run. They don't tell me, but sometimes the shipment doesn't contain drugs. It's just meant to look like drugs. They track it and make sure it gets to its destination, then wait to see if any DEA boys show up. A basic internal witch hunt."

Cade said, "So when the cartels give you an assignment, how do you know which of your drug runs are just a test?"

"I can't explain it," Stone said. "I just get a funny feeling inside."

"Let's get back on point," Jana said. "Tell us about Kyle."

"Kyle found out I was a mule before he knew I was working undercover. He befriended me. Figured I'd be a good way to get to the inside. Damn, he was good. I had no idea who he was, and that's saying something. Normally I can smell those guys out."

"He *is* good," Jana said.

"What?" Stone replied.

"You said he *was* good. He's not past tense. Kyle is alive and we're going to find him."

Cade said, "How big are the cartel's operations here?"

"A lot bigger than you'd think. It's because they're keeping such a low profile. I don't have numbers, other than what I've witnessed, but they move a lot of product," Stone said.

"How can you be so sure?" Cade said.

"Look, as far as the cartels are concerned, they know one thing about me—I always deliver on my promises. That kind of loyalty goes a long way. The Los Rastrojos cartel in particular has taken a liking to me. All this to say, I get more access to see what's going on compared to other, low level, mules. That puts me in places that others cannot go."

"But how do you know how big it is?" Cade said.

"I don't just move drugs. Sometimes it's cash. Last month I transported a tractor trailer. It was filled to the brim. I'm talking about shrink-wrapped pallets of greenbacks—hundred-dollar bills. The semi was packed to the roof, all except a stack of pallets that were positioned against the rear doors. That was a roof-high load of white flour, intended to hide the cash from prying eyes. Sometimes the Antiguan police stop trucks to inspect them."

"So Kyle was successful. He had penetrated deep," Jana said.

Stone looked at Cade this time. "You bet your ass he was in deep. Like I said, he was the best I've ever seen. When I was at the Oficina de Envigado escondite, I'd see him come and go. He was obviously investigating them."

"The Oficina de Envigado what?" Cade asked.

It was Jana that answered. "*Escondite* is Spanish for *hideout*."

"Alright," Cade said, "so you'd see him at the Envigado place here on the island. When was the last time you saw him?"

"It was about five days ago. He was there, apparently in a meeting. I walked by and he was having breakfast on the balcony with . . ."

Jana stepped toward Stone. "With? With who?" When she received no reply, she said, "Who was Kyle meeting with?"

Stone looked at her then Cade, then looked down and let out a long exhale. "Montes Lima Perez. Word on the street though is that he was snatched by the other cartel, Los Rastrojos, the one run by Diego Rojas."

17

Rojas's Background

Upon hearing the name Diego Rojas, Cade shut his eyes. Jana looked from Stone to Cade. "Okay. Will somebody tell me what the big deal is?"

Cade rubbed his neck and let out a long exhale. "He's bad news, Jana."

Stone said, "That's putting it mildly. He's Los Rastrojos's number one on the island. But not just on the island. He's a big-time player. And, he's as ruthless as they come."

"Be honest with me, Stone," Jana said. "What are the chances that Kyle is still alive?"

"If it was anyone other than Rojas, he'd stay alive just long enough for them to get whatever information out of him they wanted. But with Rojas, you never know. His temper is legend. He'd be dead by now."

"NSA has been involved on and off for years in surveilling the Colombian cartels. Cade said Rojas isn't just high in the organization, he's the new young blood. And, he's got a pedigree."

"What's that supposed to mean?" Jana said.

Cade replied. "It started with the Cali cartel. Cali was founded by the Rodríguez Orejuela brothers in the town of Cali in southern Colombia back in the early '80s. In those years, it was an offshoot of Pablo Escobar's Medellín Cartel, but by the late '80s the Orejuelas were ready to branch out on their own. They were led by four men. One of them was a man named Hélmer Herrera, known as 'Pacho.' Pacho and the others led the cartel to a point in the '90s where they controlled ninety percent of the world's cocaine supply. We're talking billions of dollars."

"So why the history lesson?" Jana said.

"Los Rastrojos is the successor to Cali. Diego Rojas is Pacho's son," Cade said.

"Yeah," Stone said, "his last son. The others were killed. So, apparently, Pacho changed Diego's last name in order to protect him."

Cade said, "After the murder of his older brothers, the kid grew up with vengeance on his mind. His psychological profile is thick, Jana. The US has been trying to get at him for years."

"DEA hasn't been able?" Jana said.

Stone said, "It's more complicated than that. The DEA has had a lot of pushback that's prevented them from shutting Rojas down."

"Pushback from who?" Jana said.

It was Cade that answered. "Pushback from the State Department. They've been afraid that if Rojas was killed, a power vacuum would start in Colombia. You see, so much of the government of Colombia has remained swept up in corruption. If the balance of power shifts, State is concerned the country will become unstable. And if that happens, you've got a hot new place for terror organizations to set up shop without anyone bothering them."

"I don't think I want to hear this," Jana said. "It makes me sick. Anyway, if the State Department doesn't want Rojas taken down, what is Kyle doing trying to penetrate their cartel?"

"Disruption," Stone said. "Likely they want to continue disrupting each new route of drug shipments to slow the flow into the United States."

Jana's impatience boiled over. "I don't care about all this background crap. I want to know how we're going to save Kyle."

"You've got to know," Cade said. "You've got to know who Rojas is and just how ruthless he is before you go in there."

Stone stood. "Before who goes in there? Goes in where?" He looked at Cade. "Wait a minute, *she's* not going in there," he said as he pointed.

"She has to go in there," Cade said. "She's our only chance to get Kyle out alive."

Stone's volume increased. "He's dead, I told you. You don't know what you're talking about. You don't know these people."

"I know all about these people," Cade spat back.

"Oh really?" Stone said as he crossed his arms. "From your cubicle at NSA?" He turned to Jana. "Baker, don't do this. I've been on the inside for a long time and I'm telling you, not only is Kyle dead, but even if he weren't, they'd sniff you out. And don't even ask me what they would do to you if you were discovered."

She put a gentle hand on Stone's arm. It was only then that she realized her hand had begun shaking. "I've got a perfect way in," she said as a shiver rode her body. "They're going to ask me in, in fact."

Stone shook his head.

"Johnny, it's something I have to do." She crossed her arms in an attempt to hide her shaking hand. "I have to. I have to. I have to."

"Yeah," Stone replied, "you sound real convincing."

18

Nightmares

Jana knew she'd be up late and decided to take a power nap. It wasn't long before she nodded off. Her pupils raced back and forth across her closed eyelids. She had already cycled through the first four stages of sleep and rapid eye movement began in earnest. Her breathing deepened then slowed. But as the dream began to unfold, visions of light popped into her mind's eye. She began to discern a particular shape, the telltale silhouette of Waseem Jarrah. Those awful scars. They were always there, a constant reminder of his power over her, and they had a mind of their own.

Her breathing accelerated. She had killed Jarrah in the moments before he was to detonate a weapon of mass destruction. The visions flickered and popped in her mind. It was as if she was watching footage from an old newsreel. Her pupils darted left then right in ever-increasing speed as Jarrah emerged from his silhouette. It was as if he had stepped out of her memory of that fateful day, high on a cliff, deep within YellowstoneNational Park.

Jarrah, now clear and in sharp focus, walked out of the silhouetted background of the newsreel footage and approached Jana. At the time, she had been badly injured and was lying on top of the rocks, faceup. Blood and scrapes covered her face, arms and legs—badges of honor earned after a two-mile sprint through the woods and rugged terrain in pursuit of Jarrah. Jarrah had knocked her to the ground, slamming her head into the rocks. The resulting concussion had made things even fuzzier.

This was another recurring nightmare, and one she could not escape. She would relive the same terrifying ordeal several times each week. And now the edges of her own sanity were beginning to weaken. It was like an earthen dam that had become saturated, the massive volume of water starting to seep through.

In the dream, Jana watched the newsreel play out behind Jarrah, who now stood before her with crystal clarity.

"It is fun to watch, is it not, Agent Baker?" Jarrah said through a sickening grin. He put his arm around her shoulder. "Let's watch it again, shall we? It's the ending that I love so dearly." Jana's breathing accelerated.

On that day, when Jarrah had reached down to pick Jana up and throw her body over the cliff, she had plunged a knife into his chest. She then slashed his throat, spraying blood across the pine needles before barrel-rolling him over the edge. Jarrah had died and Jana had thwarted the attack.

But here, in her nightmare, the memory had been altered and Jana faced her worst fears. She watched as Jarrah picked her limp body off the ground, tossed her onto his shoulder, then walked to the edge of the cliff. With Jana's torso dangling behind him, he turned around so Jana could see over the edge and into the canyon below. Sharp rocks on the bottom pointed up like fingers of death. Her body was wracked in pain and her weakened arms dangled at her sides. Jarrah laughed a monstrous laugh and said, "Oh, come now, Agent Baker. When you were a child, did you not want to fly like a bird? Let's see if you can fly." He threw her over the edge.

As she fell, she could hear Jarrah's laughter from above. Her body slammed into the rocks at the bottom of the canyon and she was left in a crumpled heap. Jarrah then casually strolled over to his backpack, reached inside, tapped a button on the device, and watched as a digital screen blinked to life. He tapped a coded sequence onto the tiny keyboard and armed the device. Without hesitation, he flung the eighty-pound pack over the edge. It landed not far from Jana's body. Five seconds later the ten-kiloton nuclear weapon detonated.

A mushroom cloud rose into the atmosphere, but that was just the beginning. The canyon where Jana lay sat just above the largest volcanic magma chamber in the world. What followed was a cacophony of primary and secondary volcanic eruptions.

Back in her bedroom, Jana's right hand began to twitch.

In the dream, Jana heard the warnings from a government geologist they had consulted during the investigation. "If that device detonates just above the magma chamber," he had said, "it will cause a volcanic eruption unlike any on record. It will devastate the western United States and cover much of the country in ash. It will blot out the sky. There will be a year-long winter . . ."

The Jarrah in her dream turned to face Jana and she could see death in his eyes. Her dream-self was frozen, unable to fight. He pulled out the same knife and plunged it into her chest.

On the bed, Jana's breathing stopped and the post-traumatic stress episode took control. Her body began to convulse and there was nothing she could do to stop it.

19

Goes Undercover

Touloulou Bar, 5330 Marble Hill Rd., St. John's, Antigua
Jana's little black dress fit snugly against her trim form. It was just enough to attract attention but not enough to be flashy. Her target was here, and she knew it. When she walked in, she couldn't help but notice Rojas sitting at the corner of the bar and it was all she could do to avoid making eye contact. *That's him,* she thought.He was looking right at her and his eyes traced down her distinct curves. Jana's heart beat faster and she exhaled, an effort to blow out jittery nerves. She felt like she was walking into the mouth of a lion.

Music thumped from five-foot speakers and bodies pressed tightly against one another, bouncing with the beat. It was a strange concoction of African rhythms bolstered by the unique sound of steel drums—an authentic blend of the island's West African heritage that had been softened by the salty air, gentle breezes, and a relaxed attitude known to locals as "island time," a low-stress approach to life.

She walked to the bar and leaned an elbow onto its polished wood. Rojas wore an expensive blue blazer atop a crisp white button-down shirt. She flicked her blue eyes at him and in response the side of his mouth curled up. She returned the grin but in more of a polite way.

The bartender, an islander, wiped the bar with a white towel and said, "Ma'am?"

"A mojito please," Jana said.

Rojas stood. "May I make a suggestion?" His Latin accent was softer and his eyes more captivating than she'd expected. He looked at the bartender. "Bring her a Guyanese-passion-fruit rum punch, and use the Ron Guajiro." He stepped closer. "I hope you don't find me too forward, but I think you'll like it. My name is Diego Rojas." He extended a hand.

"I'm Claire. That's a very expensive rum," Jana said. "About two hundred dollars a bottle as I recall."

Rojas's smile revealed perfect, pearl-white teeth. "A beautiful woman who knows her rum. You're just visiting our exquisite island?"

I can't believe I am this close to him, she thought as goose bumps formed on her arms. To be this close to a psychopath, the one man that had the key to finding Kyle, was terrifying. A bead of perspiration ran down her side.

"Most islanders prefer either Cavalier or EnglishHarbour," she said, "but that is for the average local. The Ron Guajiro distillery did its finest work in the '70s, but that's no longer in supply. But the 1980s, like he's pouring now, produced a very respectable bottle."

"I'm impressed. Have you ever tried Guajiro from the 1970s?"

She dropped an innocent hand on his arm and peered into his dark eyes. "One mustn't covet what one cannot have. Don't you agree?"

He laughed as the bartender mixed the punch in front of her. "To covet is to yearn to possess or have something. And what makes you think you can't have what you covet?" His eyes wandered down her top to what pleased them.

"Here you are, ma'am," the bartender said as he placed the rum drink in front of her. She tasted the colorful punch.

"What do you think?" Rojas said.

"Let's see. Although a sacrilege to hide a rum as fine as Guajiro behind the other flavors, I detect traces of clove, pipe tobacco . . . espresso, a bit of tawny port, and orange."

"How did you come to know so much about rum? Did your family own a distillery?"

Keep him talking. Jana believed Kyle was alive and knew his life depended on her ability to penetrate Rojas's organization. She scanned for the slightest sign of deception. A flicker of facial muscles, the eye darting down and to the left, but she could detect nothing.

"No, I come to the knowledge more honestly. I work in a bar."

He laughed louder this time and returned her touch. When his eyes landed on her hand, his dazzling smile retreated and he said, "But what have you done to your hand?"

If he knows I beat the shit out of his rival last night, he's doing a good job hiding it. She allowed a protracted silence to punctuate the moment. "I cut myself shaving."

He laughed and tossed down the remainder of his drink. "My, my. But there are cuts on the knuckles. Yet no bruising. How very interesting. Hmmm . . ." He took her other hand. "Marks on both hands. Yes, shaving is a dangerous business. One must be more careful." This time, the Latin flavor of his accent betrayed a slight English quality, like that of a person who has spent a great deal of time in the United Kingdom.

Jana shifted positions and another bead of sweat fell. "But why be careful? Life is too short, Mr. Rojas."

"Indeed," he said as he nodded.

***

From a darkened hillside about fifty yards away, Cade squinted through binoculars into the open-air bar. Even at this distance, the music was clearly audible. "Well that didn't take her long," he said.

Stone, lying on the ground next to him, replied, "Did you expect it to?" He adjusted the tripod on his Vortex Razor HD monocular spotting scope to better align his view, then cranked the reticle to zoom in closer. "I mean, how could you not look at her."

"Are you trying to tell *me* she's beautiful? We dated for a year, you know."

"So I've heard."

Cade squirmed and shook his head. "Let me ask you a question. Are you the biggest dumbass on the island?"

Stone continued watching through the scope. "Okay, I'll bite. What is that supposed to mean?"

"You had her. I mean, you had her. But you let her go? What were you thinking?"

"It's not as simple as that."

Cade put down the binoculars. "It's exactly that simple."

"Let's drop it, alright? I don't like talking with Jana's ex-boyfriend about Jana."

Cade shook his head again.

Stone said, "She'll have this guy wrapped around her fingers in a minute. Look at him."

"Sure wish I could hear what they're saying. Makes me nervous as hell with her being in such close proximity to this scumbag."

"No way I'm sending her in there wearing a wire. But that's one thing we can agree on. Rojas is a psycho. He's got no remorse. It took a lot of people to die for Rojas to become Rojas."

***

Jana leaned back and laughed. She was surprised at how easily things were unfolding. "So where were you raised?"

"You tell me," he replied.

"Let's see. Dark hair, dark complexion. But not just from spending too much time on the beach. You are Latin."

"Is that good?"

Jana grinned. "I'd say somewhere in Central America. Am I right?"

"Very good," he said as he nodded. "I was raised in Colombia. My parents owned a large farm. We produced coffee and sugarcane."

She took his hand and flipped it over, then ran her fingers across his palm. "These don't look like the hands of a farmer. And the Guajiro? One doesn't often find a man of such sophisticated tastes. They must have been very special people."

"They were the second largest coffee exporters in the country. A most exquisite Arabica bean."

"You didn't grow up harvesting sugar cane in the fields, did you?" Her grin was playful.

"Far from it. I was sent to the best private boarding schools. Then to Oxford for university."

"A classical education, no doubt."

"And here I am."

"Yes, here you are. And what do you do now?" She knew the answer but wanted to hear his cover story.

"Let's not talk about me. I want to hear more about you."

Like how to separate me from my panties? Jana's expression changed. "I can see you coming from a mile away, Mr. Rojas."

"My name is Diego," he said with the soft elegance of a Royal. His eyes locked onto hers. "And because a man finds beauty in a woman, there is something wrong with that?"

"You are only seeing the surface. You don't know me."

"Nor you I," he said. "But what fun would life be if we couldn't discover new people." His hand found his chin. "But your statement sounds like a warning. Is there something I should know about you?" His smile reminded Jana of a Hollywood leading man.

She had a hard time withdrawing from his gaze, but finally looked away. "It's not pretty on the inside."

Another well-dressed man with distinct Latin features walked with briskness toward Rojas then whispered something in his ear.

Who is that? Jana thought.

"Will you excuse me for a moment?" Rojas said with a gentle touch to her hand. "Business calls."

Jana watched the men walk onto the balcony. Rojas was handed a cellphone. *He knows. He knows I'm the one who put his rival in the hospital. Now I'm in this deep.* Jana's right hand began to tremble. *What am I doing?* Her breathing accelerated. Flashbacks of her horrifying ordeal in the cabin with Rafael popped into her vision.

***

From the hillside behind the bar, Stone squinted through the powerful monocular. "Shit, we've got a bogey."

"What?" Cade stammered as he reached for his binoculars. "Is she in danger?"

"Of course she's in danger. She's two feet from Diego Rojas."

"No!" Cade said. "Where's the new guy you're talking about?" Cade searched from one side of the club to the other.

"Hold on," Stone replied. "I know who that is. That's Rojas's intelligence man. Looks like he and Rojas are going out on the balcony."

"I can't see Jana! Where's Jana?"

Stone looked over at Cade.

His expression reminded Cade of his first days working at NSA. He was so green he'd felt like such an idiot.

Stone said, "Christ, you really are a cubicle jockey, aren't you?" He pushed Cade's binoculars a little to the left. "She's right there. Same place she's been sitting."

"Fine. Alright." Cade's breathing settled. "And I'm not a cubicle jockey," he muttered.

"Oh, no?" Stone said.

"I've been in the field before."

"Uh-huh."

"Fine, don't believe me." Cade tried to come up with a real zinger. "Besides, you misused the word."

Without losing focus on Jana, Stone said, "What word?"

"Bogey. A bogey refers to a phantom blip on a radar screen. It originates from an old Scottish word for 'ghost.' You misused the word."

"Oh yeah," Stone said. "You're perfect for fieldwork. It's also a World War II reference to an unidentified aircraft that is presumably hostile."

"Do you know the security guy?"

"Yeah," Stone replied. "More of an intelligence consultant though. His name is Gustavo Moreno."

"Gustavo Moreno?" Cade parroted back. "Why do I know that name?" Cade closed his eyes and began searching his memory for the name that would not come. "Moreno . . . Moreno, now why do I—" His eyes went wide. "Shit, shit, shit," he said as he jammed a hand into his pocket and withdrew his phone.

20

Panic Sets In

In the vast NSA command center, Knuckles saw that it was Cade calling and answered his phone. "Cade. Go."

From the hillside in Antigua, Cade stuttered. "Knuckles, Uncle Bill, get him. We've got . . . there's a problem."

"Well I guess so," Knuckles replied. "Dude, calm down."

Uncle Bill, the grandfatherly section chief, walked to Knuckles's desk with a grin on his face. "Is that Cade? Put him on speaker."

"Yes, sir."

The speaker phone blared. "She's . . . she's . . ."

"Just calm down, Cade," Uncle Bill said as he wiped a few crumbs from his beard. The tiny bits of orange cracker disappeared into the tight-weave carpeting. "Let me guess. Jana's in a bar? Perhaps surrounded herself with drug lords?"

There was a short silence. "How did you know that?" Cade said.

"Come on, buddy," Knuckles said. "We can see the location of your cellphone. It doesn't take a rocket scientist to figure out you're staked out on a hillside, probably surveilling the, let's see, a bar called Touloulou?"

"There's a couple of security cameras inside the bar," Uncle

Bill said. "We hacked them. If you're seeing what we're seeing, she's been talking to Diego Rojas, right?"

"Rojas is bad enough, but it's this new guy—"

"Gustavo Moreno?" Uncle Bill said. "Yeah, that's not good. Been looking for him for a long time."

"Dammit," Cade said, "Why didn't you guys tell me we had eyes inside?"

"Dude," Knuckles said. "What fun would that be? We just wanted to see how long it would take before you called us in a blustery panic." Knuckles handed Bill a five-dollar bill. "And I lost the bet."

"Yeah, hysterical," Cade said. "Moreno, he's the guy that used to work for Pablo Escobar? Do I remember that right?"

"He's the one," Uncle Bill said. "He was head of Colombia's National Intelligence Directorate. We haven't seen him for over a year. I'm impressed you remembered his bio."

"Didn't he used to work on our side?" Cade said. "But then took up with the Medellín Cartel?"

Knuckles jumped in, always eager to assert his knowledge. "Looks like he's changed teams. Our workup says he spent the first ten years of his career at Langley, took his intelligence experience to Colombia's NID, then disappeared."

"How does the CIA have another mole?"

Uncle Bill answered. "He wasn't a mole, Cade. He worked legitimately for the CIA. He resigned and went back to his home country to work intelligence there. It's after that that he decided the pay was better working for a drug lord."

"Whatever," Cade said. "But if Rojas has Moreno working for him now, and Moreno is gathering intelligence for the Los Rastrojos cartel, then that means—"

Uncle Bill interrupted, "That Rojas will likely run a background check on Jana. He certainly already knows that a woman broke that guy from the Oficina de Envigado cartel into pieces last night. What we're hoping, of course, is that this *chance* encounter with her will lead to Rojas trusting her."

"Bill," Cade said, "why are you so calm? If Moreno runs a full bio on Jana, they'll no doubt have her fingerprints. They're going to find out she was FBI. And if they know she used to be a federal agent, they're going to suspect she's working undercover."

"We're prepared for this eventuality, Cade."

"What?" he yelled into the phone.

"For a man with the intelligence-gathering capabilities of Gustavo Moreno, it's not surprising he would be able to find she's a former fed."

"And you're okay with that?"

"No, I'm not," Bill said, "but I'm prepared for it, and so is Jana. Look, the only thing she's going to do tonight is pique the interest of Rojas, right? Our only hope of finding a clue to Kyle's whereabouts is for Jana to get on the inside. We're assuming Rojas will find her identity and Jana will not deny it. In fact, she'll embrace the fact that she was Bureau and threw away her badge. Moreno's background check will confirm she's been living in a tiki hut on the beach ever since, under an assumed identity."

"The story is plausible, Cade," Knuckles added. "It's not unlike the story of Gustavo Moreno himself. He also worked at high levels within the US government, but became disillusioned and left."

Uncle Bill said, "When she gets back to the safe house tonight, you guys go over the story."

Cade rubbed his eyes. "Fine." He exhaled. "I can't believe we're using her as bait."

"Cade?" Uncle Bill said, "Jana is a grown woman of high intelligence, and she's especially loyal to her friends. We're not exactly using her."

"How do you figure?" Cade replied.

"Would you want to be the one who *didn't* tell her Kyle was suspected as missing? If anything happened to Kyle and she could have done something about it, she'd kill the three of us for not telling her. We may be using her as bait, but she knows exactly what she's doing."

"Bill?" Cade said. "Kyle is not *suspected* of being missing. He's missing."

"We're on the same team, Cade. But at this point, Kyle is still assumed to be under deep cover. Unless we have proof he's been abducted, we'll never get authorization for a strike team. I want you to understand the magnitude of what we're talking about here. If we send in a team to extract Kyle, and it turns out he's not been abducted, we'd not only be effectively ruining six months of undercover work, we'd be violating international law. You're not in the United States down there. Antigua is a sovereign nation. It would be viewed as an incursion, and the repercussions on the world stage would be disastrous."

Cade rubbed his eyes. "Fine. But, Bill, when this is over, I'm going to tell *Mrs.* Uncle Bill Tarleton about the secret stash of orange crackers under your desk."

21

An Island Arrival

V. C. Bird International Airport, Pavilion Drive, Osbourn, Antigua.
The man walked up the Jetway and into the terminal like any
other passenger would. He was in his early sixties, but years of
tough living had taken their toll. Such signs of outward wear
are often the result of years of drug and alcohol abuse. But for
this man, it was the result of something different.

For him, the wear and tear showed in two physical areas. First,
there was constant tension in his shoulders, as though he might
need to react at any moment. It was tension that would not
abate, the result of years of being on guard, never knowing what
direction the next attack may come from. And the second was
written in his eyes. They decried a deadness like those carried
by soldiers who had endured a long, intense war. Often referred
to as the "thousand-yard stare," the wartime gaze might come
and go. But this was different. His eyes carried in them crushing
defeat. It was like looking into the soul of a person who had
died inside, yet been forced to carry on.

Across from Gate 14, he stopped and reshouldered his carry-
on then stared out the massive windows onto the tarmac and to
the buildings beyond. It was a bright, clear day and the blueness
of the sky hearkened something from deep within. He withdrew

a photograph from his shirt pocket, inadvertently dropping his American Airlines boarding pass in the process. He stared at the photo of a young woman at what appeared to be a graduation ceremony. She was shaking hands with a much taller man in a business suit. To the man's thinking, her eyes seemed to be staring back at him, as if she was watching his every move. Yet he knew his mission. He knew his goal. He flipped it over and read the words etched in pencil on the back. It said simply "Jana Baker."

22

Back at the Safe House

Safe house, Gray's Farm Main Road, Hawksbill Bay, 1:14 a.m.

"Here she comes," Cade said.

"Will you calm down?" Stone replied. He swept his hair back and flopped onto the couch. "I'm telling you, she's good."

"Good?" Cade barked. "Good at what?"

Stone shook his head. "Man. I wasn't even talking about that. I mean she's good to go. She can take care of herself." He pointed at Cade. "You need to get that shit under control. We've got a man missing."

"I know Kyle's missing!" Cade yelled.

As Jana walked across the crushed coral driveway, Stone jumped up. "Don't bark at me! She can take care of herself. I've seen it. Hell, I trained her. She can almost kick *my* ass. And another thing. She and I had something good going. And if you have a problem with that—"

They both turned and saw Jana in the open doorway.

"What's all this?" she said. Her voice was hoarse.

Both men looked down.

Jana said, "And I thought this was going to be awkward."

"Sorry, babe," Stone said. "It's not important."

Cade stepped toward her. "Do you know who that was with

Rojas tonight?"

"The man that pulled him outside? No."

"His name is Gustavo Moreno. He works intelligence for Rojas."

Jana let the thought play forward. "It was bound to happen. There's no way my background was going to go unnoticed."

"How did you leave things with Rojas?" Stone asked.

"He invited me to his villa."

"Yeah," Cade said. "I bet he did."

"Cade. For God's sake. I'm not going to sleep with him."

Cade shuffled his feet and muttered just under his breath, "At least that's one person you're not going to sleep with."

"What was that?" she blurted.

"Nothing," Cade replied.

"What time?" Stone said.

"Lunch." She glared at Cade. "If I play this right, he's going to trust me."

"How are you going to get him to do that?" Cade said.

"I can take care of myself, you know? I don't need you to come to the rescue."

He walked to her. "Let you handle it? Got it under control?" He reached down and pulled up her hand. "Then why is your hand shaking? The PTSD isn't gone. It never left you, did it?"

She yanked the arm back. "Stay out of my business."

Cade said, "On this op, your business is my business. What you know, I know. What you hear, I hear. I'm in charge."

"You're in charge, huh? I don't work for the government anymore. And I don't work for you. I'm doing this on my own."

Cade's voice rose. "Kyle MacKerron is a CIA agent and this is a government operation."

Jana said, "If this is a *government* operation," the word spat out like spoiled vinegar, "where is the government to save him? You can't even convince people he's missing!" She started to pace. "You've got no support. There should be spec-ops teams crawling this island. The president should be on the phone threatening the Antiguan government. There should be a half dozen F-18s streaking over the interior ministry, just to scare the shit out of them!"

"I told you we had no support when we started this!" Cade yelled back.

Stone jumped between them. "Let's everybody just calm down. We're on the same team here. And all this bickering isn't going to get us closer to finding Kyle."

"I'm going in," she blurted. "I'm going all the way in, with or without support. Kyle is alive." The vibration in her hand intensified and she turned away from Cade. "I have no choice." The periphery of Jana's vision began to blur and her breathing became erratic. "I can handle myself, Cade." She walked into the first bedroom and shut the door behind her. She planted her hands onto the dresser and leaned closer to the mirror. A cold heat flushed across her face and, for just a moment, her knees weakened. She exhaled hard and shut her eyes. But the harder she tried to purge the terrors pinging her psyche, the brighter the terrors became.

She pictured herself back at the cabin, tied to the wooden chair. Rafael leaned over her, the knife in his hand. *Come on, Jana. Get a grip on it. Don't let it pull you down.* But further down she tumbled. Rafael cracked her face with the back of his hand and she tasted salty wetness in her mouth. *Stop it. Stop thinking about it. Think back to the fort. Everything will be okay if you can just get to the fort.* She crushed her eyes closed and thought back to her childhood, to the little path in the woods. She pictured the tall pines, the bright sun gleaming between the branches, and the sight of the ramshackle fort. With Rafael and the cabin fading into the background, in her mind's eye she walked toward the tangled mass of vines and sticks that made up the fort's door and tried to conjure the ever-present smell of fresh earth, jasmine, and pine needles. She took a deep breath. She was in. She was safe. And nothing could hurt her in the fort.

She opened her eyes and looked at herself in the mirror. Her hair and makeup were disheveled, her eyes, weary but not defeated. She stood tall. "Rafael is dead. I killed that son of a bitch. He got what he deserved and he's not going to hurt me anymore."

23

The Highest Bidder

Jana pulled up to the security gate and waited as an armed guard approached. She glanced at the mirror one more time and blew out the jitters. Her long blond hair was smoothed back in an elegant bun and she wore a flowing sarong skirt that blended into the island atmosphere. The guard leaned toward her open window and his eyes glided across her exposed leg all the way up to the hip. *That's right*, she thought. *Get a good look.* He may not have been the person whose attention she sought, but the effect was exactly what she had intended.

"Step out of the car, please," the guard said as he adjusted the shoulder strap on his submachine gun and slid it to his side.

Jana got out and the guard motioned for her to place her arms out wide. He used a handheld wand and waved it up and down her legs and torso. "Think I've got a Glock tucked somewhere?" she said. Her inference was not lost on the guard—her garments were form-fitting and left little to the imagination.

"This isn't a metal detector," he said.

Good thing I'm not wearing a wire, she thought.

Back in her car, she proceeded up the long drive, a manicured entranceway paved in finely crushed pink corral and surrounded by ornate tropical landscaping on all sides. As she crested the small rise, the panoramic view of MorrisBay unfolded before her. Turquoise-blue waters and white-pink sands were common of Antigua's natural beauty, but from the hillside, it was breathtaking.

The estate itself was palatial and sat in beachfront seclusion. The property was on a hilltop but was nestled in somewhat of a valley; there was not another structure in sight. And if one ignored the two armed guards walking the shoreline, the beach itself was completely deserted. Jana pulled the car to a halt in front of the entryway, a set of hand-carved glass-and-teak doors that spanned beneath a massive sandstone archway.

Rojas pulled both doors open and walked out. He wore a loose-fitting button-down shirt and gray linen pants. He took Jana by both hands and held her arms out wide to look at her.

"Your beauty is in parallel to the beauty of this island." There was a refinement in his enunciation. "I am glad you decided to join me. Welcome to my rancho."

As they walked inside, Jana took in the breathtaking view of the bay through the wall of glass that lined the rear side of the home. About a dozen of the huge glass panels had been drawn back, an open-air span of about forty feet. Gentle island breezes carried with them the faint scent of jasmine.

He led her onto a balcony where they sat at a table cloaked in white linen.

He smiled. "I think we both know you lied to me last night."

A wave of jitters raced through Jana's stomach, and although the statement caught her off guard, she did not flinch. "As did you," she replied.

He sat back in his chair. To Jana, it was an acknowledgment that the tables had turned. "You first," he said.

"My name is not Claire."

"No, it is not." His accent was enticing, seductive. "Your name is Jana Baker, and you were formerly an—"

"FBI agent," she said. "Does it surprise you so?" Her hand shook ever so slightly.

"I do not like surprises, Agent Baker."

"Nor do I, Mr. Rojas. But I do not go by that name any longer. You are free to call me Jana or Miss Baker, but the title of agent has come to repulse me." She nodded at him. "I suppose a man of your means ran a background check on me. And what else did you find?"

"I found a short but storied career with the United States government. Quite the little terrorist hunter, weren't you?"

"Perhaps."

"But you seem to have taken up shop with us here on Antigua. Working as a bartender for the last year or so?"

"I'm never going back," Jana said as she stared out into the bay's tranquil waters. "I've had a change of heart, you might say. But let's talk about you. You're not just a successful businessman, are you?"

Silence accentuated a sudden interruption in breeze.

He crossed one leg over the other. "And what makes you say that?"

"I know who you are."

"Yet you still came?"

Jana replied, "That's *why* I came."

He sized her up a moment.

She continued. "Do you think it's an accident that I broke Montes Lima Perez into little pieces?"

Two well-appointed servants walked to the table and placed salads plated on fine china on top of the larger china already on the table.

When they departed, Rojas said, "Are you telling me you targeted the unfortunate Mr. Perez?"

Jana said nothing.

"You did more than break him to pieces, Miss Baker. From what I understand, he will never walk correctly again."

Referring to the gunshot to the groin, Jana said, "That's not the only thing he'll never do again."

"Indeed."

They sat quietly a moment before Rojas said, "I find it hard to trust you, Miss Baker. One doesn't often find a federale from your country defecting."

"Oh no? Yet you employ the services of a Gustavo Moreno. Surely you are familiar with his past. The first ten years of his career were with the CIA, yet you trust him."

"Of course I am aware of Mr. Moreno's past. But I am curious, how do you come to such information?"

A nervousness descended upon her. "I learned a lot in my former life, Mr. Rojas."

He exhaled. "Yet you say you have left that life behind. Convince me."

"Are you of the belief that the US government would send an undercover agent to work in a tiki bar on the beach for a year, just as a cover? Perhaps Mr. Moreno also told you that the FBI, NSA, and CIA have been looking for me that entire time. And do you know why? Because I threw my badge at them and walked away. I changed my identity. I've been off the grid, learning a few things about myself. Things I didn't know, and I've never felt more alive."

"Go on."

"Did Moreno also tell you my former employer wanted to charge me with murder?"

"The shooting death of a man known internationally only as *Rafael*." His Colombian accent was enticing.

"They can go screw themselves," she said. As the breeze picked back up, Jana leaned across the table. "My entire life has been a lie, Mr. Rojas." She allowed her eyes to drift down the open buttons of his shirt. The look was seductive yet her insides were beginning to churn. "I have learned my interests lie elsewhere. I will not serve a self-serving government. An ungrateful lunatic with an appetite that has no end. My path lies on the other side now."

"Does it?"

"Let's just say I have certain talents, and they are available to the highest bidder."

"And if the US government is the highest bidder?"

"Then I will take their money and turn them upside down in the process. I've thought of few other things over the last year than doing just that."

"Retribution is a most dangerous bedfellow, Miss Baker."

"I'm sure Montes Lima Perez would agree with you."

He laughed. "Your intelligence is a wonderful pairing to your beauty. Like this wine." He held up his glass. "A perfect match to the bitter sweetness of the salad. One without the other is good. But when brought together, magic."

They both sipped the deep-red wine.

Rojas said, "I take it the police reports of your arrest are accurate then. The vile Mr. Perez sought to harm you?"

She looked away. "He was not the first."

"A chip on your shoulder, no?"

Jana ignored the statement. "Let me sum it up for you. After I took bullets for my country, stopped two bombings, was abducted and nearly tortured to death, they falsely accused me of murder. So do I have a chip on my shoulder? You're damned right I do. I don't give a shit about your business. My distinct talents are available to the highest bidder."

Rojas looked out into the bay and his eye landed on a seagull. The bird swayed effortlessly in the breeze. Rojas took another sip of wine and leaned toward her. "You caused a lot of damage to Montes Lima Perez. Don't get me wrong, he is a rival and I am glad to have him out of the way. But I don't need high-profile bloodshed like that. Not here. It draws attention." He exhaled. "This is not a game, Miss Baker. If you come to work for me, I demand the highest loyalty."

"I already took out the Oficina de Envigado cartel's top security agent on the island. The cartel may still be here, but I would think you should already know where my loyalties lie."

"I need to quiet Oficina de Envigado. I need the senior-most elements of their cartel to vanish from the island silently. I cannot afford to have local law enforcement or others like the CIA take notice. Are you interested in helping me with my problem?"

Jana smiled but her hand shook harder. She held it in her lap, just out of view. "Money," she said.

His eyes became stern. "Don't worry about that right now. Just tell me how you intend to carry out your assignments."

24

Fishing Tales

The man squinted into the bright Antiguan sun then pulled out his phone and opened a map application. He again removed the photograph and stared into the eyes of Special Agent Jana Baker. The photo had been taken on stage at the FBI training center on the Marine Corps base in Quantico, Virginia. It was her graduation from special agent training. She was shaking the hand of Stephen Latent, the then director of the FBI.

The man studied the map, which indicated a single ping located not far from his position. "Still in the same place," he said to himself, then walked toward Heritage Quay and followed signs to the Nevis Street Pier. "Need to rent a boat," he said to a man on the dock.

The man had weathered ebony skin and was shaded beneath a straw hat. He did not look up. "How big a boat?" His accent was tawny with a distinct island flavor.

"Just need to cruise around. Maybe a twenty-footer."

"Doing some fishing?" the vendor asked.

"Yeah, something like that," the man said as he stared up the coastline.

Twenty minutes later the man turned the key and dual outboard engines roared to life. He let them idle a moment, then threw ropes off the bow and stern and pushed back from the dock. He wedged his phone tightly between the windshield and dashboard so that he could see the map, then propped the photograph next to it. He motored out of the harbor, following the direction of the ping. "Won't be long now," he said as his smile revealed yellowed teeth.

25

Fire in the Belly

Jana stood and walked just beyond Rojas's chair, placed her hands on the balcony's handrail, then stared out at the bay. She gripped the rail tightly so as to obscure the vibrations in her hand. Rojas turned to watch and his gaze did not go unnoticed.

"I want an answer, Miss Baker. I want to know how you intend to carry out assignments such as these. These people would need to simply disappear with no one being the wiser."

Jana grinned. "Already proving my point," she said.

"And what point is that?" He rose and stood beside her.

"Your eyes. When I stood and walked over here, you could not keep your eyes off of me." She turned to him.

"And what is wrong with that? I told you before. My eyes are drawn to beauty."

"How do you think I lured Perez out of the bar and down an abandoned alley?"

Rojas nodded. "There is no room for mistakes, Miss Baker. When a leading member of Oficina de Envigado disappears, there better not be clues lying about or a body for them to find. Or they will find *your* body, and do things to it." The inference was vile, but Jana held her tongue.

"You leave that to me. You'll find I know quite a bit about how to make people disappear. And how to hide a crime scene." She looked into the shimmering waters. "A hundred thousand."

"One hundred thousand dollars is a lot of money, Miss Baker. What makes you think your services are worth that much?"

She leveled eyes at him. "That's half. That's what I take up front. The rest is due upon delivery."

He took a step closer and looked at her chest without embarrassment. It was as though he was at an art gallery admiring a statue. But after a moment, his eyes settled on the three gunshot wounds on her sternum. He raised his hand and ran the backs of his fingers on the centermost one.

A sharp, burning sensation caused Jana to pull back as flashes of Rafael's face popped into her vision. "Hands off," she said with more intensity than she had intended. "I may be on your payroll but I don't do *that* for money. And I never mix business with pleasure. My price is two hundred thousand. Take it or leave it."

"No business with pleasure? What a pity. It is of no concern," he said as he turned and waved his hand dismissively. "I have all I need of beautiful women at my disposal."

There was something in his tone that gave Jana pause. It was as if he was describing a broken cell phone or pair of torn slacks—an object to be thrown away and replaced. A tiny voice whispered from somewhere deep, a place of darkness. *Show her again*, the voice said as pain flared on the scar. *Show her how much like her father she really is.* Flickers of her nightmares popped in her vision, her father's mugshot, the arrest warrant. Her hand shook harder and the edges of her vision began to blur, but she fought back and the voice quieted.

A servant appeared with a platter in his hand and placed two glasses on the table.

"But let us sit and drink."

"And what are we drinking?" Jana said as she eased herself into the chair.

"Guaro. It means *fire water*, a Colombian specialty. Many like Aguardiente Antioqueño, but I prefer this," he said as he held up a small glass of clear liquid and crushed ice, "Aguardiente Del Cauca."

Jana held her shaking hand in her lap and used the other to bring the drink to her lips. To her, it tasted something like delicate vodka, only sweeter.

Rojas said, "Do you know what my men said when I told them to expect your arrival?"

"What?"

"*Ya vienen los tombos.* It means—"

Jana interrupted, "The cops are coming." She shook her head. "After I nearly killed one of your rivals, you still thought I worked for the US government, didn't you?"

"You continue to surprise me, Miss Baker."

"And upon my arrival, you had me swept for listening devices."

"In this line of business, one cannot be too careful."

"Show me the rest of your rancho."

Rojas walked her from room to room and described the history of the expansive property. He concluded the tour on the lowermost level, the immaculately appointed daylight basement, where dozens of wine barrels were stacked in a closed room. "The wine travels here from Colombia and is aged against the coolness of the earth."

"Very impressive," Jana said. "Yet there are two rooms you have not shown me. The first is the room in which most men choose to end the tour."

Rojas grinned. "You made your feelings about the master

113

bedroom crystal clear. And the other?"

Jana pointed at a steel door off to one side. It appeared to lead to a hallway.

"Ah, well, one can't reveal all one's secrets."

"Something to hide, Mr. Rojas?" She grinned.

Rojas ignored the assertion. As they ascended the wide, brightly lit glass staircase to the first floor, Rojas said, "I have many information sources, Miss Baker, and I will be passing certain pieces of information to you. Information about your assignments." He placed a hand on her arm. "You have earned your way into my rancho. The question remains whether you have what it takes to stay."

She started back up the stairs then turned and looked down at him. His eyes were on her backside.

He laughed. "Very well played. You continue to surprise me. Please, don't ever lose that quality."

"And you will tell me the source of your information. I do not accept facts blindly," she said. Rojas sized her up, but she continued. "I know it takes a lot of intel to do what you do, but that doesn't mean I trust it." Once upstairs, Rojas led her to the front door. Gustavo Moreno stared at her from down a long hallway. His arms were crossed. "And I do not trust that man," she said.

Rojas glanced at Moreno. "The source of this information is mine and mine alone."

"This is not a negotiation," she said.

"You will find what you seek already waiting for you on the front seat of your car. We can discuss the source later. I want this to happen quickly, Miss Baker. *Time* is of the essence. Your assignment must be carried out tonight."

She walked outside, down the steps, and onto the crushed

coral of the drive. She got in her car and thought about the one thing she had not expected: Rojas was on a timetable. Prior to entering the estate, she had felt incredible pressure to find Kyle and find him quickly. But now she suspected Rojas had another agenda, and the thought gave her pause.

She picked up a large manila envelope, then opened it. Four thick bundles of brand-new one-hundred-dollar bills were inside along with a dossier. The dossier looked identical to an FBI file. It was made of the same file-folder material she was accustomed to seeing in government reports. When she opened it, she saw that it appeared to be identical to a government intelligence service report. A glossy black-and-white photo of a man Jana knew to be her target was affixed to the left panel. On the right were several sheets of background material, all neatly bound across the top with bendable metal strips.

Where did they get this? she thought. *This target is obviously a member of Oficina de Envigado.*

Just before she started the engine, she heard a sound about twenty feet behind her, like that of someone pounding a glass window. When she turned, she saw a woman at a window. Both of her hands were splayed against the glass and a look of terror painted her wide eyes. Her mouth opened into a scream and Jana's heart rate accelerated.

A hand jammed across the woman's mouth and yanked her away. She was gone. A feeling of rage erupted in Jana's gut and she reached for the door handle. But an unfamiliar Latin voice called out from the front steps, "So glad you could join us today, Miss Baker." She turned to see Gustavo Moreno pointing toward the front gate. "It is time for you to depart our company." Two armed guards flanked him.

Jana knew the woman was being abused and the rage that had

started in her gut spread. She started the car, then shifted it into gear.

As she drove away, she tried to suppress thoughts of the woman but could not. She passed the entrance, where the guard had already opened the gate. He was standing, waiting for her to pass. The little grin on his face sickened her.

Moreno may have placed a tracking device on my car, she thought. *I can't go back to the safe house.*

26

Back to the Bungalow

Side Hill Bay.

Jana drove in the direction of her tiny beachside bungalow. If Gustavo Moreno had a detailed dossier on her, they certainly already knew where she lived, so driving there wouldn't be a problem. She wove her way down Gray's Farm Main Road and turned left toward the water on PerryBay, then turned up the dirt road before stopping at Little Orleans, a dilapidated market often frequented by locals. The sun-beaten paint had once been the colors of peach, pink, and teal. The store blended into the surrounding village with ease. She hopped out and picked up the one working pay phone and dialed Stone.

"Hey," she said. "I'm out."

"Thank God," Stone replied.

"I'm at Little Canton. Why don't you come pick me up at my place?"

"On the way."

"And make sure you're not tailed."

Stone laughed. "It wasn't too long ago that you were *my* student."

"I knew plenty before coming to you, jackass," she said with a sarcastic tone.

Her one-room bungalow was nestled in a halo of banana and coconut trees. It was more of a shanty than anything else. But the tropical colors that adorned the interior helped alleviate the notion of poverty in the surrounding area. The house, if one could call it that, sat within fifty yards of the water on a private ranch owned by a British family. The rent was beyond cheap. When Jana had arrived on the island the year prior, she'd sought out a simple existence, and simple was what she'd gotten. Compared to the average islander, Jana had money, so furnishing the sparse space had come easily.

Ten minutes later, Stone's Jeep arrived and she hopped in. "You didn't go to Rojas's place dressed like that, did you?" Stone said as he pulled away.

"No, I just changed," she said. "Kyle is alive."

He locked the brakes and the Jeep skidded as a plume of dust rose from underneath. "You saw him? Why didn't you say so? If we'd have known that, we would have put the DEA team on standby."

"I didn't see him."

He slowly accelerated. "Then why do you—"

"A hunch."

"NSA isn't going to order an incursion on a hunch."

"He's there. I'm telling you."

"Because of a hunch?"

"Perhaps you're not aware, but a lot of crimes are solved because of hunches."

"Yeah," he chided, "but a lot are solved by actual evidence."

They pulled up to the safe house and walked inside.

"Cade," she said, "what makes you think the safe house isn't being surveilled?"

"Nice to see you too," he said as he looked up from his laptop.

He turned back to the monitor, where he was in the middle of a secure video conference with NSA. "Hold on, Uncle Bill. She just walked in."

Then from the laptop speakers, Jana heard voices. "Yeah," the voice said, "we know. We could see her coming up the road."

Jana leaned over the monitor. "Hey, Uncle Bill. What do you mean you could see me? You have monitors on the road?"

On the video, Knuckles leaned in. "They're called satellites, Agent Baker. We're watching."

"Knuckles," Jana said as she stood tall and crossed her arms, "call me agent one more time and I'll . . ."

"Yes, ma'am," he said.

Cade said, "And that answers your question about why we know we're not being surveilled here. Knuckles has a team with eyes in the sky at all times. We'll know if anyone comes within a quarter mile."

"They use kilometers down there, Cade," Knuckles said.

"Know-it-all," came Cade's reply.

Stone shook his head. "Jana thinks Kyle's still alive."

"What evidence do we have?" Uncle Bill said as he drew a hand to his cavernous beard.

"None," Stone said.

"He's alive," Jana said. "How do you think we got this?" She held up the dossier. "It's a complete workup of one of the members of Oficina de Envigado. They want me to take out a man named Carlos Gaviria."

"That name would have come from Gustavo Moreno," Knuckles said. "We know he's a heavy hitter in the intelligence community."

Jana shook her head. "Not where did the background information come from, where did the *name* come from in the first place." She looked at the others. "None of you geniuses know, do you?" She was met with silence. "Rojas wants to remove Oficina de Envigado from the island, but these cartels have been doing business like this for decades. They know what they're doing."

Bill said, "What are you getting at?"

Jana said, "Even Gustavo Moreno would have a hard time finding out who was on the island from Oficina de Envigado. He would need to get that information somewhere."

On the video monitor, Uncle Bill leaned back in his chair. His fingers buried themselves deep into his hair, which had become more salt than pepper. "Kyle. Kyle was interrogated and that's where they got the name Carlos Gaviria."

"Finally," Jana said.

"Oh, come on," Cade said. "I don't buy the fact that Moreno wouldn't have known who from Oficina de Envigado was on the island. It's his job to know stuff like that."

Stone put a hand on Cade's shoulder. "Spent a lot of time working as a DEA Agent, have we?"

"Well, no, but—"

Stone continued. "Spent much time on the front lines? Making contacts? Doing undercover drug buys? In the line of fire, perhaps? Penetrating into the upper echelons of a drug ring?"

"No, but—"

"Believe me," Stone said, "It's a lot harder than you think. These people don't just show up on an island and announce themselves. They come in quietly, under false identities. The whole thing happens slowly. The quality of the passports is unbelievable. Then, when the entire crew is assembled, they open up shop in perfect anonymity."

"Run a bio on that name," Uncle Bill said to Knuckles.

Knuckles smiled. "It's already up, sir," he said, pointing to screen number four. "Carlos Ochoa Gaviria, he's the son of the commander of the MAS."

"Shit," Uncle Bill muttered.

"What's the MAS?" Cade asked.

Knuckles was all too happy to assist. "The Muerte a Secuestradores. It was a paramilitary organization. Started out as security to stabilize the region. In those days, it was comprised of members of the Medellín Cartel, the Colombian military, the Colombian legislature, small industrialists, some wealthy cattle ranchers, and even the Texas Petroleum."

Jana said, "Texas Petroleum? A US company? What the hell is a US company doing involved with the drug cartels?"

Uncle Bill replied. "Cocaine had just become a bigger export than coffee. It takes a lot of land and workers to produce that much product. And locals were being attacked from all sides. The MAS was formed to fight off guerrillas who were trying to either redistribute their lands, kidnap the landowners, or extort money. Companies like Texas Petroleum needed the region to be stable."

"But the MAS changed its charter, didn't it?" Cade said.

Knuckles said, "It became an arm of the Medellín Cartel. They did enforcement, if you know what I mean. Stability of the region was no longer a problem. Anyone that got in the cartel's way was dealt with."

"Okay," Jana said, "So my target, Carlos Gaviria, was the leader's son. So what?"

"Remember," Uncle Bill replied, "we're talking about Colombia in the early '80s. As the son, he would have gone with his father. He would have been witness to dozens or hundreds of killings. He was raised in that environment."

"Yeah," Cade said, "wouldn't doubt if he participated in some.

Making a ruthless guy like that disappear isn't going to be easy."

Jana turned her back. "Who says he has to just disappear?"

"What was that, Jana?" Uncle Bill said.

"She said," Cade replied, "why does he have to just disappear? You don't mean that, do you, Jana?"

"I'm getting Kyle out of there. I don't care what it takes."

Cade stood. "You can't possibly mean you would be willing to commit murder."

Jana's eyes were like stone.

Uncle Bill spoke next. "If your grandfather was standing next to you, you wouldn't have said that, Jana."

"It wouldn't be murder," she said.

"Oh no?" Cade said. "And what would you call it?"

"Someone getting what they deserved," she said.

There was venom in Uncle Bill's voice this time. "There will be no assassinations on my watch. The subject is closed. Now drop it." It was the first time any of them had seen the typically stoic man become angry. "Besides, we have more information," Uncle Bill said. "Tell them, Knuckles,"

"Tell us what?" Cade said.

Knuckles stood. He was in his element now. "You won't believe what we found in Kyle's CIA file."

27

Kyle's CIA File

"What's in Kyle's CIA file?" Jana asked.

Knuckles replied, "They've obfuscated his federal identity."

"What does—"

"They've falsified his file," Knuckles said. He loved being the one who knew something others didn't.

"I know what it means," Jana said. "I was going to ask, what does it say?"

Uncle Bill said, "They've got him set up as if he's a DEA agent."

Cade stood. "Why would they do that? Do they want to get him killed?"

Jana turned and took a few steps as she processed the information. "They don't want to get him killed, they want to save his life."

"That's right," Uncle Bill said. "And the data log shows this new identity went into the system four days ago."

"That's about the time Kyle disappeared."

"Makes sense," Jana said. "If Kyle was undercover investigating a drug connection, and he missed his check-in, CIA might have assumed he'd been compromised." She turned to Cade who was

123

still catching up. "I told you. Rojas got the name of my first assignment from Kyle. And the reason he knew Kyle would have that kind of information is because Gustavo Moreno ran Kyle's background."

Cade closed his eyes. "And found he was DEA. So now we know he's alive."

"Bill," Jana said, "You've got to authorize it. You've got to send a team in here to get him out."

"Tried that already," Uncle Bill replied. "It's more complicated than that."

"Dammit, Bill!" Jana said, "How complicated can it be? Kyle is being held by a drug lord and we've got to get him out."

"Jana," Bill said, "I just got off a call with the national security advisor. I got stonewalled."

"Politics," Stone said as he shook his head.

Bill continued. "Jana, I believe you. But that isn't enough. Something big is about to happen and I have no idea what it is. No one is going to upset the balance."

Jana's face began to pale. "Bill, I'm not going to sit here and let Kyle die. I don't give a shit what the political stakes are." Her breathing accelerated.

"You alright, Jana?" Cade said.

She walked toward the monitor and leaned in. "I'm not leaving him, Bill. I'm not leaving him."

Cade took her by the shoulders and eased her into a chair.

"I'm on your side, Jana," Bill said. His voice was calm, reassuring. "I am. But there's nothing I can do. My hands are tied."

There was a certain anger in her tone. "Don't you do that, Bill," she replied. "He's one of us. This is Kyle we're talking about."

Bill looked away. After a moment, he spoke. "I know who

we're talking about. Kyle is family to me."

Jana's jaw muscles tightened. "I'll do this alone if I have to," she said. "But it won't look like a surgical team went in and pulled him out carefully. It'll look like a damn car bomb went off."

Bill squinted into the monitor. "Something happened, didn't it? Something else happened when you went to see Rojas."

The woman at the estate screaming from behind plate glass flashed in Jana's vision, but she said nothing.

Stone said, "Bill, we're going to have to access the teams regardless."

"Why is that?"

"Jana's been hired by Rojas to take out the head of Oficina de Envigado. She can't go murder the guy. We have to activate an extreme rendition protocol. Jana will lure him somewhere private, and the team will sweep in and take him."

But, from behind Uncle Bill and Knuckles, a man in the NSACommandCenter walked forward. He wore a dark suit and tie. "There will be no rendition," the man said as Uncle Bill turned to him.

Jana squinted at the monitor. "Son of a bitch."

28

CIA Spoilage

"Who the hell is that guy?" Stone said, but Jana and Cade knew.

"Nothing like another Virginia farm boy to brighten a girl's day," Jana said as she crossed her arms.

The man's hands remained in his suit pockets, as if he were talking to friends at a wedding reception. "There will be no rendition team. Nor will there be a team to extract Agent MacKerron."

Stone threw his arms into the air and yelled at the monitor. "Who the hell do you think you are?"

"And you, Agent Baker," the man said, "You will stand down. There will be no bombs going off inside the estate of Diego Rojas."

Uncle Bill removed his glasses and rubbed his eyes. "Stone, let me introduce you to Lawrence Wallace, the recently appointed CIA assistant deputy director, National Clandestine Service, CounterTerrorismCenter."

"This is a CIA agenda?" Jana barked. "You're the one stonewalling this? What could be so important you'd leave a man behind? What is it this time? CIA wants to run coke for the Antiguan rebels? Sell arms to Al Qaeda so they can fight ISIS? Launder money for the—"

"That's enough, Jana," Bill said.

Lawrence Wallace's smile was polite yet condescending. "I'll not grace your comments with a reply, Agent Baker."

"I'm not an agent anymore. If you call me that one more time," Jana said behind a pointed finger, "I'm going to fly back there and rip out your Adam's apple and hand it to you."

Wallace smiled. "A pleasure to see you, as always." He walked out of view of the monitor.

Stone glanced at the others. "What the hell just happened?"

Bill replied. "It's like I said. There's something else at play here, and I intend to find out what it is."

29

Best Laid Plans

NSA War Room, Fort Meade, Maryland.

"Sir?" Knuckles said as he burst into the room. Uncle Bill stopped midsentence. He and a dozen other men, all military commanders seated around the long, oval table looked up. "Oh, sorry."

Bill exhaled. "Well that's okay, son. It's not as though this briefing is about national security matters. In fact, we were discussing knitting patterns."

Knuckles swallowed. "Yes, sir. There's something you should see. Right now, sir."

Uncle Bill said, "Won't you excuse me, gentlemen? Duty calls."

Bill kept pace as Knuckles speed-walked into the vast command center. "It's here, sir, on monitor seven," he said as he pointed to one of the myriad of oversized computer screen suspended from the high ceiling. "There, in the center of the screen."

"What am I looking at?"

"Laura?" Knuckles said to a woman across the room. "Can you zoom that up a bit?"

As the satellite view on the monitor zoomed closer, it revealed a small boat about seventy-five yards from a shoreline.

"Nice Whaler," Bill said, "I don't suppose you called me out of a meeting with the joint chiefs to show me your vacation plans."

"No, sir," Knuckles replied. "These images are coming from one of our spy sats, the NROL-55, codenamed *Intruder*. It's in geosynchronous orbit with a cover mission of ELINT or ocean surveillance, but we repurposed it to—"

"Knuckles!"

"Yes, sir. We're looking at Hawksbill Bay, Antigua."

"And?"

"Laura? A little closer please." The image on the monitor zoomed until it appeared to hover about fifty feet above the craft. The resolution was impeccable. The bright white of the boat's deck shone back at them as it bobbed in the calm surf. The sole occupant, a male, raised a long set of binoculars to his face. "He's doing surveillance, sir."

"Wait, Hawksbill Bay? Our safe house?"

Knuckles said nothing but the inference was well understood.

"Christ. Knuckles, get me a secure uplink to the safe house."

"That's just it, sir. I've tried that already."

"No joy?"

"It wouldn't even go through. The comlink is offline."

"That's impossible," Uncle Bill said as he walked to a laptop station and sat.

"Right here," Knuckles said as he pointed to the computer monitor. "I tried the satellite three times, and then I ran this. Take a look at the diagnostics."

Bill studied the readout. "The satellite is there alright. And look, it's operational." Bill studied the information further. "All systems are online. And we were on a call with the safe house, what, an hour ago? What's the problem?" But then Bill sat upright and slammed a fist onto the desk. "That son of a bitch."

"Sir?"

Bill stood. "Those pricks have cut the uplink."

"Who? Who cut the uplink?"

"No one outside the highest levels of our intelligence services have access to it." He picked up a phone, dialed a number, and said to Knuckles, "They've cut the uplink and now we've got a rogue on our hands." He spoke into the receiver. "Get me DEA Special Response Team at Point Udall, US Virgin Islands." He waited a moment as his call was connected. "Commander? This is William Tarlton, NSA clearance code kilo alpha one one niner six zulu eight. I've got a priority target on Antigua. Put your assets in the air and expedite. You'll receive routing and an assignment package in flight. This is not a drill, Commander. Affirm?" He hung up the phone and looked at Knuckles.

"I still don't understand who cut the uplink." But the moment the question left his lips Knuckles knew the answer. "Oh my God."

30

A Rogue

NSA Command Center.

"CIA?" Knuckles said. "But why would CIA cut our comsat?"

Bill was way ahead of him. "Knuckles, I need a flight plan for DEA and our estimated time to intercept."

"Sir, we're really sending a team in? We're going to need authorization from the president to invade Antigua, aren't we?"

"You let me worry about that. And it's not an invasion, it's one team."

"Try telling that to the Antiguan foreign ministry." The kid banged away on his laptop. His keystrokes sounded like gunshots. "It's two hundred and twenty nautical miles from the DEA station on the US Virgin Islands to Antigua," Knuckles said as he began talking to himself. "Let's see, DEA has a Gulfstream IV down there, so . . . max V-speed is 0.88 Mach, which is, what is that? About 488 knots, right? But I doubt they push it quite that hard, so, say 480 knots, give or take. That's 552 miles per hour, which puts them at V. C. Bird International in Antigua about forty minutes after takeoff, depending on how fast they get to max. Plus we'd have to account for the time it takes them get to the plane in the first place—"

"That's way too much time," Uncle Bill said. "If the rogue in that boat is a spotter, he could have already called whichever damned cartel he works for, and they could have people on the way. Call Cade's cellphone."

"But, sir," Knuckles said, "It's not a secure line."

"I don't give a damn. I want them out of that place right now." Bill began to pace. "That asshole could be anybody."

"The other possibility—" Knuckles offered before again being cut off.

"What if he's working for Rojas?" Uncle Bill continued, oblivious to the boy. "That would mean Cade and Stone would be compromised, not to mention the fact that Jana's cover would be blown for sure. You still got eyes on him?"

"Of course we do, sir. But there's one thing you're not—"

"If we have to do a hot extraction, there's going to be hell to pay, but at this point, I really don't give a shit."

"Sir!"

"What is it, Knuckles. Dammit, son, spit it out."

"What if the DEA strike team grabs the guy in the boat, but it turns out he's CIA?"

31

Unintended

Safe house, Gray's Farm Main Road, Hawksbill Bay.

Stone pushed his shades onto the top of his head and flopped onto the couch. "This is a real hassle. Who is that prick?"

Jana had had enough and disappeared into a back bedroom.

Cade said, "Lawrence Wallace is a company man. I've had dealings with him in the past."

"Yeah?" Stone said. "Without a rendition team, how are we supposed to make Jana's assignment, Carlos Gaviria, disappear? I mean, the three of us? It can't be done."

"I thought you were a hotshot Army Delta Force operator, no less."

"I'm serious. You stopped and thought about what it takes to pull off something like this? With a rendition team, it wouldn't be so bad. Jana could lure the guy into a private room where he thinks he's going to get a little ooh-la-la with her. They'd pop in and jam a needle in his neck so fast, by the time he felt the sting, the drug would have him halfway to unconsciousness. Then the team would whisk him into a van and he'd be gone. Next stop, Guantanamo Bay. But this . . ." Stone shook his head.

Cade shrugged. "I don't know. It's got to be something we can do ourselves."

"How long have you been sitting in that cubicle?"

"Hey, Stone, screw you," Cade said. "I've been in the field before."

"Good, because we're going to need it. But you're not thinking this through. Gaviria won't be alone. He's the Oficina de Envigado's number one on the island. He'll have protection. And by *protection*, I don't mean he'll be carrying a condom."

Jana stood in her bedroom doorway and said, "Two ex-boyfriends talking about condoms. Can this get any worse?"

Stone stood. "Jana, you don't look so good."

"Thanks a lot," she replied. "Cade, I had to rush out of my bungalow. You have any Advil?"

"Sure. My stuff's in the other bedroom. Outside pocket of my bag."

She disappeared into Cade's room.

Stone walked closer and lowered his voice. "It's getting worse."

"I know it is."

"No, man. I mean, I've been with her for close to a year and I've never seen it this bad."

"She didn't show signs of PTSD before?"

"Sure she did. It's just that she had better control of it. But this, it's like she's going to blow at any second. You can see it in her eyes."

"You some kind of psychological expert?" Cade's assertion was condescending.

"Happens to a lot of guys. I've seen it. We'd come back from a long deployment. It's a tough thing to cope with. The human being is not meant to handle a war zone. What happened to her, anyway?"

Cade crossed his arms and squinted. "You were with her a

year and she never told you? Doesn't sound like you had much of a relationship."

"Kiss my ass. She left *you*, as I recall. And that had nothing to do with me. You know, I'm tired of your crap. When I met her, she was eager to learn. So I taught her. She would never quit, and that's when I knew. She was driven by something she'd been through. Now what was it?"

"If she didn't tell you, I'm sure as hell not going to."

"I'm not the enemy, Cade. We're on the same team, if you hadn't noticed."

"I don't have time for this," Cade said. He looked at the laptop. "And why hasn't NSA called in again?"

Stone looked at his watch. "Maybe they're busy."

"Uncle Bill is the best there is. He doesn't get *busy*." Cade sat at the laptop and clicked a few keys. He squinted at the monitor. "What the hell?"

Stone leaned in. "What's wrong?"

"The satellite," Cade said as he pointed to a tiny icon of a spinning globe in the upper-right corner of the screen. The globe was dark.

"What about it?"

"When the connection is hot, the globe is bright green. It's like it's not there. Shit, we've lost connection."

"Well," Stone said, "if it's anything like Wi-Fi—"

"It's *nothing* like Wi-Fi. A stable connection like that doesn't just drop. It's in geosynchronous orbit. The satellite stays in the same position at all times. And it's not like we're mobile, or there's interference from a storm system. Let me run diagnostics."

"You bite my head off like that again, and you and me are going to have a problem. Geosynchronous orbit. I'll show you geosynchronous orbit."

"Hey, Delta Force boy, you just stick to your side of the mission, I'll stick to mine." Cade then muttered something under his breath.

"What was that?"

"I said, you wouldn't know your Wi-Fi from your Bluetooth from your BGAN from your VSAT."

"What a pencil neck. Think you know your shit, do you? Let me ask you a question. In an M84 flashbang, is the pyrotechnic charge a subsonic deflagration or a supersonic detonation? No? What's the muzzle velocity and max range of the .338 Lapua Magnum when fired from an M24A3 Sniper Weapon System?" Stone waited but Cade just looked at him. "Yeah, you know jack shit."

Cade squared off in front of Stone, his jealousy and anger having gotten the best of him. Then from the back bedroom, Jana yelled, "What is this?" The men turned to find her standing in the doorway.

Stone said, "Nothing, babe. Just a gentleman's disagreement."

Her eyes were locked on Cade. "I said, what is this?" In one hand she held a box of candy. In the other, a stack of standard-sized envelopes bound together with rubber bands. The bundle was about four inches thick.

Cade's mouth dropped open.

Jana marched up to him and shoved him into the chair. "Speak."

"Uh, those?" he said. "I was going to tell you about those."

"When?" she barked. "This isn't just a box of candy. This is marzipan. You know I love these. You know I used to get them when I was a kid. What did you think? That because you brought me marzipan, it was going to bring up all those memories, and

136

we were going to be a couple again?"

He sat stunned.

"And these?" She held out the stack of letters. "These are letters from my father! When were you going to tell me about these?" She tore into the stack. "And look at them. From the postmark, he's been writing me letters for the last nine months. And I'm just now finding out about these?"

Cade stuttered but then his voice turned. "You were gone. You disappeared, remember? You left. Stopped paying rent on your apartment, no notice of where you were going or when you might come back. What did you think would happen to your mail?"

"I didn't give a shit what might happen to my mail or the lease on the apartment or any of it."

"Then stop screaming at me about a stack of letters from your father. You never told me you were in touch with him in the first place."

Stone said, "Wait, why wouldn't she be in touch with her father?"

A salty silence permeated the space.

Cade finally replied, "Because he's been in the federal pen her whole life."

32

US Code Section 793

Safe house, Gray's Farm Main Road, Hawksbill Bay.

Jana threw the box of candy to the ground and her jaw muscles flexed. "I'm not mad at you for collecting my mail. What I want to know is why did you bring these letters here? What makes you think I have any interest in that man? He's dead to me. He's been dead my whole life! But wait a minute," she said as she thumbed through the envelopes. "These are all opened. You've been reading them, haven't you?"

"FBI has been reading your mail since you disappeared. I told you before, you killed the most-wanted terrorist in the world and that puts you in danger."

"Oh," Jana replied, "*the FBI* has been reading them. What about you?"

Cade looked at his feet. "No one knew what to do with your mail, so I've been collecting it."

But Jana was fixated. "Yeah? Just what I thought. Did you share these around the office? Everybody get a good laugh? Ha ha. *Agent* Baker's dad is in the joint!"

"It's not like that," Cade said.

Stone interrupted. "Hey, I don't mean to jump in the middle

of something, but your father is in the pen? What did he do?"

Jana's face froze. "US Code, section 793," she said.

Stone thought for a moment. "793? But that's . . . espionage."

"Yes," Jana replied. "My father committed treason against the United States." Her lower lip quivered but she recovered quickly. "I was two years old. They told me he'd died, cancer. As an adult, I found out the truth."

"Jesus," Stone said.

"And Cade here thinks bringing me marzipan and these letters is going to, what? Get me to open up? Find my roots and all that crap?" She moved to within an inch of his face. "You think this is going to change me back into the girl you used to know? What a bunch of psychobabble bullshit!" She threw the letters to his feet.

"Kelly Everson—"

"You talked to Kelly?" Jana blurted. "About me? What gives you the right?"

Stone said, "Who's Kelly Everson?"

"Headshrinker," Cade replied. "Counseled Jana through the PTSD. Yes, of course I talked to Kelly. We all did. And she feels—"

"Don't talk to me about what she feels. I love Kelly, but I don't want to hear it. Get it through your head. I'm not going back. I'm never going back." Jana walked into her bedroom and slammed the door behind her.

Stone looked at the mass of envelopes at Cade's feet and the candies spread across the floor. He said, "Well, that went well. Good job."

33

Of Rogues and Danger

Safe house, Gray's Farm Main Road, Hawksbill Bay.

Cade collected the envelopes and candies and dropped them onto the desk next to his laptop. He studied the monitor again and shook his head. "Where is that satellite?" His cellphone buzzed. "Cade Williams?"

"Cade," Knuckles said. "Hold on, here's Uncle—"

Uncle Bill came on the phone. "Cade, we've got a problem with the satellite."

"No kidding. I can't make a connection. I'm going to reposition the NROL-55 to see if I can get a better signal."

"That won't help. The uplink has been cut, purposely."

"Bill, what are you talking about?"

"Don't worry about that right now. We don't have much time." Bill was almost speed-talking. "There's a spotter on your twelve o'clock. You've got to get—"

The phone call clipped into silence. Cade pressed it against his ear. "Bill? You still there?" The only thing he could hear was silence. No background noise, no shuffling feet, no breathing. He looked at the phone. The call was dead. "What the hell?"

"What is it?"

"I don't know. The call dropped." Cade was still staring at it. "And now I've got no cell signal."

"No signal? Are you sure?"

"Bill was saying . . ."

"Saying what?"

"God, he was talking so fast. I don't know. Twelve o'clock?" Cade looked at his watch.

"What else did he say?"

"Why would my cell be dead? What? Oh, he said something about a spotter."

"A spotter?" Stone said as he turned and looked out the large windows. "Wait, he said twelve o'clock?"

"Yes."

"Good God, Cade," Stone rushed outside and opened the trunk of his Jeep. He pulled out a large case and brought it in.

"What are you doing?"

Stone flipped the latches on the case and opened it. Inside was an automatic weapon tucked neatly into hardened foam. "Jana?" he yelled. "We've got to bug out, right now!"

"Why do we have to leave?" Cade said.

Stone removed the HK 416 carbine, jammed a magazine into the weapon and charged a round. "Commo is out, right?" Stone said as he grabbed extra magazines and stuffed them into his beltline.

"Commo?"

"Communications equipment. You lost the secure comlink, and now your cellphone, and Bill mentions twelve o'clock and a spotter?"

"Right, but—"

"Look out the window, nimrod. At our twelve o'clock. Guy in a twenty-foot Whaler with a pair of binoculars."

"What?"

Jana ran into the room and Stone handed her a Glock. She took it from him and checked to ensure a round was in the chamber. It was as if she was on autopilot.

"We're going out the back," Stone said.

Without another word, the three went into Jana's room. Stone threw the window up. They climbed out and disappeared into the dense tropical foliage.

34

Orders Countermanded

NSA Command Center.

Knuckles ran to Uncle Bill, who was nose-first in a laptop monitor. Bill looked at the boy. "What?" Bill said.

"DEA Special Ops, sir. Something's wrong."

"The flight? What happened?"

"They went wheels up sixteen minutes ago, but they just turned back."

"Turned back? What for? Mechanical? Get me the commander."

Knuckles scrambled to put on a headset. He pecked away at his laptop, then said, "Commander Brigham? Stand by for NSA, William Tarleton."

Bill took the headset. "Special Agent Brigham, radar track shows you've turned due west."

A crackle across the headset initiated the reply from the DEA commander. The plane's engines roared in the background. "Sir, just received the abort command. We are standing down."

"Abort command? I didn't authorize any . . ." But Bill stopped a moment. "From where did the order originate?" Though he had his suspicions.

"Not at liberty to say, sir."

Uncle Bill covered the mic. "Son of a bitch!" He then said to the commander, "Roger that. This is NSA, out." He turned to Knuckles. "Wallace must have found out I ordered DEA onto the scene. CIA has countermanded my orders."

"Sir, the cellphones of Cade, Jana, and the contractor, John Stone, have all been cut. We have no way to reach them." The kid began to look frantic. "Are you telling me CIA cut all our comms with our own team?"

"Damn right that's what I'm saying."

"Uncle Bill, they're down there all alone, with no support. What are our options? Can we call local authorities?"

"Can't risk it. It wouldn't be uncommon for one or both of the cartels to have penetrated the police forces there. We'd be giving them away. No, we've got to pray that our message got through."

Knuckles took his laptop and began to walk away.

Bill said, "Think up a way we can raise them."

35

The Approach

Jana held the Glock and pushed Cade between her and Stone.

"Why do you keep looking behind us?" Cade said to her.

"Checking our six, dumbass."

"Quiet," Stone said. "Both of you." He held the carbine forward and led them out the back of the property through the tropical foliage, a mixed thicket of banana, jumbie soursop, and apra trees. They moved away from the house and toward the unpaved road until Stone held up a fist, the signal to stop. They took cover in the dense undergrowth and looked in the direction of the boat.

"Who is that?" Jana said.

Stone replied, "I don't know, but this can't be good."

"How much ammo you got?" Jana said.

"A thirty-round mag and two in reserve," Stone said. "Yours is full. Sixteen plus one in the pipe."

They scanned the surrounding area, then focused on the boat and its sole occupant. "The Glock 34 holds seventeen in the mag, not sixteen," Jana said.

Stone shook his head. "Starting to regret I trained you, Baker."

Cade said, "Sixteen rounds, seventeen rounds. Does it really matter? Can we focus on the issue here? Like, who is that asshole and why is he watching us?"

"I can think of a couple of possibilities," Stone said, "and none of them are good. We're going to have to get out of here."

"Wait!" Jana said. "Look."

The man put down the binoculars and threw a second anchor into the water. The first was off the bow, and this one, thrown off the stern, would serve to stabilize the boat.

"He's staying for a while, that's for sure," Stone said.

The man secured the line tightly then slid his legs over the railing and dropped into the deep turquoise water.

"Are we sure this has anything to do with us?" Cade said. "Guy could be just a tourist out for a swim."

"A tourist with a pair of Steiner binoculars trained straight onto our safe house? We lose commo and all three of our cellphones go dead? Simultaneously? Bullshit. He's a spotter and we've been made. The cartel knows we're here. The only question is, which one."

"Agreed," Jana said. "But look, he's swimming to shore."

"I say we get out of here," Cade said.

"No," Jana replied. "Let's see who it is."

They watched as the man came out of the water onto the beach. He removed his T-shirt and wrung it out.

"He's not carrying a weapon," Stone said, though he held his rifle on the man.

"He's coming this way," Jana said. "Christ, he's walking right toward the house!"

36

To Thwart an Attack

To Thwart an Attack

The man walked straight for the safe house as the trio watched. He walked up the drive to the Jeep and paused as he looked inside. He walked farther and his footsteps crunched into the crushed coral. When he got to the house, he peered into the bay window with his hands around his eyes.

"What does he think he's doing?" Jana said as she again scanned the area behind them. Her eyes were in constant motion.

"Looking for us," Stone replied. He thumbed the safety on his carbine into the off position.

The man walked to another window and looked inside.

"Okay, here's how this is going to go down," Stone said. "I'm going to sneak up there and take him down. Jana, keep an eye on our six. If he's got a crew on the way, they could roll in any second. If he gives me a fight, I'm going to knock his ass out. Cade, if anything happens—" He stopped. "Jana where are you going?"

"Watch and learn," she said before quietly pushing through the undergrowth and toward the man.

"Jana!" Cade whispered.

"I've created a monster," Stone said as he watched Jana approach the subject from behind. He turned and looked down the unpaved road to ensure an attack was not coming.

"Stop her!" Cade said.

"Relax, cubicle-boy. Watch this."

Jana was within four feet of the man and had tucked the Glock into her jeans. When he stepped just past the window, Jana blasted a shoulder into him like a linebacker. His body smashed into the side of the house in a shocked mass and Jana wrenched him to the ground.

Stone and Cade leapt from their position and ran to her but Jana was atop the man, with one knee in the back of his neck. She held one of his arms behind him in a wristlock as the man gagged in an effort to return air to his lungs.

Stone crouched into a cover position and pointed his weapon toward the road—he was preparing for an attack that did not appear to be coming. "Nice takedown." He reached up and grabbed Cade and yanked him down.

"I rather enjoyed that," Jana replied. "Now, let's find out who this asshole is." Jana paused as the man coughed and began to regain his composure. She said, "You, talk."

The man's chest heaved as he tried to breathe under her weight. "I . . . I . . ."

"Alright, old man, what are you doing walking up on us like that? And while you're explaining that, why don't you help me understand why you're anchored off the beach, conducting surveillance on us?"

"It's not like that. I'm, I'm looking for someone," he said.

"Well, you found someone," Jana said. "So before I thump your skull for you, who are you looking for?"

"Her name is Baker," he coughed. "Jana Baker."

Stone turned and looked at Jana. To him she appeared to be

148

lost in a distant thought.

Jana shook it off and her brow furled. "Who do you work for?"

"No one!" the man said. "It's not like that."

"Then why are you looking for Jana Baker?" Stone said.

"Because she's my daughter."

37

Federal Identification

There was something about the voice. Bits and flashes of long-lost memories popped into Jana's vision. The aroma of sizzling bacon, sunlight glistening on the tips of dew-covered stalks of corn, and the smell of aftershave.

Jana rolled the man onto his back. She stared into his eyes and her mouth dropped open. It was her father. She hadn't seen him since she was a toddler. Yet here he was, in the flesh. His skin was wrinkled and red with sunburn. But the eyes. The eyes were weary and haggard, yet they removed all doubt. He was her father.

Jana stood. She looked like someone who had seen a ghost. Her voice became guttural. "I can't . . . what are you . . . I don't understand."

"Jana?" the man said. "Is that really you? My God . . ."

Jana's breathing deepened. "What are you doing here?"

"I came to find you. I came to find you and tell you I'm sorry."

"You're sorry?" Jana barked. "Sorry for abandoning me when I was a baby? Sorry for getting my mother killed?" Jana stepped back. "I grew up without a father or a mother. Do you know what that's like? And you're sorry? Stay away from me." Yet more memories flashed before her eyes. The greenish glow of sunlight passing through foliage into her childhood fort, the jingle of change is someone's pocket, and the smell of marzipan—dark chocolate and almond paste. She backpedaled and almost tripped.

Cade and Stone stood speechless.

"Jana, wait," her father said. "Please let me talk to you."

He began to step toward her when Stone held out a stiffened arm.

"No, no," Jana said as her head shook. "You can't be my father. You can't!" she screamed.

Cade went to her. "Come on, let's go inside."

"Jana, please," her father said as Cade led her away.

Stone turned on him. "Turn around. Hands on your head. Interlock your fingers." He spun the man against the house. Once he had frisked him, he said, "Break out some ID."

The man removed a small, wet, leather wallet and pulled out an orange-colored identification card. On it was a photo of the man along with a barcode. The card read,

US Department of Justice
Federal Bureau of Prisons
09802-082
AMES, Richard William
INMATE

"So you're Jana's father, huh? Then why does this say your last name is Ames?"

But the man was fixated on Jana as she disappeared inside. "That is my last name."

"Her last name is not Ames."

"Baker was her mother's maiden name. After I went to the pen, her mother disavowed all knowledge of me." His voice shook. "She changed Jana's name to Baker. Please, I have to talk to her."

Stone held him back but reengaged the safety mechanism on his rifle. He called out, "Cade?" Cade popped his head out the door. "Man claims to be Jana's father yet his last name is—"

"Ames. Yeah, I know." Cade shook his head. "John Stone, meet former CIA case officer Richard Ames. Arrested in 1998 for treason against the United States, and the father of Jana Baker."

Stone took Ames by the collar and led him to the door. "Time to have a little talk, Mr. Ames."

"Jana doesn't want to see him," Cade said.

"I know, but there's a few things we're going to have to find out, like how Mr. Ames here found us."

38

Not That Type of Music

Stone led the man inside and pushed him into a hard wicker chair.

Ames looked for Jana, but saw only a closed bedroom door.

"Alright, old man, talk," Stone said.

"What?"

"You know what," Cade said.

"I, uh. Well, I've been out a few months."

"And what about that?" Stone said as he examined the ID card. "When I run you through NCIC, am I going to find you're a fugitive now? "

"No! No, I served my time. Twenty-eight years and thirty-six days. I paid my debt to society. I've been released."

Cade said, "Paid your debt? They should have buried you under the prison."

Ames looked at his feet.

Stone was all business. "Out with it. How did you find us?"

Ames shifted in his chair.

"Hey!" Stone yelled.

"I, uh. I found you . . ." He looked directly at Cade. "It was him."

"Him?" Stone said. "What do you mean it was him?"

Ames looked back at the closed bedroom door. This time he saw the shadow of two feet underneath the door. Jana was standing just on the other side.

"When I got out, all I could think about was her. Actually, she's all I thought about on the inside as well. I hadn't seen her since she was a baby." His voice became choked with emotion. "I had to find her. But no one would tell me. No one would tell me anything."

"And?" Cade said.

"I started doing internet searches, looking for her. It took no time to find all the articles. FBI agent, stopped those terrorist bombings. She's not exactly a private figure, you know?"

"Yeah, well aware," Cade said. "But there's nothing online that would lead you to her home address, phone number, workplace, nothing. And there's sure as hell nothing that would lead you here."

Stone towered over Ames and crunched a stiff hand onto his shoulder. Ames winced. "I'll ask you nicely. How did you find us?"

"I placed a music box on him," he said as he nodded to Cade.

"A music box?" Cade said.

Stone squinted at Ames. "The term *music box* is CIA parlance for a radio transmitter. How in the hell did you place a radio transmitter on him?"

"Not so much a radio transmitter. A tracking device. It wasn't that hard."

Stone clamped harder. "Why don't you explain it to me before I become impatient?"

"Jesus, alright," Ames said. "I started sending Jana letters a good six months before I got released. I didn't have her address so I sent the first one to FBI headquarters in DC. I figured they'd send it to whatever field office she worked. But the letter got returned. They marked it as 'no longer at this address,' presumably meaning she didn't work at the FBI anymore. I didn't know what to do so I sent another letter. This time they forwarded it to her apartment address."

"How do you know that?" Cade said.

"Because they got something wrong. They forgot to include the apartment number. So when it got there, the post office just marked it 'return to sender' and the letter came back to me at the United States Penitentiary at Florence. Now I had her home address, minus the apartment number. I started sending letters there and those were never returned."

"Yeah," Cade said, "I was looking after her place when she disappeared. I had worked with the apartment manager and asked the postal-delivery guy to flag all her mail. I was collecting it. Holy shit."

"That doesn't explain how you found this place," Stone said.

Ames continued. "When I knew the letters weren't getting returned, I figured I had the right address. I kept writing. Then when I got out, I sent a box of candies."

"The marzipan," Cade said.

Ames looked at the bedroom door. "They were her favorite when she was a little girl."

"And?" Stone said.

"Inside the box I hid a Tile."

"A Tile?" Stone questioned. "What the hell is a Tile?"

Cade's eyes flared at the familiarity. "A *Tile*?"

"Yeah. Little Bluetooth tracking device," Ames said. "Bought a couple of sets on Amazon. They're great for locating your missing wallet, finding your car in a giant parking lot, or . . ." He looked at Cade. "Placing in the bottom of a box of candy."

Before Stone could ask, Ames said, "It's not always easy to locate your Tile because they don't use the cellphone network for location tracking. If they did, it would be easy. You'd just pop open the application on your phone and find the device's location. Instead, they use Bluetooth. Everyone who owns a Tile installs the Tile app. There are millions of users. If you need to locate one of your Tiles, you tell the system to locate it. Then, all the users become a network of devices that look for your Tile automatically. If someone comes within a hundred feet of it, their device sends a notification. In this case, I got lucky."

"How so?" Stone questioned.

"When I mailed the marzipan to Jana's apartment complex, I didn't locate it on the tracking app at her apartment. I located it when this guy," he pointed to Cade, "took it back to his own apartment, which is a different complex from where I believed Jana lived. At first, I didn't know what that meant, but assumed maybe she moved or something. I traveled from Colorado to Maryland and staked out the apartment, hoping to see Jana. But all I ever saw was him. I staked out her apartment complex as well, but she never showed up."

Cade scrambled to keep up. "Wait a minute. You were the one that sent me the package of—"

"That's right," Ames continued. "Like I said, it isn't all that easy to locate a missing Tile, even with millions of users out there. The ping showed up on my Tile app probably because someone in your apartment complex had it. But I had to make sure you installed the Tile app on your phone. That way, if you ever hand-delivered the candy to Jana, your phone would ping its location."

"What package? What did he send you?" Stone said to Cade.

"I received a free package of Tiles in the mail. It said it was a free sample. Hell, I thought it was cool."

Stone rubbed his eyes. "So you installed the app on your phone so you could track your cute new little tracker devices? Let me guess. You put one in your car, one in your wallet, and one, wait, in your satchel in case little Timmy stole it from you at recess."

"Kiss my ass, Stone," Cade said.

"And when he flew here," Ames said, "and the box of marzipan came with him. I could easily track where he was. It was only a hope, a long shot, that he would deliver the candy to Jana." He looked at the bedroom door again, the feet were still there.

Stone slung the rifle behind himself and crossed his arms. "What were you thinking, sneaking up here like that?"

"I didn't know," Ames said. "I mean, it's a tropical island. It's not as if I thought she was on an op or something. She doesn't even work for the FBI anymore. I figured she was on vacation."

Stone said, "You almost got yourself killed."

"I'm going to be sore in the morning, that's for sure," Ames said as he rubbed his ribs. "I take it you guys are on an op? But I don't get it. It's just the three of you?"

"We can't discuss anything with you," Stone said.

Ames shook his head. "Doesn't sound like much has changed. Back at the Agency, I'd set up operations all the time. Damned if someone wouldn't screw the pooch though. Somebody would pull the plug and my guys would be on their own. No support."

"Screw the pooch?" Cade said with a smirk. "You really have been out of circulation. I don't think anyone has used that particular phrase in a couple of decades."

"If it's just you three," Ames continued, "maybe I can help."

From behind the bedroom door, Jana's voice boomed. "I want that man out of this house, right now!"

"Doesn't sound like you're invited. Time to go, sir," Stone said as he pulled Ames to his feet.

Cade walked him down to the beach toward the boat. "Looks like your anchor came loose," Cade said. The stern of the boat had slid closer to shore and bobbed gently against the sand.

"Yeah, guess I'm not much of a captain," Ames replied.

The two spoke for several minutes. He handed Ames back his wallet. "Let me help you get this boat pushed back out."

Once they were done, Ames began to climb aboard. Cade said, "You went to a lot of trouble to find her."

Ames looked down at him and spoke through a tightened throat. "She's all I have left. She's all there is."

Cade shoved the boat and Ames fired the engine and motored out.

39

Shell Game

Cade walked back to the safe house and waved for Stone to come outside.

"What did you two talk about?" Stone said.

"It doesn't matter."

"Uninstall that ridiculous app from your phone before someone else uses it to track us."

Cade said. "Not that he doesn't already know where we are."

"Can you believe that old nutjob? Sneaking up on us then asking us if he could *help*?"

Cade said nothing but his expression spoke volumes.

"Wait a minute. You want him to help us? Are you out of your mind?"

"Think about it. You said yourself it was going to be impossible for the three of us to make Carlos Gaviria disappear. Maybe you were right. We need more men. He's ex-CIA."

"He was last at the Agency when Jana was a baby. It's out of the question. We can't put some rogue civilian in the middle of this. He's a liability and can't be trusted."

"You know we're running out of options. If Kyle is alive, he won't last in there much longer. What was your plan? For the three of us to go in with guns blazing? We wouldn't stand a chance. The only way to get to Kyle is for Jana to be successful taking Gaviria out of commission. After that, she'll have gained the trust of both Rojas and Gustavo Moreno. I agree that the last type of person I'd trust is one who'd committed treason. But did you think he was going to do anything to put Jana in harm's way? He's her father. And nobody on this island even knows he's here. He looks worn out, but so do a lot of these tourists. He'll be able to get in close with no one having any idea. And," Cade paused for effect, "he's got a boat."

"What are we going to do with a boat?" But Stone thought about the idea for a moment. "A boat. That's it. If Jana can lure Gaviria into a compromising position in some place right next to the water, we can whisk him away."

"It'll be nighttime. Cover of darkness," Cade added. "You've got to admit, it's the best plan we have."

"It's the *only* plan we have," Stone admitted.

"Why are you looking at me like that?"

Stone shook his head. "Surprised, that's all."

"Oh screw you. I told you, I've been in the field before."

"Oh, then you'd know what a freshly cut M112 block demolition charge smells like."

"What? There's no time for this. I've got to—"

"Lemon citrus."

"Well that's just lovely, Stone," Cade said with a sarcastic tone. "You should work for a potpourri company."

"And if we need to, we're using Ames."

"I disagree," Cade said.

"You're not in charge!" Stone barked.

"Hey! This is an NSA operation."

"NSA doesn't run field operations, cubicle-boy."

"We can argue about this later. Right now I've got to find a way to establish comms with FortMeade again."

"We're going to rent our own boat. And if we go after Gaviria tonight, we need as much background as possible. Where's that file Jana brought back?"

"In the house."

The two walked in. Stone picked up the background dossier and said, "You think Jana's up for it?"

"Never seen her back down from anything," Cade said as he sat at the laptop.

"Good," Stone said as he began studying the dossier.

Cade began working the laptop again.

Jana emerged from the bedroom and the two looked up. "I don't want to talk about it," she said. "The first person to mention my father is going to hobble away from here. What were you two talking about outside?"

Stone said, "Gaviria. How to get Gaviria. We need a plan."

"It's happening tonight, so make the plans quick," she said. "Anything useful in that file?"

"Not much. Just that he's got a metric crap-ton of bodyguards. Looks like his address is in here, not that it will do us any good. We can't go pull a raid on his villa with all that firepower. We've got to get him off-site somewhere."

Cade sat up. "What the hell?" he said as he pecked at the laptop. "The satellite uplink, it's back." But before he could punch in a call to the NSA command center, a ringtone pulsed on the laptop. It was an incoming video call. A moment later a new window appeared and CIA Deputy Director Lawrence Wallace's face stared at them.

"Don't bother trying a call to NSA, Mr. Williams, the comlink won't be online long enough."

Jana and Stone hovered over Cade's shoulder and glared at the monitor.

"What is wrong with you?" she blurted. "What are you playing at?"

"It is a pleasure to work with someone of your stature, Agent Baker. Considering the success you've had killing terrorists, that is."

Cade spoke. "Why is CIA interfering? Kyle MacKerron is being held and you're blocking us at every turn. He's CIA for God's sake!"

"Don't concern yourselves with that right now," Wallace said. "You need to focus on Agent Baker's assignment, Carlos Gaviria."

"How do you know about that?" Jana yelled.

"It's my *job* to know, Agent Baker," he said. "And it's your job to worry about Gaviria. What you are missing is the *where*, am I right?"

Before Jana could speak, Stone put a hand on her arm. "Let the prick finish."

"One thing you won't find in the Gaviria dossier is the fact that he owns a local nightclub. That's because it's registered to one of his shell corporations. I'm sending you the information packet now."

Jana said, "That's a *CIA* dossier, isn't it?" But the video connection terminated. "What is CIA up to? They were the ones that supplied that file to Diego Rojas."

Cade said, "Well, there goes the uplink again," referring to the satellite connection.

The three looked at the monitor at the new information packet that Wallace had sent. It outlined the complex series of banking connections that linked one of Carlos Gaviria's shell corporations to the local nightclub.

Stone said, "Well, we could do it there, at Bliss. That's the club down from my place."

"But I thought it was called Rush Nightclub."

"Bliss is in the front of the club, close to the water, Rush is in the back. Lots of people and noise," Stone replied. "If Gaviria is there, you're going to need to separate him from his bodyguards."

"What is this place?" Cade said.

Jana answered, "Busy nightclub down on RunawayBay. But Stone, what does it matter that Bliss is closer to the water?"

"Cade's idea," Stone said. "Bliss sits up on the hill, closer to the water, right? It's just up from my cabana."

"So?" Jana replied.

"If you lure him there without his bodyguards, we might be able to get him into a boat."

"A boat? I get that your place is right at the dock, but how am I going to get him into a boat? And he'd never separate from his bodyguards."

"You won't lure him into the boat. You'll lure him into my place. It sits out over the water, right?"

"Yeah?"

"There's a trapdoor under the bedroom floor," Stone said.

Jana squinted at him. "A trapdoor? I've been in that bedroom a hundred times and I never—"

Cade rubbed his eyes.

She continued. "I never saw a trapdoor."

"It's under that grass-cloth rug," Stone said.

"Stone?" Cade said. "Why is there a trapdoor in your place, under the grass cloth rug, that's in your bedroom, that Jana's been a hundred times?"

"I put it there. I work deep cover, cubicle-boy, and wanted a way to skin out if something went sideways."

Jana said. "Okay, great, so there's a trapdoor. What do you

want me to do, knock him out with some rohypnol and dump him into the ocean underneath your bedroom? Where are we going to get a drug like that?"

"Rohypnol wouldn't be a bad idea," Cade said.

"No time for that crap," Stone said. "You don't need roofies to knock him out." He let her think about the statement.

A moment later, she smiled. "You're right, I don't."

"What's that supposed to mean?" Cade said.

"She's more than a little effective at applying a choke hold. If she gets her arm around his neck from behind, he'll go out like a light. Never mind," Stone said, "you just work on the commo. Jana can handle herself."

Cade shook his head. "Is it just me, or does anyone else see the big elephant sitting in the room?"

"Cade," Jana said, "I've told you before, Stone and I were together. If you can't handle the fact that I've slept with other men since you, that's your problem."

"Not that," Cade said. "It'll be set up to look like a chance encounter, right? Just like when you 'bumped into' Diego Rojas at Touloulou Bar? You plan on meeting Carlos Gaviria the same way. I get how you're going to lure him from the club into Stone's place, but how do we know he's going to be at the night club in the first place?"

40

To Lure a Drug Lord

"Gaviria will be at the club," Stone said.

"Oh really?" Cade questioned. "And how do you know that?"

"It's my job to know these things. You've been on this island five minutes. I've been here five years, remember?"

Cade said, "Okay, so why don't you explain it to those of us who just work in cubicles."

"The Oficina de Envigado cartel hasn't been here long. And Gaviria himself apparently arrived very recently. Remember how I told you that these cartel members sneak onto the island quietly, under assumed identities? It's almost impossible for us to know when someone new gets here. But about a month ago, I overheard a couple of Los Rastrojos members talking about the arrival of some new Oficina de Envigado cartel leader. They didn't have an identity, but they were aware that they'd sent in someone new, someone big."

"So how does that make it easy to get Gaviria to the club?"

"Right after that, the club changed. It's right up the hill from my cabana, so the change was obvious."

"How so?" Cade said.

"The music, the clientele, the ownership, all of it. Dammit, why didn't I see that before?" Stone said.

"See what?" Cade asked.

Jana nodded and smiled. "He owns the club now. And if he owns it, he's almost undoubtedly the guy who made all the changes."

"So he owns the nightclub? So what?"

Stone said, "They're always interested in covering their tracks with legitimate businesses. Besides, he probably loves that nightlife crap."

"Alright," Jana said, "here's the plan. We'll assume he's going to be there. If so, I'll meet him and try to bring him to Stone's. Where are you two during this time?"

"I'll be close," Stone said. "You won't see me, but I'll be there. If anything goes wrong, I'm coming in and coming in hard."

"And if all goes to plan, what?" she said. "If I get Gaviria in the cabana and knock his ass out, I'm going to lower him through the trapdoor?"

"I'll be in a boat directly underneath you," Cade said.

"You?" Jana said.

"Is that such a surprise?" Cade replied.

"You're not so good for fieldwork," she said.

"I wish you people would stop saying that," Cade said. "I'm going to rent the boat now."

"There's not much time," Jana said. "You two sure you know what you're doing?"

"Hey," Stone said as he placed a hand on her, "have I ever let you down?"

"Yes," Jana said. "You disappeared for a month and didn't say a word."

"That's not going to happen this time."

Jana shook her head. "And where are we going to rent a boat?"

"Leave that to me," Cade said. He went out and got in the rental car. What he didn't realize was that he'd left his cellphone on the desk.

41

Sanctioned

Jolly Harbor Marina, Lignum Vitae Bay, Antigua.

Police Lieutenant Jack Pence got the call at around 8:00 p.m. He was at home.

"This is Pence," he said into his phone.

"L. T., this is Detective Okoro. Sorry to bother you at home, sir, but I've got a uni that says he's got one of your subjects in play."

"Tell him to stay on it. Send him some backup and grab the little prick. Then call me and I'll meet you at the station."

"Roger that, sir."

About thirty minutes later, Lieutenant Pence's phone rang again. He picked it up and listened, then said, "Uh-huh. Uh-huh. Good work. No, let's let him sit in the tank a while."

At around 10 p.m., Pence walked into the interrogation room at the precinct. "Well, well, well, if it isn't my good friend from the NSA. How are we today, Mr. Williams?"

"What time is it? I've been sitting in this shithole for hours. I've got to get out of here, right now! I'm on official US government business. What gives you the right to hold me?"

"The right? It's my island, Mr. Williams. You're not on US soil. But why so impatient? Can I call you Cade? Sure, why not.

After all, we're friends, right?"

Cade glared at him. "Answer the question. What am I charged with?"

"I'd watch your tone, Mr. Williams. But let's talk about that, shall we? You know what I don't like?"

"When you step on gum and it sticks to your shoe? I have to get out of here!"

"Ah," the lieutenant said, "a smart ass." He leaned over the table. "You want to know why you're here? I don't like being lied to, that's why."

"Look, Lieutenant, you need to call the US embassy. They'll call the State Department and then probably your interior minister, who I'd venture to say, is going to be pretty pissed off."

"I did call the US embassy. And they did call the US State Department. And you know what? They don't know why you're here. You're sure as hell not on official business. I should have never released Jana Baker to you. I want to know where she is, and you're going to tell me."

"That's impossible," Cade said. Then he thought, *CIA! The damned CIA screwed me.* "I never lied to you," he said.

"Oh no? You know who else I called? The US attorney's office."

Cade's face went pale.

"Yeah, the assistant US attorney was never on his way to Antigua, was he?" Pence grinned. "That was a good one, by the way." He lunged forward and slammed his fist onto the table. "Where is Jana Baker? Her little *incident* is looking more and more like assault with a deadly weapon, and probably worse."

"She was attacked!"

"That, my friend, is crap. Did you think I was an idiot? Her story is more than a little flawed. For example, in her statement, she said she was walking home from the club when, allegedly, the attempted assault occurred. But she went a little out of her way. Six blocks out of her way, in fact."

"What are you accusing her of?"

"You should be more concerned with what we're accusing *you* of. But as for Miss Baker, attempted murder, for starters. She wasn't attacked. She lured her victim down that darkened back alley and shot him twice, not to mention all the compound fractures. Left him there to bleed out. I'm charging her, and it's going to stick. So let me ask you this. Did your little *asset* go out of control, or was she on assignment?"

"I'm not saying a word. You let me out of here right now."

The door opened and a uniformed officer walked in. He handed the lieutenant a clear plastic evidence bag. Inside was a firearm.

"And the weapon she used," Pence continued as he dropped the bag onto the desk with a thud, "did you supply it to her? You know what I find interesting about this weapon?"

Cade laid his head on the desk. "No, and I don't care!" he yelled.

"I find it interesting that when one runs the serial numbers, nothing comes back."

"So what?" Cade said. "So the hell what?"

"This is a Glock 43. A highly customized Glock 43, to be exact. Note how the handle has been cut down. It requires a handmade magazine to fit it. And the silencer. That's a nice touch. But let's talk about the serial numbers. All the parts are stamped with matching serial numbers, just like we'd expect. And the manufacturer registers every weapon it produces. Funny how this one doesn't show up on the registry. It apparently was never manufactured."

SANCTIONED

"Let me out of here."

"That's a pretty good trick, isn't it?" Pence continued. "For a gun to disappear from the national database? I'd say it would take a government to pull off something like that." He circled behind Cade. "I don't just want to know where Jana Baker is, I want to know what she's doing pulling a US-government-sanctioned hit on my island."

"She's not an assassin."

"She sure as hell isn't a kindergarten teacher, is she?" Pence walked to the door. "I tell you what. Why don't you sit in your cell a while longer? Maybe by morning your memory will come back to you." The door slammed behind him.

Shit, Cade thought. *How am I going to be in a boat underneath Stone's bungalow later tonight if I'm stuck here?*

42

Storm of Fury

Stone looked at his watch, it was already 10 p.m. "We've got to go, Jana." He picked up Cade's cellphone from the desk where Cade had left it, then glanced at the tracking application on the screen. On the map, a single blip pinged, indicating Cade's location. *What are you doing? Come on*, he thought, *get in position.*

From the back bedroom Jana responded, "Would you relax? You think we're going to get there and Gaviria will have gone to bed? You know as well as I do these clubs don't get started until late."

Stone heard her footsteps and jammed the phone into his pocket. He didn't want her to know Cade wasn't in position. When she walked out, his facial expression turned to *wow*, but he made no comment.

Jana smiled. "Where's Cade?" she said.

Stone faltered a moment. "Oh, he'll be ready." He tapped the cellphone in his pocket. "The boat will be there." His voice, however, didn't sound convincing.

Jana hopped in the open-air Jeep as Stone threw his gear in the back. A stiff night breeze blew against her long ponytail and she looked out at the moon rising across the bay. The moonlight illuminated the chop that had begun forming on the dark waters.

Lightning flickered in the distance.

They took off down the beach-side road and drove in the direction of the club.

"If all goes to plan," Stone said, "I'll be hidden in my bungalow when you get inside with Gaviria. You won't know I'm there."

"Don't worry," she said as her hands tightened on the wheel. "If anything goes wrong inside the bungalow, I'm going to take his ass out."

"This isn't a sanctioned assassination. This is just a rendition, got it?"

But Jana said nothing.

Stone looked at her as they sped down the gravel-like roadway. The Jeep slid into the curves. She was focused on something.

"Hey," he said, "you in there? You need to remember, we're on our own down here. And that doesn't just mean that we have no backup. It also means if this goes sideways, the US government is going to let us twist in the wind. They'll disavow all knowledge. And you know what? They won't even be lying."

"Uncle Bill would move heaven and earth to help us. And nothing is going to go wrong. Stop obsessing," she said. "You just do your part. Gaviria is mine."

When they got within six blocks of the club, Stone said, "Alright, this is good. Let me out here." She pulled the vehicle to the side. The roadside was dark and surrounded by dense, tropical foliage. A strong gust of wind blew and Stone hopped out then grabbed his gear. He looked up at the storm clouds, then disappeared into the thick.

Jana turned her gaze forward, the mission clear in her mind. She jammed the accelerator and crushed-coral dust kicked up from behind.

Just down the hillside, a wave crashed into the shoreline. The impending storm was getting closer.

43

Thunder Harbor

Stone took up position on the hillside just above the club. He was still surrounded in dense foliage. He threw the carbine's sling over his head and looked through a set of miniaturized binoculars and began to count bodyguards. "One, two . . . shit, three." The well-dressed Colombian men were stationed outside the club at various points. Stone exhaled and looked further down the hill to his bungalow. "That was three bodyguards outside the club, how many inside?" He scanned the parking lot. The Jeep was not there, but then he noticed Jana as she pulled up to the valet. Even in the tension of the situation, he couldn't help but notice how beautiful she was.

He shook his head and returned his focus to the bodyguards. He zoomed the view closer and studied each man individually. "Uh-huh," he said as he located a large bulge hidden beneath the coat jacket of each. "Automatic weapons, just like I thought."

He pulled out Cade's cellphone and looked at the map. This time the ping had closed the distance. "What is taking so long? Get the damned boat over here." But then a wave crashed into the dock and the boats tied into slips rocked against their bumpers. *Damn this weather*, he thought. More lightning flashed and in the flicker of light, Stone saw the boat approaching.

He looked just past the club at the boardwalk and staircases that led from the club down to the dock and in front of his bungalow. As the boat entered the harbor, it rocked across waves of increasing size. The storm was getting worse. *Time to get into position.*

44

Bad Vibrations

Before Jana walked into the club, she could feel the thumping of music. When she and Stone had been dating, they had never frequented the place because it wasn't their scene. Loud music, strobe lights, and throngs of humanity huddled together in a sweaty mass.

The club was huge but she knew Gaviria would be here somewhere. If she could just spot him. She nudged her way through people jammed together until she could see the dance floor. It was lit from underneath and bursts of color popped from one section to another, a throwback to the 1970s.

After about fifteen minutes, she spotted a well-dressed man who looked as if he could certainly be Colombian. It wasn't Gaviria, but perhaps he was close by. The man walked up a thin set of stainless steel stairs overlooking the vast dance floor and disappeared through a set of hanging beads.

Just then Jana felt a hand rub across her backside and she turned and snatched it. Behind her was a half-drunk man. She tightened her grip. "Get a good feel?" she said.

"Hey, you're pretty strong. Maybe you and I—ow, shit," he said as Jana twisted the wrist and the man crunched down in pain. "Damn, babe. What's with all the hostility?"

She released his hand and he stood. "I'm not your babe."

He looked at her chest. "Well, you should be."

She thumped him in the softest part of the throat so fast he didn't even know he had been struck until the choking sensation overwhelmed him. He coughed and grabbed at his neck.

"Were you going to ask me to dance?" she said. The man clutched his throat and coughed. She shrugged then said, "Nothing to say? Hmmm, how disappointing." She walked toward the stairs. When she got to the first step, she looked up. An oversized bodyguard shrouded the top landing. A wave of nausea shot through her stomach but she did her best to ignore it. She ascended the staircase as if she owned the place.

The man held up a hand but Jana continued. "Carlos sent for me."

The man thought a moment then said in an accent thick of Central America, "Wait here." He glanced her up and down and smiled, then walked through the beaded divider. As he disappeared into the adjoining room, Jana followed. A second guard just beyond the divider put a hand on her just as she saw Carlos Gaviria across the room.

He had a girl on each side and gold rings on his fingers. His button-down shirt was opened. "I didn't send for any girl," he said. But as he caught sight of her, Jana could tell he was intrigued. His head leaned to one side as he looked at her. "But please, I don't wish to be rude," he said with enough volume for Jana to hear. "Have her come join me." He nodded to the two women beside him and they stood and disappeared into a back room. As the door swung open, Jana saw that it led to an outdoor balcony on the beach side of the club.

She walked to Gaviria and held out her hand. He kissed it gently. Another wave of nausea swept her. *Get a grip*, she thought. *Probably the gold chain around his neck that's making you sick to your stomach.* She smiled at her own humor.

"What an exquisite creature. Please, join me."

The guards retreated to their posts.

Jana sat and crossed her legs.

"My name is—"

"Gaviria," Jana interrupted. "Carlos Gaviria. Yes, I know who you are."

"I find myself at a disadvantage. You know who I am but I do not know you."

"A friend of yours from home sent me. Does it matter who I am?" Jana said with a playful smile. "A gift, you might say, for a job well done."

He sized her up a moment. "I *have* done my job well," he laughed, referring to his success in establishing the island as a new drug route. "But this is most unusual."

"You are not accustomed to such rewards?"

"Oh, I have my rewards," he said. "But you, how can I say this? You are not what I would have expected."

She traced a finger across his forearm. "You do not like me?"

"Quite the contrary," he said. "It's just the blond hair, the accent. You are an American, no?"

"Born and raised." Her tone was disarming.

"And very direct, I see. But tell me, how is it that a woman of your distinct . . . gifts finds yourself on our island and working in such a capacity?"

"Perhaps I'm more curious than other girls." She looked down his chest and let her hand rest on his thigh.

"Yes, I can see that," he grinned. "And you know, I wouldn't want to disappoint my friends. After all, they've been very generous." He looked at her and Jana knew the time was right.

She leaned to him and whispered into his ear. "It's not just talents I possess. They're more like *skills*." She nibbled his ear and stood up then walked through the door onto the balcony. Here, more guards were positioned, flanking a staircase that led down toward the water.

A strong gust of wind buffeted her tight dress, and lightning cracked out in the bay. Gaviria was not far behind and Jana walked past the guards and down the stairs. When she got to the bottom landing, she looked over her shoulder. There was a wide grin peeled across his face. He handed his drink to one of the guards and followed.

The boat was lashed into position underneath the bungalow, but Stone looked at it one last time. It was too dark to see Cade behind the wheel but Stone knew he was there. The waters were angry and the wind had begun to pick up in earnest. A loud crack of thunder rumbled as the approaching storm announced itself. He shook his head and yelled underneath the bungalow, trying to make himself heard over the crashing of the waves. "Just hang on. It won't be long now." He slipped around the side and peered up the hill. "That's her!" he yelled. "She's coming."

Stone was just about to hop through an open window on the side of the bungalow but took one more glance back. He watched Gaviria close on Jana.

Gaviria hugged her from behind and pulled her to him. She smiled and feigned a most flirtatious laugh. Stone could just hear their voices. He put one leg through the window but stopped as he heard footsteps pounding. Two bodyguards thundered down the boardwalk in their direction. Then, Stone heard yelling.

"What?" Gaviria yelled back to the guards. "You two are paranoid."

"Patron," one said, as he panted to regain his breath. "She is not as she says."

"What are you talking about?" Gaviria said.

The other guard grabbed Jana. "It is her, Patron. She's the one that put Montes in the hospital."

A burst of adrenaline rocketed into Stone's veins and he hopped off the platform and onto the sand below. His first thought was to shoot both guards and then go after Gaviria. *But Kyle? The instructions were clear. Gaviria must be taken quietly.* 5.56 mm NATO rounds were the exact opposite of quiet. The gunfire would draw a flood of bodyguards and a firefight would ensue. Kyle could not be rescued this way.

Gaviria looked at Jana. "Is that so?" He grabbed her throat while the bodyguards muscled her arms behind her back, then bound her wrists. Jana struggled futilely. Gaviria yanked her ponytail and said to the guards, "You two wait out here." He looked at the cabana which was only twenty feet away. "She and I are going to have a little talk." He wrenched her kicking and screaming into the cabana.

45

Predicting the Unpredicted

Thunder cracked in the mouth of the bay and the wind gusted harder. Heavy waves crashed against the boats and shoreline. Stone looked from one guard to the other and tried to devise a plan. *I've got to think, dammit!* Whatever it was, it had to be silent and it had to happen right now.

He slung his HK416 over his shoulder and crouched below the boardwalk. Then an idea occurred to him. *It's the lightning*, he thought. He shut his right eye and held his left open, a technique used by special ops troops to allow the soldier to see his own rifle sights right after a flare-parachute illuminates a darkened battlefield.

Come on, come on! Stone thought as he waited. But then it happened. Lightning flashed just overhead. The resulting pulse of brilliant light followed by immediate darkness provided the perfect cover. Stone leapt over the railing behind one of the bodyguards. In a blinding blur, he reached from behind and placed a hand across the man's jaw and back of his skull. He wrenched, then twisted with a sudden, violent jerk. The spine crunched under the dual forces. But even before the body could drop, Stone leaned into him and forced the man's torso to flop onto the side rail. Stone flipped the man's feet over the railing.

The clap of thunder was so cacophonous it covered the sound of the body crashing onto the ground.

Stone leapt over the railing and yanked his carbine into position and prepared for the worst. Just above the crashing of the next wave, he could hear Jana scream again. *Shit! I've got to get in there!* The other guard peered into the cabana window. He had not seen Stone's action.

Going to have to get lucky on this next one. He heard something shatter inside the cabana, like the sound of a coffee table being crushed. He pulled off a paracord bracelet and unwound it into its sixteen-foot length. He'd used it in survival situations for everything from fishing to tying a tourniquet. But now, he had a different use in mind. He shuffled beneath the boardwalk closer to the cabana. In the darkness, he tied one end to a side rail, then tossed the length across the boardwalk to the other side. He shuffled underneath and pulled the cord taught, then tied it off.

Lightning flashed again followed by a huge thunderclap. This time, the other bodyguard looked up. When he noticed his partner was nowhere to be seen, he took off in a blind run. He tripped across the paracord and went airborne. Before he could crash onto the hardened planks, Stone leapt the side rail. But no sooner had he pounced did the man blast Stone across the face with an enormous fist. Stone flipped over the railing and crashed onto the ground. He leapt up just in time for the man to jump down on him. They thrashed in the reeds in a blinding brawl.

46

Adrenaline Infused Terror

Jana pulled against the bindings on her wrists but Gaviria shoved her into the cabana. She tripped across the entryway and crashed into the bamboo coffee table. It shattered beneath her. All the air in her lungs abated.

"So you're the little bitch that tried to take out Montes, huh?"

It was all happening so quickly and Jana struggled to catch her breath.

"Who hired you?" He yanked her to her feet as she struggled to bring air back into her lungs. He shook her violently. "Who hired you?" he screamed then back-handed her across the face. As her body spun around, she jammed a back kick into his chest and he flew into the wall. But he reacted like lightning, throwing a right that impacted her jaw and sent her to the ground.

Gaviria laughed. "Did you think, doing what I do, anyone would respect me if I was just some pussy? Now you're going to tell me who put the contract on Montes, and you're going to tell me right now."

Jana was blinded by pain in her jaw. Her vision blurred. It was hard to tell the difference between an impending PTSD episode and pure, live terror. Lightning crashed outside and the thunderclap shook the tiny bungalow. She struggled to form a plan, any plan. Before she knew it, he was atop her, his hands crushing her throat. He yanked her head up and down as he choked her. He screamed, "Who hired you?"

Jana saw a blurred figure appear behind Gaviria just before everything went black. She had lost consciousness.

47

The Awakening

Jana's eyes flicked open but everything was so dark and loud. She was half conscious and pain permeated her body. She found her hands were still bound. Thunder exploded from somewhere above and she was being pelted with driving rain. The surface beneath her rocked violently and her body bounced up and down. Her consciousness faded and she again blacked out. In her mind's eye, she found herself running through the woods toward her special hiding place, her fort. If she could only get to her fort, everything would be okay . . .

The floor below her bounced again and her body slung against something. The noise above was deafening. She looked in one direction and saw Stone crouched. He was pointing his rifle in the direction behind them and Jana could now recognize they were in a boat. *The boat. Cade got us a boat.* It all made sense to her.

Bolts of lightning shot horizontally across the sky, accompanied by a boom so loud she thought they had been hit. They were in the heaviest rain she'd ever experienced. She looked toward the front of the boat and squinted into the raindrops but could barely see. Though her hands were still bound, she felt the tremors. They started in her right hand but quickly spread across both arms and torso. The PTSD episode took a violent turn for the worse. Soon, she was convulsing. The last thing she remembered was a dark, murky liquid rolling across the white deck toward her. It sloshed together with rainwater to form a slurry, and there was no question, it was blood.

48

Gagged and Bound

Jana awoke in a sea of darkness. She was disoriented and sat upright and looked around. She was in her bedroom at the safe house. Her hands were free but her jaw hurt. She touched it, and what felt like an electric shock pulsed. She could feel the swelling.

She stood and steadied herself. In the distance, thunder rumbled—the storm had moved past. She heard voices and opened the bedroom door, then squinted into the brightness of a lamp.

"Oh, come on, you big baby," a voice said. "It's not that bad."

"Ouch, dammit, that hurts," she heard Stone reply.

In the blur of her vision, it looked as though Cade was applying a set of butterfly bandages above one of Stone's eyes to seal a gash.

"Hey," Stone said, "you're up. You feel okay?"

Jana placed a gentle hand on her jaw and rubbed her neck. "Well, I've felt better. What happened? The last thing I remember was—"

But she stopped midsentence. Cade turned around, only it wasn't Cade. It was her father.

Jana's mouth opened. "What are *you* doing here?" There was

anger in her words but, speaking against the swelling in her throat, her volume was hushed.

He didn't answer, but instead turned back to Stone to apply the last butterfly.

"Dammit, old man, that hurts," Stone said.

Ames wiped a stream of blood that had made its escape. "You'll be fine," he said as he pulled Stone up. "Here, take a look." He pointed at a mirror on the wall and Stone examined the work.

He turned to Ames. "Hey, this is pretty good. You've done this before?"

Ames exhaled and shook his head. "Not my first time."

"I don't understand," Jana said. "How did he get here?" Her voice was shaky. "Kyle! Oh my God. Did we ruin our chance to get Kyle?"

Stone said, "Relax. We still think everything is okay as far as Kyle goes. When Rojas is told that the target he assigned you is now gone, he'll be pleased."

"But, but . . ." Jana stuttered. "The bodyguards! It was supposed to be so quiet. Gaviria was to be taken out without anyone knowing what happened! Rojas will know."

"As far as they'll know, it *was* quiet," Stone said. "The other bodyguards at the club never saw a thing. The storm covered our tracks. It's all handled."

Jana pulled a chair closer and sat. She turned her attention to her father. "Then explain that," she said as she pointed.

Stone examined her neck and jawline. "There's going to be some swelling, but your jaw isn't broken." He looked at Ames. "It if wasn't for him, you'd be dead right now. In fact, both of us would be dead right now."

"What?" her voice had softened.

"Late yesterday, after Cade went to rent the boat," Stone said.

"What about it?"

"I don't know how to tell you this. But yesterday Cade disappeared. I didn't know where he was. He went to rent the boat and that's the last I heard from him. When I called his cell, it rang here at the house. He'd left it. I didn't tell you because I knew you'd lose your shit."

"What happened to Cade?" She stood. "Where's Cade?"

Stone put his arms on her shoulders. "Right now, we don't know. But we'll find him, okay?"

"There's two missing now?" Jana said as her thoughts swirled. "He's been gone this whole time? Did he get taken?"

"I know, I know," Stone said. "Here, sit down. When I couldn't find him, I looked at his phone. I don't know, I was looking for anything. But I did find one thing I'd suspected. The little cubicle jockey hadn't deleted the Tile tracker app from his phone like he told me he had. At first I was pissed, but then thought that it might be the one thing that could help us find him. He has a Tile tracker on his key chain. So I opened the tracker app to see if it would locate him. It did. It showed his position on the map at the marina."

"So you found him?" Jana said.

"Not exactly," Stone said. "But it made perfect sense at the time because he appeared to be right where he was supposed to be, renting a boat. But when I saw the storm approaching, I got nervous. I wanted him to get the boat under the cabana as fast as possible. Otherwise the surf may have gotten too rough for him to get into position without banging into the piers that support the place. So I pinged him."

"But he didn't have his cellphone," Jana said.

"I didn't ping the cell, I pinged his tracker device. Tiles have a tiny speaker in them. You can use the app on your phone to cause an alarm to sound across the speaker on the tracker. That way, you can find your lost keys or whatever. I was hoping Cade would hear the alarm and get to a landline to call me so I could warn him." Stone turned and looked back at Ames. "But it wasn't Cade that called. It was him."

Jana covered her eyes. "I don't understand."

Stone continued. "Cade apparently didn't trust Mr. Ames here, and had taken the Tile from his own keyring and threw it in Ames's boat so he could keep an eye on him. When I pinged the tracker, Ames called Cade's cell and I answered. It was your father who brought his boat to help us. He's the one that took out Gaviria. He's the one that pulled that gorilla off me. He's the one that got you into the boat, along with Gaviria, and that's how we got out of there. He saved our lives."

Jana doubled over, it was as if she had a sharp pain in her stomach. She closed her eyes and began breathing very deeply, an attempt to thwart the demons. "We've got to find him. Oh God, how are we going to get both Cade and Kyle?"

Jana's father spoke softly. "Operationally, when faced with overwhelming odds, we take one objective at a time."

Jana glared at him then sat upright. "We? Are you supposed to be some kind of expert? And besides, you don't get to do that," she said. "You don't get to disappear for twenty-eight years and then show back up and everything's alright."

He waited. "There's nothing I can ever do to make up for the sins of my past. There's nothing I can do that would make it right. But maybe you can put that aside, just for a little while, until we get your friends out. I can help."

"I don't want to hear it!" she said. "I don't want to hear another word. Now leave and don't ever come back. I never want to see you again."

Stone said, "Jana, none of us know what your life was like growing up without your parents, but he's right. Look at our situation. We've got two men missing. We need his help. Not only is he willing to help, but he's got operational experience."

"Yeah!" Jana yelled. "Experience in selling classified information to the Russians!"

Stone continued. "As much as I agree with you, we need his help. He saved our asses out there tonight. Do you know what your father did at CIA before he became a case officer? He was a field operative."

Jana looked up.

"That's right," Stone said. "His experience might date back to the Cold War, but the field is the field. I couldn't get to you inside the cabana because of the two bodyguards. I thought you were dead for sure. But your dad, he came down on that guard. He didn't hesitate. Before I even knew what had happened, your dad yanked a knife from my belt and jammed it into the guy's neck. But he came for me only after he had saved you. It's you, Jana. Your dad risked his life to save *you*. And look at him. He's sitting there, ready and willing to do it again."

Jana shook her head and stood to walk into the bedroom. "In a couple of hours it will be daylight. I've got to get ready to tell Diego that Rojas Gaviria is dead. And I've got to have a plan to get Kyle out. After that, we'll start looking for Cade." She glanced at her father. "And you stay away from me. Don't speak to me, don't look at me."

"Jana, wait," Stone said. "We've got a problem."

"What now?"

Stone walked to the other bedroom door and opened it. Lying on the floor was Carlos Gaviria. His hands were bound behind his back and he was gagged.

49

A Hidden Agenda

"What is *he* doing here?" Jana said. "He's not dead?"

The duct tape across Gaviria's mouth muffled his angered screaming.

"But, there was blood," Jana said. "Blood was all over the boat."

Stone said, "It was his blood alright, but he's not dead. Your dad knocked him cold though."

Jana thought back to the moments before she was choked out, the blurred figure in the cabana behind Gaviria.

Jana said, "What are we going to do? Just leave him on the floor? I thought you had dumped his body. We can't keep him here."

"It all happened so quickly," Stone said. "I was pretty out of it." He pointed to the gash above his eye. "But without a rendition team, this is our problem now."

A ring tone emitted from Cade's laptop and Jana walked over to it. "I can't believe it. It's that son of a bitch."

"Jana, wait," Stone said. "Ames, get out of sight of the video camera. I don't want anyone to know you're here."

Ames walked behind the table so he could not be seen.

She clicked a button on the secure video conference window. "Wallace? What the hell do you want?"

"To offer my help, as always," Lawrence Wallace said from the screen. His expression was smug.

"Help? Yeah," she said, "CIA has been so helpful so far."

"You would have preferred to locate Gaviria yourselves? And how would you have done that? As it is now, you have accomplished what you set out to."

"Really?" Jana said. "What we want is to get Kyle MacKerron out of harm's way."

"The path to Agent MacKerron is through Carlos Gaviria."

Jana leaned into the monitor. "That was your agenda, wasn't it? You provided Diego Rojas with a full dossier on Carlos Gaviria and he then gave it to me. Something is up, and I want to know what it is. What does the CIA want with a drug lord?"

Wallace ignored the question. "As I said, I am here to offer my assistance."

"What makes you think we need any help?" Stone joked.

Wallace said, "First, I congratulate you on taking out Gaviria. I am impressed."

"Great," Jana said. "It's been my lifelong goal to impress you."

"But you have quite a problem, don't you?"

"And what's that?" Jana said, though she knew the answer.

"Gaviria isn't dead, is he? You can't possibly hold Gaviria while you try to free Agent MacKerron. You need me to take him off your hands."

Jana looked at Stone then back to the monitor. "How do you know that?"

"I know a great many things, Agent Baker," Wallace said. "I can take Gaviria. A rendition team is what you've needed all along, am I right?"

"I don't trust you, Wallace. So I'll ask you again. What does the CIA want with a drug lord?"

"You let me worry about that."

Jana crossed her arms and waited.

Wallace continued. "I have a team in route to your location. They'll be there within two hours. Gaviria will no longer be a problem."

"And what if I won't give him up?" Jana said.

Wallace laughed. "You have no choice."

"I don't work for you," Jana said.

"I tell you what, Agent Baker. You hand over Gaviria and I'll tell you what you want to know."

"You're going to tell me the CIA's agenda?"

He laughed again. "No, but I'm going to earn your trust. I'm going to tell you where Cade Williams is."

Jana's mouth dropped open but her words came out laced with anger. "What did you do with him?"

"I assure you, he's not in CIA custody. Consider the information a gesture of good will."

"Dammit!" she screamed. "Where is he?"

"Do we have a deal?"

"Yes."

"After Gaviria has been turned over to us, you'll receive instructions."

The call went dead.

Jana slammed her fists into the desk. "Prick!"

From behind the laptop, Jana's father said, "You are right not to trust him. There's an agenda. There's always an agenda."

Jana's jaw muscles clenched as she glared at her father, but then Stone spoke. "What are they playing at?"

"I don't know," Ames said. "But it's always a level above."

"Meaning?" Stone said.

"Well, you were a Delta Force operator, right?"

"Yes."

"You were given missions, and those missions made sense on your level, didn't they?"

"Normally, yes. Our clearances were high, so we typically knew what we were doing and why."

"But there's always a level above. A higher priority, a grander scale. That's what you didn't know. For example, where's one place you were deployed?"

"I can't talk about that," Stone said.

"Of course not," Ames replied. "Let's see, okay, here's an example. Let's say it's 1985 and you're on Delta Force. You get tasked to do a weapons transfer to the Iranians. Now, at that time, Iran was under weapons embargo, so none of this was legal. But you are told that the US is going to sell Hawk and TOW missiles to the Iranians in exchange for the release of seven American hostages being held in Lebanon by Hezbollah. And since Iran has a lot of influence over Hezbollah, we'll get our guys back. You follow?"

"This is sounding awfully familiar," Stone said.

"What you wouldn't have been told was the higher agenda, the next level."

"Which was?"

"Getting the American hostages made sense on your level, but the real goal was the exchange of cash. The US needed a massive, untraceable cash hoard to fund anti-Sandanista rebels in Nicaragua. Their goal? To overthrow the Sandanista government."

Jana murmured, "The Iran-Contra Affair."

"That's right," Ames said. "A higher priority agenda. And that's not the half of it. You've no idea how far CIA will go. Ever heard the name Kiki Camarena?"

"Sure," Jana said. "Cade talked about him. Said he was a DEA agent that was murdered in Mexico."

"Murdered because CIA didn't like him disrupting their drug trade," Ames said.

"Oh, come on," Jana said. "CIA isn't going to have a federal agent murdered. Why would they be involved in a drug trade of their own?"

"Look it up if you don't believe me. Same reason," Ames said. "They were raising funds for the anti-Sandanista rebels."

Stone said, "Alright. We're getting off track here. So that takes us back to square one. What is the CIA agenda here on Antigua?"

"I don't give a shit," Jana said.

"You don't sound very convincing," Stone replied.

"I want Kyle and I want Cade. That's the priority. If CIA wants in on the drug war, they can have it. After this is over, I can hunt down Wallace and kick his ass."

A few hours later, just as sunlight had begun to form a glow in the eastern sky, a rap on the door startled the trio.

"Pizza delivery guy?" Stone joked.

"I don't think the Company delivers pizza," Jana retorted.

"But they do a nice pickup service I hear," Stone said as he glanced outside. Four Kevlar-laden operators flanked a casually dressed man. "Go ahead, it's them."

Ames slid aside in an attempt to stay out of view.

But when Jana opened the door, she couldn't believe who was standing on the other side.

50

A Surprise Visitor

"Hello, Jana," the man said.

"What are *you* doing here?"

The man nodded to the operators and they made entry with weapons forward. Stone pointed to the bedroom door. The four hulking men grabbed Gaviria off the floor and drug him out as he thrashed. They disappeared toward the water, where an inflatable F470 Combat Rubber Reconnaissance Craft idled just off the beach.

The man passed a stern look at Stone but then turned to Jana. "Sorry, had to wait until they were clear."

"What's going on?" she said.

"I don't know, but I'm going to find out."

"What do you mean you don't know?" Jana said.

The man said, "I have a message for you. Apparently Cade got pinched. When he went to rent the boat for your operation last night, the locals grabbed him. He's still in custody."

"The local police?" Jana said. "Why?"

"They're looking for you, Jana. They've been scouring the island. Since you didn't report back in, they consider you a fugitive, and Cade an accomplice. They want to charge you with attempted murder for the attack on Montes Lima Perez."

Jana shook her head but before she could say anything, the man extended his hand. Jana shook it and felt him pass her something. He disappeared toward the water and was gone.

She closed the door and Stone said, "Who was that?"

"Pete Buck, CIA. We've worked with him before. Kind of comes off as an asshole at first, but once he gets to know you, he's a good guy."

"Yeah, seems very warm," Stone said. "What did he hand you?"

"You don't miss much," Jana said. She opened her hand to reveal a tiny manila envelope. She opened it and dumped the contents into her hand. Three unmarked digital chips spilled out.

"SIM cards?" Stone said. "The CIA cuts communication from the US to our cellphones, but now they're giving us new SIM cards?"

"Buck wouldn't have given these to us without a reason," Jana said.

"It doesn't make sense," Stone continued. "They can listen in on our cell calls whenever they want, so why give us new SIMs?"

Jana was entranced in thought. "I don't think the CIA gave us these. I think Buck did."

"But Buck is CIA."

"I know," Jana said, "but there's something going on. He wouldn't do anything to harm me, of that much I'm sure."

Stone said, "You think the CIA doesn't know what the CIA is doing?"

"Wouldn't be the first time," Jana replied.

From against the wall, Ames said, "I think he's trying to communicate with you."

Stone looked at the angered expression on Jana's face then said, "Mr. Ames, I think you should sit this one out." He turned to Jana. "I think he's trying to communicate with you."

"Very funny," Jana said.

"Do you trust him?" Stone said.

"Yes."

"Then you should trust him. Put the SIM in your phone. I'm betting that not only will it receive calls from the US mainland, but that Buck will be calling you soon."

"Fine, but we've got to get ready for Rojas. He owes me a hundred K."

51

Obstruction of Justice

Office of the Commissioner, Royal Police Force of Antigua and Barbuda, American Road, St. John's, Antigua.

"I'm sorry, who did you say is calling?" the secretary said into the phone. When she heard the repeated response, she cringed. "Oh, one moment please." She pressed a button on the desk phone and said, "Commissioner? I think you're going to want to take this."

"I'm in the middle of a briefing," Robert Wendell, the newly appointed Commissioner, said.

"Sir, I just really think—"

"Fine, patch it through. Good Lord," he said to the group of twelve senior inspectors assembled in his office. "New secretary," he said with a smirk. "Still not quite sure who she can tell to leave a message." He picked up the blinking phone line. "This is Commissioner Wendell."

The other men in the room could hear muffled yelling coming from the phone receiver.

The commissioner stuttered into the phone, "Yes, ma'am. We have a what? Well hold on now, ma'am. I don't even know—I see. No, ma'am, I'm sure we haven't detained a—I understand that you're saying he's a US citizen but on Antigua—" The commissioner waited as the person on the other end of the line continued.

The inspectors heard a banging sound across the phone as the party on the other end hung up.

The commissioner placed the phone receiver down then rubbed his eyes. He looked up at the inspectors until his eyes landed on one in particular, Lieutenant Jack Pence. "Pence? Do we have a US citizen in custody?"

"Yes, sir. His name is—"

"His name is Cade Williams. Yes, I know. And he's charged with?"

"Obstruction of an investigation."

"So, in other words, he's committed no crime. Am I right?" He slammed a fist onto the desk. "Do you want to know how I know his name?" He was met with silence. "Well I'm going to tell you." He rose from his seat so quickly his swivel chair slid into the wall. "That was a very pleasant woman named Linda Russo on the line. Want me to give you three guesses who Linda Russo is?" He leaned his fists onto the desk. "She's the damned United States ambassador to Antigua! Why in the flying fuck do we have a US citizen in custody? And not just some random tourist, but apparently an employee of the United States government. Jesus Christ! I haven't been in this chair for four months, and I'm about to get my ass canned! Call your people and cut him loose."

"Sir," the lieutenant stuttered, "we believe he's—"

"Harboring a fugitive. Yeah, the ambassador was kind enough to share that little fact with me. Look, you want to bring in the actual suspect and charge her with murder, that's one thing. But harboring a fugitive?" The commissioner shook his head. "Cut him loose, right now."

Twenty minutes later, Cade walked out of police custody. He hailed a cab and watched behind them to ensure the vehicle wasn't being followed. The cab dropped him a mile from the safe house. He waited to further ensure he did not have a tail then walked across the street and offered a kid ten dollars for a bicycle with no tires. He rode the rest of the way back on steel rims.

When he pulled up to the house, Stone came outside. "Hey, nice ride."

"Very funny. Where's Jana?"

"Inside. You enjoy your little time in the slammer?"

"Oh, it was lovely." Cade walked in and Jana hugged him. It was more than he had expected.

"I'm sorry," she said. "We had no idea what happened to you."

"How'd you find out?" he said.

After she explained the previous night, the CIA's revelation that he'd been arrested, Gaviria being taken away, he nodded.

"They're going to charge you, Jana. I'm sorry."

She said, "They really consider it attempted murder?"

"Apparently so," he said. "They know about your route home. That you walked out of your way. To them, it looks like you lured him down that alley. And since they know about your special-agent background, the training . . . well, they think it was planned."

She crossed her arms. "Screw them. Besides, we don't have time for this. We've got to get set up for my visit to Diego Rojas."

"You think you're ready?"

"I can get past the gate. But how to get Kyle out of there, that's the problem. I know he's being held. And I'm betting he's somewhere behind that steel door in Rojas's wine cellar."

"I believe you, by the way. That Kyle's alive. It makes perfect sense. Even though we don't know why CIA is involved, it makes sense that Kyle was the one who told Rojas that Gaviria was now on the island."

Stone walked in and listened.

Jana said, "We can't get distracted with CIA. We've got to focus on our one objective, Kyle." She looked around then out the bay window. The boat was gone. "Wait a minute. My father is gone?"

"Left a while ago," Stone said.

Cade said, "I know you don't want any advice about your father, Jana, but you need to give him a chance."

"He doesn't deserve a chance. If he wanted to be there for me, he had that chance when I was born."

Cade let the subject drop. He looked at Stone. "We need a plan to get Kyle out. Stone, you were a hot-shot Delta Force operator, and you've been inside Rojas's estate. What do you suggest?"

"I'd go in with a team of eight operators. Come in under cover of night, put guns in position to cover, take the guards out quietly. Have our electronics expert disable any alarm systems. Get inside and breach the door Jana described. Grab Kyle up and get him out of there. We'd have a vehicle in front waiting for us and a CRRC boat in the back, just in case we need to get out that way. Helicopter gunships in reserve in case it got ugly."

Jana said. "That's nice, for a team of eight."

"I know," he said. "There are four of us."

"Three," Jana said.

"We need his help, Jana," Stone said.

"Look, there's only a few of us," she said. "You're talking about killing these guards quietly, in cold blood. If that goes wrong, we'd probably be in a firefight. Have you ever done this before?"

"Many times," he said, though his voice was distant.

Cade shook his head. "We don't have that type of support. Gunships in reserve, boats? It's just us."

"Then we walk in the front door," Stone replied. "Jana walks in, anyway. I'd be set up just off-site. I've got a sniper rifle with an AMTEC suppressor. If things go sideways, I'll take out the guard at the gate and the one at the front door without anyone knowing."

"Wait, wait," Cade said. "We don't stand a chance trying to take Kyle by force. Not the three of us. How can we get him out without all that?"

"We use Jana," Stone said. "Jana on the inside is better than eight operators on the outside. But she's going to have to be prepared in case things go bad."

Cade said, "How is she going to be prepared if they search her again, which, they're sure to do?"

"I'm going in armed," Jana replied.

"Armed?" Cade said. "How are you going to sneak a weapon past the guards?"

"I'm not. I've proven myself to Rojas. I'm carrying a weapon on my person and he can kiss my ass if he thinks otherwise."

Then, Jana's phone rang.

52

Origins

The caller ID on Jana's phone said simply "Unknown." She placed the phone to her ear but said nothing. A garbled, computerized voice said, "Your mother had a favorite candy. Meet at the place of their origin, ten minutes. Come alone."

"What?" Jana said, but the call had gone dead.

Cade said, "Who was it?"

"Somebody wants to me to meet."

"Well, it has to be Pete Buck. He's the only one with the number to this new SIM card."

"Yeah," Jana said, "but where? And why would he disguise his voice?"

"He disguised . . ." Cade said. "He obviously doesn't want anyone to know he's in touch with you. He slipped you the SIM cards, and now this. Where did he say he wanted to meet?"

"I have no idea," she said.

"You just talked to him," Stone said, still looking out the windows.

"He said to meet *at the place of origin of my mother's favorite candies.*"

"What the hell does that mean?" Cade said.

Jana began to walk as she thought. "She loved marzipan too.

That's where I got it from. But they're made in New Orleans. He said to meet at the place of their origin in ten minutes. Now how am I supposed to meet him . . ."

"Jana?" Cade said.

"I know exactly where," she said and then walked out the door. "He means the Little Orleans Market."

Cade and Stone began to follow but Jana held up a hand before getting in the car. "I'm doing this alone."

When she drove away, Stone said to Cade, "Don't worry, she knows what she's doing."

"That's what bothers me."

53

The Question is the Answer

The Little Orleans Market, Antigua.

A few minutes later, Jana pulled her car behind the market and parked next to a dumpster. She went in the back door. Inside the ramshackle shop was the owner, a little old lady named Abena. She didn't look up from her sweeping. Pete Buck was seated at a tiny round table, one of three set up for anyone enjoying Abena's cooking. Jana walked to the table but paused, her eyes glued on the old woman. Abena had stopped where she was standing, her broom in hand. It was almost as if she was frozen.

Jana walked to her and placed a gentle arm around her waist and took hold of the broom. The woman smiled at her through Coke-bottle-thick glasses and the two walked in shuffle-step behind the counter where Jana helped her onto a stool.

Then Jana sat at the table. "She gets stuck sometimes."

"I know you're going to ask, Jana. And I don't know."

"What am I going to ask?" she said, though she knew the answer.

"Why," he exhaled. "Why is the Company knee deep in drug cartels."

"And?"

"I told you, I don't know."

"You're going to have to do better than that, Buck."

He said nothing.

Jana continued. "Let's start with what you do know. And don't hand me that classified bullshit. It's Kyle we're talking about."

"We've been doing a lot of background work on Colombian cartels, the new ones. Again, I don't know exactly why, but when an ops package comes in, you work on it, you don't question it."

"Thanks for reminding me why I fled to a tropical island," she said with a smirk. "God, I hated all that."

"Can I continue?" he said. "At any rate, there's something big going down."

"They sent you into an operation and didn't tell you the objective?"

"Same old Jana." He shook his head. "Maybe there's something in the history. Look, in the '80s, the Colombian cartels used to be comprised of the Medellín and the Cali cartels. The Medellín was Carlos Escobar's brainchild, and the Cali spawned off of it. None of that exists any longer. Hell, even the cartel *structure* Escobar put into place is gone. That organizational structure controlled everything. All the links in the drug chain from production to retail were owned by him. When he was killed, it fell apart. So over the last twenty years, Colombia's drug trade has reorganized, but it's fragmented."

"What's all this got to do with Antigua? Or with Kyle, for that matter?"

"Keep your pants on."

"I plan to," she said.

"A new generation of drug trafficking groups were born, under an entirely new structure."

"Okay, I'll play along. What's this new structure?"

"The BACRIM is the newer organization. It's so named by

the Colombian government to mean 'bandas criminales.' The BACRIM is a group *of groups* of drug traffickers. They *had* to decentralize because any person that climbs too far up the ladder is quickly identified by the Colombian police or the DEA and brought down. Today, there can't be a new Carlos Escobar. There are two main groups within BACRIM, Oficina de Envigado and Los Rastrojos. And that's where Antigua comes into play."

"How so?" she said.

"The Oficina de Envigado is the successor to the Medellín Cartel, and Los Rastrojos succeeded Cali. Again," Buck continued, "these are highly fragmented groups, nearly impossible to take down."

"Why?"

"DEA has tried, believe me. Each group is broken into many smaller parts. Many of these nodes are individual drug traffickers with a small band behind them, and they use the BACRIM as protection to take advantage of routes and departure points. The removal of any single node doesn't lead to the fall of the other nodes. It only results in a temporary disruption. Then the flow of drugs continues as the network reforms itself. And," Buck continued, "they've set up shop on Antigua. It's the new drug route to move product to the Mexican cartels, and then into the US."

Jana leaned in. "Then why don't you people identify, then take out, the head of each little node all at once?"

"It's not our job!" Buck snapped.

"If it's not CIA's job, then what are you doing on my island?"

"When did you become such a pain in the ass?" Buck said.

"When I threw my badge and credentials at the director of the FBI and started a new life. Before you people dragged me back in."

"Identifying these people is not that simple. The nodes are practically invisible. These guys are more likely to be armed with an iPhone than an Uzi. They look like businessmen. They blend in. And, they keep things quiet. Not to mention the fact that it's harder than it used to be. We can't just follow the flow of cocaine backwards and get to the source. These guys have a far more diversified criminal portfolio—extortion, illegal gold mining, gambling and microtrafficking, like dealing marijuana and synthetic drugs as well as cocaine and its derivatives."

"All I care about is getting to Kyle." Jana lowered her voice. "The only thugs at Diego Rojas's house that don't carry automatic weapons are his intelligence officer, Gustavo Moreno, and Rojas himself. It doesn't seem that hard to identify them."

Buck shook off the accusation. "Anyway, like I said, something big is coming down and I don't know what it is."

"I know who does."

"Yes, I'm sure my boss is well aware of whatever is about to happen, and why CIA is here. I brought you here for a reason. I brought you here to tell you we're going to have to move fast."

"I'm not helping the CIA do anything."

"No," he said, "I'm talking about Kyle. I'm here to help and I'm telling you, we have to move and move now."

"Or what?"

"I'm getting a bad feeling. IMGINT and MASINT reports are coming across my desk."

"Speak English."

"Imagery Intelligence and Measurement and Signature Intelligence."

"And what do these reports say?"

"There's an awful lot of satellite imagery of Rojas's estate. I mean a lot. That along with more of the same from sites across Colombia."

"If the Company is doing some kind of investigation and he's the main target, wouldn't that be normal?"

Buck looked over his shoulder. "Yeah, normal, I guess. But there's a strange amount of location-based data. GPS coordinates, longitude, latitude, precise measurements from roadways. I don't get it."

Jana stood. "I have no idea what any of that means, but it's a lovely fucking job you have. How do they expect you to do your job if so much is secret?"

"What if there's an attack planned?"

Jana gritted her teeth. "You're thinking of that team of CIA operators that picked up Gaviria, aren't you? Dammit, first they tell us we're on our own, that no backup is coming, and now you're thinking they're about to launch a raid? The US government is going to commit an act of war against a noncombatant nation?" She pointed in the direction of the estate. "There are innocents in there. Servants, cooks, cleaners. They're just locals."

Buck lowered his head. "Collateral damage."

Her voice became stilted as she thought back to the woman screaming at the window. "There's a woman in there. That prick is raping her. She's a victim of the human slave trade."

"Which one?" Buck said.

"Which one? What does that mean? I don't know. She's got long black hair."

"She's dead, Jana."

"What?" she said a little too loud before covering her mouth.

"Her body showed up yesterday," Buck said. "Rojas gets bored very quickly. There's a steady stream of sex slaves. Rojas has them shipped in. When he's done with them, they get carried out." Buck stood up. "She was easy to identify. Most of them are moved in from South America, but she was Persian, from Syria. We don't know how she got here, but I'm betting the fact that she's from the Middle East is somehow related to whatever's about to happen. I'm on your side, Jana." He looked down and noticed her hand shaking. "Don't shut down on me. Outside of Cade and Stone, I'm the only friend you have."

"The Middle East?" Jana said. "What's that supposed to mean? Are you telling me there's a connection?"

"My clearance doesn't go that high."

"Bullshit!" Jana said. "If you know he's committing kidnapping, rape, and murder, why hasn't CIA arrested him? Why is his fucking head not on a stick?"

"Jana, you know it doesn't work that way."

She slammed an open hand onto the table. "What is the Company doing on Antigua?"

"I told you, I don't know."

"Oh really? Well let me ask you this. What happened to Gaviria?"

"What's that supposed to mean?"

"You guys showed up all hot and ready to take him off our hands. You had a team prepped and waiting. And you wouldn't have done that without a reason."

"Jana, this is me we're talking about," Buck said. "I'm telling you what I know. I'm telling you more than I should. I'm taking a hell of a risk here."

"Then you better find out what happened to Gaviria before something else goes wrong."

"What could go wrong? We're the CIA."

Jana leaned back in her chair. "Yeah, sure. What else could go wrong?" She sharpened her tone. "I don't exactly get a warm fuzzy where the Agency is concerned."

Buck said, "Me and you both."

The two smiled.

54

Sting of the Scorpion

CIA covert station, location undisclosed, Antigua.

Lawrence Wallace leaned over the analyst's shoulder and peered at the man's computer monitor.

"It's right here, sir," the analyst said as he pointed to a blip on the radar screen. "That's the float-plane's transponder."

"And you're sure our target is on board?"

"That's an affirm, sir."

"ETA to Antigua?"

"Let me calculate the flight time," the analyst said as he began tapping away at his keyboard. "Depending on headwinds and airspeed, it's between fifty-six and seventy minutes, sir."

Wallace looked at his watch. "Fifty-six minutes? We're running out of time. We've got to get all parties in there." He spoke lower. "Hand me that headset. Where is *Avenger* in reference to Antigua?"

"The aircraft carrier?" He looked at his laptop. "Cruising seventeen hundred nautical miles south-southwest, sir." The analyst waited a moment.

Wallace stared at the analyst's monitor and his eyes became glassy. "Have them turn into the wind." He began to pace the room, entranced in thought.

The analyst whispered to himself, "The only reason to turn a carrier into the wind is to launch an aircraft."He glanced at the window and caught Wallace's face in the reflection. In it, he saw a strange slurry of panic mixed with satisfaction.

Wallace said, "Give me that headset." He placed the headset on and adjusted the mic. "Avenger?" Wallace said into the mic, "this is Crystal Palace, over."

***

1,766 miles away, at Fort Meade, Maryland, Knuckles yelled across the vast NSACommandCenter, "Uncle Bill! The feed is live!" He clicked his mouse a few times, and the device began recording.

The aged man came running over in a panting rush. "What is it, son?"

"They just called to the USS *George H. W. Bush*. She's part of carrier strike group two, currently deployed in the Caribbean Sea." The temptation to dispel information was too much for the young analyst. "They've been monitoring the deteriorating situation in Venezuela. She's got at least one cruiser, a destroyer squadron of at least two destroyers, or possibly frigates, and a carrier air wing of sixty-five aircraft."

Bill looked at him over the tops of his glasses. "I know what a carrier strike group is comprised of."

"Oh, yes sir."

"Hand me that headset."

***

"Go ahead, Crystal Palace," the aircraft carrier called. "This is *Avenger*."

"*Avenger*, this is Crystal Palace. Give me a sitrep."

"Asset is on the pad, Crystal Palace. Catapult locked in."

"Roger that, *Avenger*. Launch the asset. I repeat, the asset is a

216

go for launch."

***

On the deck of the aircraft carrier, the pilot of an F/A-18F Super Hornet was given the thumbs-up. The pilot charged the engines until a concentration of flame roared from the exhaust ports. The launch catapult rocketed forward and flung the plane off the deck.

"Asset is away, Crystal Palace," the voice said into the secure uplink.

"Roger that, *Avenger*. Give me direct comms."

A few moments later a crackle came across the headset as the F-18 pilot made contact. "Crystal Palace, this is Scorpion. All systems nominal, altitude two hundred and eighty-seven feet. Climbing to cruising altitude, over."

Wallace looked at the radar monitor as a second blip representing the F-18 pulsed onto the screen. "Roger that, Scorpion, this is Crystal Palace. I've got you five by five. At your discretion, come right, bearing 327.25, affirm?"

"Roger that, Crystal Palace. Making my heading 327.25 degrees."

"Weapons status?"

"Crystal Palace, this is Scorpion. AGM-84K off my starboard wing. Scorpion is fragged."

The CIA analyst looked up quizzically at Wallace. Wallace covered his mic and said, "He means the aircraft has been armed with the specific weapon ordered by the mission directive."

"What's an AGM-84K, sir?"

***

"Did he say an AGM?" Uncle Bill said as he pressed the headset against his ears.

Knuckles typed in the name of the weapon just to confirm his suspicion. He pointed at his monitor as his computer spat back:

AGM-84K SLAM-ER (StandoffLand Attack Missile—Expanded Response)

Boeing Company

Weight: 1,487 lbs.

Length: 14.3 ft.

Operational Range: 170 mi.

Speed: 531 mph

"Mother of God," Uncle Bill whispered.

"Fourteen hundred pounds?" Knuckles said. "What are they going to do with *that*?"

***

Wallace spoke into the mic, "Scorpion, this is Crystal Palace. Approach to within one hundred and sixty miles, source to target, then hold."

"Roger that, Crystal Palace," came the clipped reply from the F-18 pilot. "Scorpion out."

***

Uncle Bill's fingers descended into his thick gray hair. "We've got to warn Jana." He pulled the glasses from his face and rubbed his eyes. "How do we do that without arousing CIA's suspicion?"

"We've tried raising them, sir," Knuckles said. "Nothing is working."

"Dammit, son. I have to talk to them. I want answers."

"But . . . sir, I don't understand," the boy stammered. "What is that bomb for?"

But Uncle Bill was entranced in his line of thought. "And even if I do warn her, Jana's not going to leave Kyle in there."

***

At the covert station, the CIA analyst looked up. "Sir, I know I'm not operationally cleared, but I need to understand the plan."

Wallace squinted his eyes at the man. "You are, what, five years into the Agency? What do you believe the mission to be?"

"I originally thought it was to disrupt a new drug route for the cartels. But now I understand there's another target involved: a target that is on that floatplane, on its way to Antigua. Is the larger plan to draw all the players together?"

Wallace didn't acknowledge the statement. "You disapprove?"

"Sir, it's just that Agent MacKerron is still being held. Agent Baker needs time to get him out."

"This will not be the last time you see a throwaway."

"Sir?"

"An agent whom the company will permit to be detected."

The analyst looked down. "So you are saying Agents MacKerron and Baker are expendable."

"It's for the greater good, son. We dead-dropped intel to Diego Rojas so that MacKerron would be captured."

"But—"

"Agent Kyle MacKerron is icing on the cake. The real agenda here is not to simply disrupt the flow of drugs. The DEA can spin its wheels all it wants to that end. It's to sanitize a terrorist-cartel connection before it gets started."

"I don't understand, sir."

"This is above your pay grade." Wallace looked down his long, thin nose at him. "You are either with me or you are out."

A few moments later, the CIA analyst said, "What's the play, sir?"

"Get me Red Dragon."

"The CIA operators? Yes, sir."

Once they were on the line, Wallace spoke into the mic. "Red Dragon, this is Crystal Palace."

"Go ahead, Crystal Palace," a CIA special operator replied.

"Operation Overlord is a go. I repeat, Operation Overlord is a go." Wallace listened for a reply, but when one did not come, he said, "I say again, Red Dragon. This is Crystal Palace. Operation Overlord is a go. Affirm."

"Roger that," came the operator's stilted reply. "This is Red Dragon, out."

The analyst said, "He didn't sound very happy about that, sir."

"Well it's not within his directive to have an opinion, now is it!" Wallace yelled.

"No, sir. I didn't mean to imply . . ."

Wallace ran both hands across his scalp. "Fuck! The whole damned operation hinges on this!"

"Sir, what is Overlord?"

"You just do your job. Overlord is my responsibility."

***

In the NSACommandCenter, Knuckles said, "What was that, sir? He was on the comms with a team of operators? Operation Overlord?"

"I have no idea," Uncle Bill answered, but I can tell you one thing, I'm getting too old for this shit." He thought a moment more. "Son, get me the DEA Special Response Team at Point Udall, US Virgin Islands."

55

Living with It

Safe house.

Jana saw her father in the other bedroom. "What is *he* doing here?"

Cade looked at her. "We're a little short on numbers, and you're about to go back into Rojas's estate. Anything can happen. We might need him."

"Oh, and you think an ex-CIA case officer who has been in prison the last twenty-eight years is going to help?"

"He was apparently a pretty big help when things went sideways with Gaviria."

Jana's breathing accelerated. "I don't have time for this." She looked around the room. "Where's Stone?" But as she looked back at the crushed coral driveway, she had her answer. He was pulling back in with his Jeep.

"Reconnaissance," Cade said. "He went to Rojas's to scope out where he could set up with his sniper rifle." Stone walked in the door. "Well?" Cade said to him.

"It's going to be harder than I thought. But I think I have a spot."

"Where?" Ames said from the bedroom door.

"You stay out of this," Jana barked.

Stone shook his head. "I'm on the next hillside over. There's a lot of foliage and cover. It affords me a clear shot from that side of the compound."

"But, wait a second," Jana said. "That's a long way away, isn't it?"

"Not in sniper terms."

"How far?" Cade said.

"Eleven hundred and sixteen yards," Stone replied.

"And that's not far?" Cade said. "You've got to be kidding me. Eleven football fields away?"

Stone made no reply.

"He's right," Ames said as he walked cross-armed into the room. "When I was a handler, I arranged three ops that required shots longer than that. Believe me, if he's certified as a Delta Force sniper, he can do it."

"No one is asking for your opinion," Jana snapped. "How long is it going to take you to get into position?"

"We're going in now?" Stone said.

"Tonight," Jana said. "Shut up a minute while I make this call." She dialed a number and let it ring. She said, "I'll be there tonight at seven."

On the other end of the line was Diego Rojas. "Agent Baker, how pleasant of you to call." Jana heard a woman's muffled crying in the background. "But I have plans for tonight. I'm afraid I will be unavoidably detained."

Anger-infused adrenaline pushed into her veins. Rojas was abusing another woman. "I don't give a shit who you are entertaining. I'll be there to collect, and I expect you to have my second payment ready."

The woman screamed again, but to Jana, it sounded as if she was gagged. "You are a woman who does not know her place,

Agent Baker."

"Don't take that male-dominating tone with me, Rojas. The last man to do that ended up with his balls blown off and his face the color of purple eggplant." She paused and let the statement sink in a moment. "You had no way to get to Gaviria. If you did, you wouldn't have hired me to do the job. Now that the job is done, I expect to be paid, and paid in full. And you have other assignments for me, don't you? Things have changed. Oficina de Envigado is well aware that their fearless leader is no more, and the heat is turning up. The stakes are higher, and with higher stakes comes a higher price."

"You disposed of Senior Gaviria's body?"

"Of course I did."

"We will discuss your next assignment tonight," Rojas said. Just as he hung up the call, Jana heard the woman scream again. To her, it sounded like muffled terror.

Cade said, "Jesus, Jana, you're shaking like a leaf."

"I swear to God, I'm going to kill that son of a bitch," she said.

"What is it?" Stone said.

Ames was looking in the other direction, but said, "The killing is the easy part, Jana. It's living with it that's hard."

She reeled toward him and opened her mouth but images popped into her mind's eye. She was back at the cabin, tied to the chair with Rafael leering over her.

Her chest heaved and she brought a hand to her throat then pulled it back the way a person might check themselves for blood.

"Hey, Jana," Cade said. "You still with us?" By way of distraction, he asked, "What happened with Pete Buck?"

As she had finished recounting what she'd learned from Buck, her phone vibrated once. She glanced at the screen then held it for them to see. It was an incoming text message, which contained a single word, "Marzipan."

"It's Buck again," she whispered just above the tightening in her throat. "Christ, he must want to meet again. I just got back."

"He must have more information," Stone said.

"We don't have time for this," Jana said. "We've got to get ready for tonight."

Ames said in a low voice, "You better go find out what Buck has."

But a moment later, Cade's computer chirped and everyone looked at it.

"What?" he said. "Satellite connection coming back online. There's only one way that's happening."

They all knew what that meant, another call was about to come in from Lawrence Wallace.

56

Star on the Wall

Cade's initial thought was to try to use the reacquired satellite connection to communicate to Uncle Bill at NSA. They'd been cut off for over a day and not even the new SIM cards Pete Buck had slipped them would work to call off the island. It had been maddening. But no matter what Cade tried, his connectivity was still blocked.

A chirp came across the laptop's tiny speaker.

"Here we go," Cade said as Jana and Stone leaned over.

Ames kept his distance. He was trying to tread lightly where Jana was concerned.

Lawrence Wallace's smug face appeared on the monitor. They could see his lips moving but heard nothing. A few moments later, the sound became audible.

". . . there's not much time. You're going to have to move right now."

"Wallace," Cade said. "We didn't get that. Your connection was broken. Say again."

"If you want to get Agent MacKerron out, now is your only opportunity." Wallace fidgeted in his seat. "Do you hear me? I said you have to move now."

The three looked at one another. Jana said, "Wallace, what's the sudden rush?"

"It's nothing that concerns you. The timetable has . . . shifted."

"Timetable? What timetable? And when are you so concerned about Kyle?" she said. Her tone was accusatory.

"The sole concern of the Agency has always been the safe return of our agent."

Jana shook her head. "That's crap and you know it."

"Whatever our differences, Agent Baker, the life of Kyle MacKerron hangs in the balance. Do you want him to end up a star on the wall at Langley? You are the only asset that can get to him."

"That's bullshit too," she said. "What about that team of operators that popped by last night to pick up Gaviria? They didn't exactly look like they were on the island to pick up a little sun. Why don't you send them in?" Jana was testing him.

"Baker!" Wallace said as he fidgeted with his hands. "You are the only one that can get in that compound and pull him out. If a raid were attempted, Agent MacKerron wouldn't stand a chance. Now I am ordering you to—" He stopped midsentence and spoke to someone just out of the camera's range. "He's what? How did that plane get so far so fast?" He turned back to his monitor. "Baker, you have to trust me. If you don't go now, Agent MacKerron will be dead within the hour."

"Dammit!" Jana screamed. "How the hell do you know that? What has changed?"

"It's on a need-to-know basis."

"You want me to go into a den of drug lords and you don't think I have a need to know? I swear to God, Wallace. When I'm done with Rojas, I'm coming for you."

From the back of the room, Ames said in a low, almost reverent voice, "Hidden agenda."

Jana looked back to the monitor. "Wallace, you've got five seconds to tell me what's going on. Otherwise, get him out yourself."

Wallace became stone-faced. "Get him out now, or his blood will be on your hands." He disconnected the call.

57

To Fan the Flames

Little Orleans Market.

Jana steered the Jeep around a tight curve and stopped behind the market. Buck was waiting. "What is it?" she said. "We were just here twenty minutes ago."

Buck's voice was distant. "I just got off the phone with an informant."

"Spit it out."

"Gaviria's body was just dumped at the front gate of Oficina de Envigado."

Jana was speechless. "His body? But CIA had Gaviria in custody. He was alive. What, did they kill him?"

"I have no idea, but this is not good."

"If Gaviria's body was just dumped at his own cartel's front door, that means . . . that means Oficina de Envigado is about to declare war on Los Rastrojos."

Buck said, "Envigado will send every soldier they have. Rojas's estate is about to become a war zone. And there's more. A high-priority suspect is en route to the island. A terrorist named Karim Zahir. He's apparently coming for a meet with Rojas."

Jana's eyes sharpened. "This is it, isn't it? This is what Wallace was so panicked about. He knew. That son of a bitch did this himself. He's got something up his sleeve and this is his way of forcing my hand."

"What are you going to do?"

"I'm going to get my friend."

"Jana, wait!" Buck yelled. But it was too late. The Jeep's tires were already spinning.

58

An Object in Motion

As the Jeep slid from one side of the dirt road to the other, Jana dialed Stone. When he picked up, she yelled into the phone. "Go now! I'll be at the house in four minutes and I won't be there more than two before I head to Rojas's. You've got to be in position."

"Jesus, Jana. What happened to you tonight? Nineteen-hundred hours, remember? We have to plan."

"Move!" she screamed, then hung up the call.

When she arrived at the safe house, Stone had already left. She jammed the brakes and skid across the parking area, then ran inside.

Cade was on his feet. "What happened? Why are we going right now and not later tonight?"

She blew past him and into the back bedroom. "What do you mean, *we*? You're not going anywhere." She flung open a wooden louvered closet door which slammed into its frame and began to wobble. She then yanked a dress off its hanger.

"I *have* to go," Cade said as he stood in the doorway. "You can't expect just you and Stone are going to pull this off. What if you need help?" His voice faltered as he watched Jana throw her shirt and shorts to the floor. "What if you need a diversion or a secondary vehicle to get away?"

Jana turned her back and dropped her bra to the ground, then threw the little black dress over her head and snugged into it. Cade tried to avert his eyes but couldn't.

"Where is Ames?" she said.

"Your father? It might help if you could at least call him that."

"Where?"

"Gone. I don't know. When Stone took off, I turned around and he was nowhere."

Jana pulled out a small black purse then reached behind a chest of drawers. Her hand fumbled for a moment, then Cade heard the sound of Velcro ripping as she pulled out a fully-framed Glock 9 mm handgun.

Cade said, "You don't think you're going to tuck that thing into that tiny dress, do you?"

"No, nimrod, just grabbed the wrong handle, that's all." She reached behind the dresser again and placed the weapon back. Then she withdrew another, much smaller one. It was identical to the weapon she had used to teach her attacker, Montes Lima Perez, a lesson. She tightened the silencer and ensured a round was in the chamber, then tucked it into her purse. She pulled out a black Velcro strap that housed two extra magazines. Cade again tried unsuccessfully to avert his eyes as she propped her leg on the bed and pulled her skirt high enough so she could wrap the strap around her upper thigh. When she saw Cade staring, she said, "Get a good look?"

"You offering?" he jabbed back.

"No."

"So what's changed? I'm going with you," he said as he went out into the main room and grabbed a handgun from Stone's bag.

"Whatever, but you're going to keep out of there. I can't pull Kyle out and have to go back and get your ass too."

As they went out to the Jeep, Cade got in the driver's seat. He said, "What did Pete Buck tell you this time? Why the sudden rush?"

Jana looked into a mirror and dabbed her makeup and hair. "There's a terrorist on his way. He and Rojas are going to consummate their business relationship."

"Which is?"

"Money laundering to the tune of hundreds of millions."

"Lovely," Cade said as he accelerated. "But that doesn't explain the urgency. Why does this have to happen right now?"

"Oh," she said, "did I forget to mention that Gaviria's body just showed up at the compound of Oficina de Envigado?"

Cade nearly lost control of the vehicle. "What? He's dead? How did—"

"I don't have time to draw you a picture. But once they see that body, there's going to be a shitload of angry drug runners crashing the gates at Rojas's place. It will be an all-out war. I've got to get Kyle out now, no matter what."

"Christ, Jana. We need backup. We can't fend off fifty heavily armed men while you traipse inside to grab Kyle, from a locked cell, I might add. We need Uncle Bill. He could task a strike force down here in a heartbeat."

"Well since we still can't so much as place a damned phone call to him, that point is moot."

"How are we going to play this? I mean, you're going to, what, talk your way past the front gate?"

"When we get close, you're hopping out. I don't stand a chance of getting past that guard with someone else in the car."

"How are you going to get past him in the first place? You

aren't supposed to be there until tonight."

Jana put her lipstick away and glanced at herself in the mirror one last time. She looked down at her exposed cleavage and said, "I'll think of something."

59

Arrival

Morris Bay.

The skids of the Quest Kodiak single-engine floatplane touched down in the calm waters of Morris Bay. Water sprayed from them in protest. The plane taxied toward a small, private dock. From the rear passenger seat, Karim Zahir pressed his dark sunglasses further up. He glanced out the windshield at Rojas's estate and eyed two armed men standing on the dock.

Zahir wore a long-sleeved, button-down shirt which was open several buttons. The light-colored suit jacket and slacks stood in sharp contrast to his dark features. A beautiful young woman with bronze skin sat quietly next to him.

Zahir ran his eyes down her body and grinned. He leaned to her. "If you want to be alive," he whispered, "you will stay very, very quiet."

Her lower lip began to tremble.

"Mr. Zahir?" the pilot said when he saw the men at the dock carrying automatic weapons. "This is MorrisBay, Antigua, sir. But are you sure we're in the right place?"

"Of course I am sure. Do not let the crudeness of my business associates' security detail disturb you. It is all for show."

The pilot swallowed. "Yes, sir." He steered the craft until it

234

floated gently to the dock, where one of the guards took hold. The guard opened the plane's side door and held it.

"Stay here," Zahir said to the pilot, "and be prepared. I do not like to be kept waiting." He stepped onto the plane's float then onto the dock. The woman followed him, yet, in her high heels, she nearly slipped. "My business will be concluded within the hour, then I will depart."

"Do you mean you both will be departing, sir?" the pilot said.

Zahir looked down the woman's dress. "No, I will depart alone. My associate here has other business to conduct and will remain."

When she saw the grin on Zahir's face, she shrunk from him.

60

Jitters No More

"Here is where you get out," Jana said to Cade as they pulled closer.

Cade stopped the vehicle and hopped out while Jana slid to the driver's seat. He tucked the weapon he had taken from Stone's bag under his shirt. "Be careful," he said.

But just after accelerating away, she said, "Being careful is exactly what I'm *not* going to do."

Cade disappeared into the tropical foliage and moved in the direction of the compound.

Jana turned the Jeep up the driveway but stopped short. She took a few breaths and glanced at her right hand. She had been gripping the steering wheel so hard she had not noticed the shaking. *You've spent the last year training for something like this, something you hoped would never happen.* She closed her eyes and exhaled in one long motion. *This is it.* And with that, all the jitters left her body.

61

Flesh and Lead

From his perch on the opposing hillside, Stone focused the Leupold rifle scope. He scanned the front of the estate and down to the guardhouse at the entrance gate. Something in his peripheral vision moved and he squinted in its direction but could make out nothing. He started to move the scope to take a closer look but when he saw the Jeep approaching, he zoomed his view closer to see the guard.

Jana pulled the vehicle to a stop in front of the guard shack and assumed a playful grin. The same guard she had encountered before stared at her and let his eyes run to her chest. When he finally looked her in the eye, she returned the favor by running her own eyes down his body. After all, a little flirtation couldn't hurt.

But when he shifted his automatic weapon to the front of his body, she straightened.

His voice was salty. "You are not on the schedule until seven."

Try one more time, she thought. She leaned an elbow in the open window, propped her head onto her hand, then tilted it. "I know," she said. She reached out and let her fingers run delicately across his hand. "Things got a little busy. So I thought I'd come early."

The man looked at her hand and swallowed. "I'll have to call it in." He turned toward the guard shack.

Shit, this is not working. "Do you?" Her tone was playful. Just out of his line of sight, she felt for her purse. "I wanted it to be a surprise for Diego."

"I am not permitted." He picked up a phone but when a silenced bullet ripped into his skull, brain matter splattered onto the guard shack and he collapsed. "I guess I'm going in hot," she said as she hopped out of the Jeep. "It was a boring conversation anyway."

On the hillside, Stone watched the man collapse. He glanced to the guards at the front of the house to see if they had heard when he again saw movement out of the corner of his eye. It had come from the same place. "What the hell is that?" He trained the scope on the spot but there was too much foliage blocking his view. But then he saw color behind the dense green and caught a glimpse of Cade's face. "Rookie," Stone said. He looked back at the guards and saw one of them raise a walkie-talkie and begin to speak. Stone shifted the rifle into position and locked onto the guard. "That's not good. They know. Dammit, they know."

Jana pushed the button inside the guard shack and the massive steel gates began to lurch open. She jumped in the Jeep and drove calmly up the drive and toward the estate.

At the front door, the first guard motioned to the second and started down the steps toward Jana's approaching car.

"She'll never make it," Stone said. He exhaled and held, counted slowly, then tapped off a single round. Across the silencer, the discharged round sounded like a muffled *whump*. The sound the bullet made when it slammed into the man's skull, however, was loud, something similar to a slapping noise. The guard's body spun and flopped onto the ground just as the Jeep crested the hill.

The second guard turned at the slapping sound to find his partner in a pool of blood. Stone lined the crosshairs and began to apply light tension to the trigger. But before the weapon could discharge, he saw the man's body fling into the air. Jana had run him down with the Jeep.

Stone watched as she hopped out and without hesitation pumped one round into the man's head on her way up the steps.

"Christ," Stone said to himself, "I've created a monster. Oh shit!" he said as another guard came out of the open doorway.

Jana dropped to the ground and fired upwards into the man's throat. The .380-caliber hollow point tore into the soft flesh and exited through his spine. He was dead before the empty brass shell casing tinked onto the stone landing. She leaned against the door jam and scanned the massive, glass-lined room with her weapon forward. On the veranda, she saw Diego Rojas shake hands with a well-appointed man who had a black beard and a devilish grin. The men stood with their backs to Jana and pointed up and down at a woman standing across from them. Her long, shimmering black hair draped gently across the straps of her full-length, form-fitting sequin gown. The woman was the only one facing Jana's direction and Jana knew, she was another sex slave.

The Middle Easterner placed a hand on Rojas's shoulder and laughed as he presented her as a gift, a gesture of good will. Just the thought of what would happen to the woman caused Jana's pulse to explode, but when she saw the petrified look on the young woman's face, her eyes flared even further.

The center-most scar on Jana's chest began to burn and she heard voices. She turned behind her but the voices were distant. One towered above the others.

Do it, the voice taunted as it laughed. It sounded like the hissing of a snake. *Do it now. You know what they are going to do to that girl. You know you can stop it. Dooo it.* Jana tightened the grip on her firearm and her breathing became erratic.

The laughter from the trio of voices sent a new shockwave of nausea through Jana's system, and the edges of her vision, once crisp and sharp, began to blur. She looked down and saw the body of the last guard she had killed, then turned around to see the other two.

You killed them without hesitation, the voice said. *It was a thing of beauty.*

Jana's fingers ran across the scar and she winced in pain. She glanced back at Rojas and the other man.

Do it. Kill them, the voice taunted. *Kill them all!*

Jana's knees began to shake.

The others would have killed you. They were justified. But these two, you'll walk over and kill them in cold blood. Once it is done, your journey will be complete.

Tears began to stream and Jana struggled to breathe. The gun lowered. "Kyle, I've got to get to Kyle." She dropped to one knee and shook her head violently, then said, "Think back. Think back to the fort. You've got to find the fort." She gritted her jaw and allowed her mind to drift back to her childhood, back to her precious fort, her bastion of safety. When she was finally inside it, her breathing began to normalize.

She looked up to find the woman on the balcony staring at her, her eyes glazed in fear. Jana put a finger to her lips and mouthed *shhh* just as the woman's eyes drifted onto the dead guard in the doorway. She looked petrified, but seemed to register that Jana was there to help.

Jana grabbed the dead guard by his jacket collar and dragged him across the slick stone floor, out the door, then rolled his body down the steps.

At least he's out of direct view, she thought. She crept back to the door casing and motioned to the girl with an open hand, a signal for her to stay put. The woman blinked and a tear rolled down her cheek.

The magazines held only five rounds and Jana withdrew a full one from the Velcro strap and charged it into her weapon. She quick-stepped over to the glass staircase and began to descend. About halfway down she saw an armed guard on the lower level looking out the wall of glass at the floatplane still at the dock. She stood upright and clasped her hands behind her back, shielding the gun from view, then descended the stairs.

When he heard her approaching, he turned in an abrupt motion and spoke in a thick, Colombian accent, "What are you doing here?"

She continued toward him and said, "What is that supposed to mean? Did you not see me here the other night? I am the guest of Diego, and I will not be spoken to in that manner."

His mouth opened as if he were choosing his words.

Jana closed to within eight feet. Her hand flicked out from behind her back and she pulled the trigger. His body folded to the ground. She rifled through his clothing and jerked out a set of keys, then darted to the wine cellar and its mysterious steel door.

It took her three tries to find the right key, but when she did, it slid in easily. When she opened the door, however, the real trouble started.

62

Committed

Back at the safe house, Cade's laptop chirped once as the small icon of a spinning globe turned green. The satellite connection blinked to life. A video window opened and Uncle Bill in the NSA Command Center said to someone off screen, "Are we on yet?" He looked at the monitor. "Cade? Jana? Christ, where are they? We've got to warn them!"

Standing in the safe house, just behind the monitor, was Richard Ames.

Uncle Bill said, "Look, if you can hear me. There's something big about to happen. CIA has ordered an F-18 into the air. It's coming your way, and it's armed with the mother of all bombs. We're tracking it now. Given the fighter jet's current airspeed, flight time, and maximum range of that missile, we estimate you've got twenty-eight minutes. I'll repeat that. Time of impact is fourteen hundred fifty-six hours; two fifty-six local time. Whatever you do, don't go to that compound!" Bill looked just off camera. "Dammit! How do we know if they got the message?"

When the satellite call terminated, Ames looked at his watch. He then withdrew his phone and conferenced together the phones of Jana, Cade, and Stone. It took a few moments, but each answered the call in turn.

It was Jana that picked up last. "I don't have time for a chitchat, Ames."

"All three of you," Ames said in a calm voice, "listen closely. There is an airstrike inbound at this time. ETA is two fifty-six local."

"An airstrike? What are you talking about?" Stone blurted from the hillside above the Rojas estate.

Ames said, "I told you, there's always a higher agenda. NSA just cracked through the satellite blockage and called it in." He looked at his watch. "You've only got twenty-five minutes. There's no way you can get inside and get MacKerron out in time."

"Too late now," Jana said. "Already inside the gates. Twenty-five minutes? I'll have him out in six. Baker, out." She hung up.

"She's right," Stone said. "It's too late. We're committed."

As the call ended, Ames looked at Stone's bag sitting on the safe-house floor. He leaned down and unzipped the long duffel. When his eyes landed on an object that piqued his interest, he said, "They're going to need some help." He withdrew it from the bag and looked in the mirror. "Say hello to my little friend."

63

Incoming

Cade pushed his way through the dense foliage toward the guard shack. Speaking of the phone call, he said, "Twenty-five minutes? Shit." When he saw the open gate, he could only assume Jana had made it through. Though his heart was pounding, he crept closer to the shack. He became emboldened when he did not see anyone sitting inside. He peered into the tiny outpost. Blood was splattered along the walls. His heart pounded harder. He edged around the rear of the building and his eyes landed upon a set of black boots. Those boots were attached to a dead man, and Cade averted his eyes. He looked over his shoulder to ensure he could see no one.

If what Ames said is true, he thought to himself, *this hillside is going to be laid flat in a few minutes.* He grabbed the man by the arm and was starting to drag when his phone buzzed again. It scared him so badly he flattened to the ground. He looked at the phone.

"Stone, what the hell do you want?" he said as he looked in all directions.

"What do you think you're doing?"

"Are you watching me? I don't have time for a social call. I've got to move this body out of view. If anyone sees it, the game is

244

up."

"That body is nothing compared to the three lying around the front door of the estate. Don't bother with it. Grab his automatic weapon and get back in where you can't be seen."

"Don't tell me what to do. I've been in the field before. I know what I'm doing."

"So glad to be working with another operator," Stone jabbed. Their rivalry lived on.

Cade pulled the automatic weapon's strap from the man's shoulder but when he saw the dark blood coating the back of the strap, he leaned over and gagged.

Stone watched in the distance. To him it appeared Cade was about to be sick. "It's blood, Cade. He's dead. Sometimes it happens. But I'm glad to see you can handle it."

Cade straightened. "Very funny, asswipe. It was the brain matter I wasn't too happy about."

"Look like rotted cottage cheese?"

"God," Cade said, "that's awful," he said as he fought back nausea.

But then Stone said, "Wait a minute. I'm hearing something." Stone paused, then said into the phone. "Do you hear that?"

"Hear what?"

"It sounds like an engine. It sounds like several engines." Stone raised binoculars and scanned the road in the distance. "Cade! We've got incoming. Get that security gate closed and get out of there!"

64

Breathe

As the door scraped across the gritty cement floor, Jana scanned the darkness with her weapon forward. The stench was overwhelming. When she saw just a single silhouette, a man lying on the floor, she lunged in and pointed the gun behind the door to ensure there was no guard. She turned back and could see that it was Kyle. He was lying on a filthy mat, one arm chained to the wall. She knelt down and shook his shoulder. "Kyle, Kyle. Wake up." She shook harder and finally he began to stir.

"Hey, man. Leave me alone," he said in a groggy haze.

"Kyle! Get up, we've got to go."

Jana fumbled through the keys until she found the one that fit the padlock on Kyle's wrist. She shook him again and pried apart one of his eyelids to examine the pupil. It was dilated. She checked his arms. Both showed telltale bruising where needles had been injected. "They've drugged you." She pulled until he sat upright. "What are they giving you?" But the answer didn't really matter. She put his arm over her shoulder and struggled to her feet.

"Kyle, help me. We've got to go. We've got to go right now." She glanced at the open doorway.

As Kyle steadied himself, he said, "You're not that dude. Where is that dude with the stuff?"

"Come on, we've got to go."

She walked him forward but he stopped. "I've got to get some stuff, man. Where is that dude?"

Jana squared off in front of him and slapped him across the face. "There's no time for this! This is our only chance."

"Hey, man, that hurts. Hey, Jana? Hey! What are you doing here? Did you bring me the stuff?"

Jana rethought. "Yes, Kyle. Yes, I have the stuff. But it's outside. We've got to go out there to get it. Just come with me, okay?"

"Alright, man."

The pair stumbled forward as Kyle tried to gain his footing.

"Hey, is that a gun you're carrying, or are you just happy to see me?" He laughed. "Why the hostility? These people are awesome!"

Jana had not counted on Kyle being in this condition. She couldn't decide if it was his weight she struggled with more or if it was the terror of getting him out before a missile slammed into the roof. She held the gun in a half-raised position.

As they came out into the lower-level room, Kyle squinted at the wall of glass. Jana scanned back and forth. She looked up at the underside of the balcony. *The woman*, she thought. *I've got to get her out of here.* But with Kyle in this condition she strained to come up with an idea.

Kyle looked at the dead man sprawled against the wall. "Hey, dude. Wake up," he said. He snickered. "No sleeping on the job." But as he looked closer and saw the dark pool of blood, he looked to Jana. "He doesn't look so good. Maybe we should get him a Band-Aid or something." She started to drag Kyle away when he said, "Dude's got a boo-boo, that's for sure."

She looked out at the large, open expanse at the back of the compound. The floatplane sat at the dock and was flanked by two of Rojas's guards. *Shit*, she thought. *Can't go that way.*

She spun Kyle around and headed to the glass staircase. She steadied him then heard several voices from upstairs. She turned Kyle back toward the massive bay doors and walked him onto the patio. On the balcony above, Rojas, the Middle Eastern man, and his bodyguard still held the woman. It was then that she heard men coming down the glass stairs, speaking in Spanish. She began to panic.

She pushed Kyle to the far side of the patio and laid him down just behind a bench seat. She ran back and grabbed the dead man and dragged him onto the patio just beyond Kyle. Two sets of feet came into view on the staircase. She grabbed an oriental rug and pulled it over the bloodstain, then ducked onto the patio.

She crouched against the edge, shielding Kyle with her body, and held her weapon at arm's length. *Keep quiet, Kyle. Please, God. Keep quiet.*

The two guards ambled down the last steps in the middle of a conversation.

Jana's mind raced. *Did I close the door to Kyle's cell? Will they notice the carpet out of place?* The harder she tried to control her breathing, the harder it became.

As the two heavily armed men approached the giant bay doors, Jana glanced at silhouettes of people on the balcony above. *There is no way they aren't going to hear this*, she thought, referring to firing a silenced weapon in such close proximity.

The men stepped onto the patio. Jana clasped her lips and dared not breathe. If she were forced to kill them, Rojas would hear and she would have no choice but to try to escape with Kyle. In his condition, they didn't stand a chance. She held for what seemed like an eternity and could almost hear the ticking of her wrist watch. *The missile,* she thought. *We're out of time.* She applied light attention to the trigger.

65

Hell Hath No Fury

The men stood in the breeze. Jana was three feet away. Their conversation continued as one pointed to the floatplane. She applied more pressure to the trigger. But then in the distance, she heard popping sounds, like automatic-weapons fire. The men turned and ran back up the stairs and Jana drew a long breath. *What the hell is that? Oh, God, Stone is out there.* Her phone buzzed. It was Cade.

"What's going on?" Jana whispered into the phone. She heard yelling on the balcony above and watched as the people there emptied into the house.

"Oficina de Envigado is here!" Cade yelled over the gunfire. "And they're pretty pissed off."

"What about Stone?"

"He can't decide who to shoot next."

"Tell him to shoot them all. Wait!" Jana said. "This is the perfect diversion!" She watched the two guards at the floatplane break into a sprint.

Cade said, "It looks like they're about to breach the gate! This place is going to be overrun. Rojas's people are fighting back, but they're dropping like flies."

"Forget all that! I need help. They've drugged Kyle. I can't get him out on my own."

"Oh, shit!" Cade said. "Where are you?"

"Back patio. Ground level. Tell Stone to rendezvous at the dock behind the estate."

"And do what?"

"There's a floatplane there."

"What are we going to do with a floatplane?" Cade said.

"Shut up and move!"

66

Shards of Glass

Just over the gunfire, Cade heard a whistle. He looked up and saw Stone waving to him. Cade motioned him to move around to the back of the estate.

Stone nodded but as he saw Cade jump and run to the side of the building, he trained his rifle scope just above Cade's shoulder.

Cade was on a dead run. A guard popped out from behind the building and began firing but then his feet flew out from underneath him. He crashed to the ground. Cade stopped in his tracks trying to register what had happened. But then he knew, it was Stone. Cade ran around the back of the house to the patio.

Stone slung his sniper rifle over his shoulder and pulled the HK 416 carbine into position. He took off down the hill, weaving between tropical plants. His movement was swift. The effect would have made him both hard to see and even harder to shoot.

Gunfire from the two opposing drug cartels intensified and stray bullets tore through the air on all sides. Stone's phone buzzed and he answered it.

"We're pinned down," Cade said into the phone. "Kyle is unconscious and we've got to get to the dock!"

"Be there in sixty seconds!" Stone yelled. An instant later a bullet zipped through his right calf and he grunted.

"What was that?" Cade said.

"Nothing. On my way. Just hang tight."

Stone detached a Velcro tie-off and snugged it above the wound. "I'll have time to bleed later," he said and took off running. He stayed in the thick and when he could see the full expanse of the back side of the property, he took up position. Two guards were firing at Jana and Cade. Stone switched back to the sniper rifle and put both of them down. He spoke into the phone, "You're clear."

Cade replied, "The pilot is still at the plane! We're going down there with Kyle. Cover us!"

Automatic gunfire ripped across the manicured lawn as Cade emerged with Kyle over his shoulder. Cade shut his eyes as dirt and blades of grass sprayed his face. He turned to find Jana still crouched underneath the balcony. "What are you doing?" he yelled, then turned to see another guard drop to the ground.

"I'm not leaving her," Jana said.

"What?" Cade said.

"He's got another woman up there."

"Jana! We've got to go. This place will be overrun any second!"

She turned him around by force. "Get Kyle to the plane. Do it now!"

Cade took off running as more gunfire sprayed about him.

Stone popped off one round, then another, and the guns stopped.

Cade zigzagged across the open ground. He was struggling under Kyle's weight. More bullets zipped past his head and he tripped. He and Kyle tumbled to the ground.

Stone popped in a new magazine then tapped off another round. The shot hit home. "Move, Cade!" he yelled into the phone. Cade grabbed Kyle again and threw him over his shoulder, panting to catch his breath. The floatplane was just fifty yards away.

Jana crouched on the glass stairs and surveyed the floor above. Several of Rojas's guards were firing out windows as attackers swarmed up the front. Brass shell casings littered the marble floor near the front door, which was now shut. She heard a woman screaming from down the hallway and leapt to her feet just as bullets shattered the massive glass walls on the back side.

Karim Zahir's personal bodyguard stepped out of one of the rooms with his weapon pointed in her direction. Jana crashed against a wall for cover and snap-shot him in the chest. He fell backwards, firing wildly, and rolled to the ground. He grasped at his chest then slumped over.

Jana ran down the hall and dropped into a crouched position, then pointed the Glock upward. Zahir lunged out, firing his handgun at chest level. The bullets tore into the drywall above Jana's head and she popped off one round. It slammed into Zahir's shoulder. His gun dropped to the ground and he scrambled into another room.

Jana leaned in and saw the woman. Her sequined dress was torn and her mascara had run down her face. She grabbed the woman by the hand and pulled her toward the hall when suddenly she felt the woman yank back. The last thing Jana remembered before everything went black was the woman's screams.

67

Not Without Her

Jana's eyes opened from the blackness into a wet, scorching pain. Her head throbbed. She could tell men were towering above her but all she could hear was a bright stinging ring. Since she was facedown, she could not see which one of them had grabbed her by the hair and dragged her into the room. As her hearing began to return, she could hear gunfire coming from several directions.

She heard Rojas's voice. "Roll that fucking panocha over. I want her to look me in the eye when I kill her." Someone grabbed her again and rolled her onto her back. The man standing directly above her was Gustavo Moreno, Rojas's intelligence officer. He stood with a polished chrome pistol in his hand.

Jana reached to the back of her head and winced against the pain. Her hair was wet and when she pulled her hand back, it was covered in dark blood. Moreno grabbed her by the shoulders and yanked her against the wall to prop her upright.

"There, Señor Rojas, but we must move quickly, we haven't much time."

Rojas stood at Jana's feet. "My intelligence officer warned me about you. He never trusted you, but after what you did to Montes Lima Perez, how could I not?"

"They're on to you, you prick," Jana said.

"You've got quite a mouth for a panocha, a cunt, that is about to die," Rojas said.

Jana's head was still spinning. "I know what it means."

"So, you were working undercover for the Americans, no? A double agent?"

"I work for no one," she spat back.

"Then why come after me? Most people who come after me do not live to tell the tale."

"Patron, we must go," Moreno pleaded.

"Kyle MacKerron," Jana said.

"Yes, when my intelligence officer saw you on the surveillance camera, he told me what was happening."

Gunfire from the front of the estate intensified. Gustavo Moreno placed a hand on Rojas's shoulder. "Señor Rojas, we must get you out. I don't know how much longer we can hold them off."

Rojas said to him, "The tunnel was put there for a reason, Gustavo."

Jana said, "A tunnel. The way of the coward. I would have come for you anyway."

Rojas laughed. "And what is that supposed to mean?"

"The woman," Jana said. "When I was here the first time."

"Ah, you saw her at the window? Yes," Rojas smiled, "she served her purpose."

"Go fuck yourself."

"Ever the gentile young woman, Agent Baker. But I must know one last thing. Your timing seems impeccable. You come into my home to free Agent MacKerron just as my rivals at Oficina de Envigado start a war? That is not a coincidence, no?"

"Figure it out for yourself," Jana said.

"I wish I had time to teach you a lesson in manners."

Jana said, "It's no coincidence. The freshly murdered body of Carlos Gaviria just found its way to Envigado's front door. How do you like their response? Your operations here are at an end."

"Freshly murdered? But he was killed two days ago."

"No," Jana smirked. "We kidnapped him two days ago, right from under your nose. He was very much alive."

More gunfire tore through the walls, and the sound of a cascading sheet of broken glass crashed from out in the main room.

"Señor Rojas!" Moreno pleaded. "I must insist!"

"You kept him alive, then murdered him at the appropriate time? And dumped his body to start a war? He was my godson!"

Jana knew she had touched a nerve. "He squealed like a little girl when they killed him."

"He did no such thing!" Rojas screamed.

A stray bullet zipped through the drywall and shattered a glass statue in the corner of the room.

This time, even Rojas knew they had to leave. He said, "We have a saying in Colombia. *There is no deceit in death. It delivers precisely what it has promised.*" He nodded to Moreno, who pointed the pistol at Jana's head.

Jana glared at Rojas. "You can burn in hell."

Rojas replied. "You first."

Jana closed her eyes but they startled open at the sound of an automatic weapon firing at point-blank range. She rolled for cover as drywall dust and fragments splintered the room. Rojas and Moreno went down. Jana looked up to see the woman in the sequined dress, an automatic weapon dangling in her hand.

The woman dropped to her knees and began to sob. Moreno lay motionless, his eyes, wide. Jana began to pull the gun from his hand, but Rojas lurched onto her. She elbowed him across the face, smashing his nose. Rojas rocked backward then leapt to his feet as Jana grabbed the gun. He was across the room and out into the hallway as Jana fired. The round clipped his upper back and he was gone.

Jana struggled to her feet then looked at her watch. "Oh God," she said as she grabbed the woman's hand. "We've got to get out of here!" They ran through the house as bullets whizzed past. They descended the staircase to the floor below and ran onto the patio only to see Cade struggling with Kyle in the distance. Bullets chewed up the grass. She heard gunfire coming from the tree line to her left and looked to see Stone shoot another of Rojas's guard.

Stone yelled to her, "Go!" then began laying suppressive cover fire. She yanked the woman's hand and they ran into the fray. A bullet grazed the flesh of Jana's shoulder and she flattened to the ground. But in the adrenaline rush, she jumped up and ran with the woman. They were halfway to the dock as Cade loaded Kyle onto the plane.

The pilot yelled something inaudible above the engine noise.

Weapons fire from inside the house intensified into a pitched crescendo. Jana pulled on the woman then pushed her body into the plane. She yelled to the pilot. "We've got one more!" then motioned to Stone as he made a run for it.

Bullets tore across the dock and splinters of teak sprayed the air.

The pilot yelled, "I'm not waiting! We're leaving!"

Jana raised the pistol at him. "To hell you are!" But when she turned again, she saw Stone limp then go down. "Oh my God." She broke into a sprint and fired toward the house.

From the plane, Cade yelled, "Jana!" but there was nothing he could do.

She reached Stone and pulled him to his feet and they ran onto the dock. As Stone fell into the plane's front seat, he raised the carbine and fired at cartel members who were flooding onto the lawn. "Get in!" he yelled to Jana. But she grabbed his wounded leg and flipped it in, then pulled the carbine from his hands.

"There's something I have to do first," she said as shut the door then slapped her hand on the side of the plane, a signal for the pilot to take off.

The plane's engine roared and it lurched into motion on the water. Jana ran from the dock, firing the weapon at her attackers. She was in a sprint to the wood line. To her thinking, it was the only part of the estate where a tunnel could have possibly been fashioned. But no sooner had she begun firing did the weapon run out of ammunition. Streams of gunfire tore in front of her and she rolled to the ground.

She covered her head against the sting of flying debris. Things began to move in slow motion. The sound of gunfire was deafening. Jana could see men from both cartels firing at one another, and at her. A few bodies were strewn in the blood and chaos. Lying facedown in the grass, Jana struggled to comprehend that this was all real. She kept hearing the warning, *the air strike is imminent.*

She could barely comprehend how she would live through this, but the thought of Rojas making an escape caused her adrenaline to spike. Bullets whizzed past her head. She looked in all directions but there was no way out. *How am I going to get to the tunnel?* she thought.

Several cartel members were headed straight for her, firing as they ran. A bullet struck the ground just inches from her face and dirt and debris flew into her eyes. She curled into a ball, her hands cupping her ears and face.

Jana struggled to regain sight, when from just behind her, a man stood from the bushes and begin firing at the cartel. Bullets flew overhead and scorching-hot shell casings ejected from his weapon and landed on her.

There was something familiar about his silhouette. Her vision was blurry and she struggled to focus on the face. In the given context of a horrific firefight, she couldn't understand what she was seeing. When her vision cleared, the shock on her face was only equaled by the rage in his.

68

Not Without Him

From a remote location, Lawrence Wallace spoke into the mic. "Scorpion, this is Crystal Palace. Give me a status, over."

The F-18 pilot replied, "Crystal Palace, this is Scorpion. Heading, three one five. Angels, twenty-one. Speed, four-fifty. Just within range-to-target. Master Arm, off. Warning yellow, weapons hold."

"Roger that, Scorpion. You're at twenty-one thousand feet, speed, four hundred and fifty knots. Arm the weapon, over."

"Crystal Palace, Master Arm, on. Weapon is armed. Target is locked on."

"You are red and tight, Scorpion. Launch on my command. Launch, launch, launch."

A moment later, "Crystal Palace, this is Scorpion. Greyhound is away."

***

It was Ames. The man towering above her was Ames. Her father stared into abject death and would not relent. His actions reminded Jana of a trained operator. He would aim carefully, squeeze off a three-round burst, then retarget. It was mechanical. He moved with such fluidity that the weapon seemed to be an extension of his body, something fused to him like an arm or a leg.

Bullets chewed into the ground where he stood. In the melee, Jana could hear nothing. She was suffering from a condition known as auditory exclusion in which people in high-stress situations don't hear sounds around them. She watched as Ames's mouth moved and knew he was screaming something to her.

The more she stared at the bizarre sight, the more she began to perceive what he was yelling. He was screaming at her to get up and move. As she rolled onto her feet, Ames sidestepped in the other direction, all the while continuing his attack. He was drawing fire away from her. He continued the methodical process, dropped an empty magazine, and recharged the well with a fresh one. And the sequence started again.

Jana ran as fast as she could into the tree line. She paused a moment to look back at her father. With the air strike about to hit, she knew it would be the last time she would see him alive. She broke into a run through the dense forest toward the only direction where the tunnel could be. But her mind drifted. The pounding of her feet and heart, the feeling of brush crashing against her limbs, catapulted her back to the prior year, running through the forest at YellowstoneNational Park toward terrorist Waseem Jarrah. Fury pulsed in her veins.

The center-most scar on her chest began to burn and the trio of terrifying voices piped into her consciousness.

She will do it herself, the one in the center said. It echoed in a manner similar to a person speaking inside a cave.

How? another replied.

She will seal her own fate. Once she kills him, she will join us and will not be able to claw her way free ever again.

The trio laughed in a chilling echo.

But just as the periphery of her vision began to cloud, she shook free of the impending post-traumatic stress episode.

"You don't run me," she said across tightened vocal chords. "I run me." The voices silenced and her feet pounded harder. She ran up a pathway until she came to a brick-framed door shrouded in tropical growth. It was embedded into the hillside. Vines all but obscured the secret escape route. The huge steel door was shut but she could see fresh footprints on the ground chased by what looked like a single set of tire tracks, a motorcycle.

She pulled the door open but then a solitary fear struck her. *I don't have a weapon.* She struggled to listen above the distant gunfire and could hear something in the distance—the sound of a dirt bike's engine.

When she looked inside, the dimly lit tunnel was empty. The cement tunnel was about four feet wide and she squinted into the low light. It went straight back for about forty yards then veered to the right. "Must lead into the basement level," she said.

Just outside, a roar ripped across the sky. It was so loud it could only be described as the sound of air tearing. What followed next was the largest explosion she could imagine—the air strike. She dove into the tunnel and the ground shook as she went down. Dust and tiny fragments of cement rained down as light bulbs popped. Outside, a steady torrent of dirt and debris, intermixed with shattered wood fragments, began crashing to the ground.

As her eyes adjusted to the darkness, she saw that the tunnel had a long alcove built into one side. Three dirt bikes stood parked with room for a fourth. Each motorcycle had an electrical cord plugged into its small battery, an apparent effort to trickle-charge the batteries and prevent them from draining.

Many months ago, when they had been dating, Stone had

taught her to ride. It was often the case that they would ride tandem on his motorcycle. For most of the time, she would sit behind him and wrap her arms around his torso, but later, Jana had hopped on the bike and looked at him playfully. "Teach me," she'd said.

Thick, black smoke poured from the other end of the tunnel and toward Jana. Without hesitation she hopped onto a bike. Only then did she notice the cuts and abrasions on her legs. "No time for that now." She jump-started the bike and caught her own reflection in one of its side-view mirrors. Her face was covered in dirt, her hair was a mat of dried blood, and blood dripped from her shoulder.

She gunned the throttle and dirt exploded from the rear tire. The only question was, could she catch Rojas before he could disappear? But as she thought of all the women he had harmed entered her mind, fear and doubt abated. Whatever the outcome, she'd do anything in her power to stop him.

69

To Pursue a Madman

Jana wove the dirt bike back and forth through the jungle, stopping every few minutes to listen. In the distance she could hear another motorcycle. She pursued but knew that since she did not have a gun, she would have to keep her distance.

As she approached the winding, paved road, Jana glanced at a trail of mud the other bike had left in its wake and she followed it. She looked back toward the estate. A massive plume of smoke rose hundreds of feet into the air—the compound had been destroyed.

As she crested a hillside, she saw the bike and telltale outline of Diego Rojas cruising ahead. He had slowed in an apparent attempt to blend in.

She pursued, but the farther he went, the more shocked Jana became. With each turn his intended destination became clearer.

"How would he know where our safe house was?" She thought further. "But if he knows where the safe house is, that means . . ." her thoughts played forward, "the equipment, the NSA computer, all that classified information. He's going to try and find out what intelligence we've gathered against him.

She throttled the bike into full acceleration.

70

Memories Long Forgotten

Jana slowed the bike on the approach to the safe house and pulled off early. She did not want to alert Rojas. Once on foot, she made a quiet approach to the edge of the property.

Jana heard yelling from inside. "Tell me!" Rojas screamed. "What does the United States know about my operation?"

The questions were met with unintelligible answers but the voice was unmistakable. It was Pete Buck. Then, a single gunshot rang out.

Jana darted through the thick vegetation along the left side of the yard, then moved down that side of the house. She hugged the wall and crouched low until she came to the first window. She pulled out her phone and opened the camera, then raised it just above the level of the window sill and watched the screen. She panned the camera left, then right until she spotted Buck. He was on the floor, clutching his leg. Jana could not see Rojas—her view was obstructed by a wall. But the sight of blood was all it took.

She stayed low and moved toward the back of the house. When she came to her bedroom window, she flung it open and climbed in. She rolled onto the hardwood floor with a thud.

***

The sound of her body crashing to the ground caused Rojas to duck. Momentarily startled, he regained his composure. "That fucking bitch," he said. He took one glance at Buck, raised the handgun into the air, and pistol-whipped him across the face. Buck's unconscious body splayed across the floor and blood pulsed from his leg without impunity.

***

Jana lunged toward the chest of drawers on the far wall. She ripped at the Velcro and withdrew the Glock from its hiding place.

Rojas burst into the room. It took him no longer than a millisecond to snap-fire his weapon at her. The bullet grazed the length her right forearm, tearing a gash across the flesh.

Everything again went into slow motion and a voice reverberated in Jana's mind. It was the voice of her shooting instructor from Quantico. *Double-tab, center mass, then one to the head.* Without thinking, she sidestepped and fired. The round struck Rojas in the right shoulder.

Just before Jana fired again, she saw Rojas's arm go limp as the gun fell from his hand. It bounced across the hardwood floor and landed at her feet. She kicked it underneath the bed and Rojas fell on his knees.

With her finger still on the trigger, Jana took two strides toward Rojas and placed the muzzle against his temple. With it, she pushed his head into the door jam. Her jaw clenched, her eyes flared, her breathing accelerated, and her focus sharpened. Had anyone else been present, they would have described her face as that of a beast. She applied tension to the trigger.

"No, no, wait," Rojas said as pain wracked his face. "You need me. Think about it. You need me."

Jana's right hand began to shake but in the heat of the moment, she could not tell whether it was from an impending PTSD episode or the unadulterated rage coursing through her system. She jammed the muzzle harder and spoke through gritted teeth, "You tortured those women, didn't you? After you finished raping them?"

Rojas began to laugh maniacally. "I taught them their place, that's for sure," he said as his body rocked into the laughter.

"I need you? What I need is to see your brain matter sprayed all over the floor. Say goodnight, you prick."

He crushed his eyes closed, bracing for the gunshot, when a soft voice called out. "Jana? Sweet Pea?"

Jana instinctively jerked the gun toward the voice and lined up on the silhouette of a man standing in the front door. She nearly pulled the trigger, but realized she recognized the form. Her mouth dropped open—it was Ames. She turned the muzzle back to Rojas's skull.

"Jana? It's me. It's your dad."

"But . . ." she said, "You were at the estate when that bomb hit."

"Please, baby, don't do this thing. He's unarmed." His voice felt like a cold glass of milk on a hot summer day. Memories exploded into her mind—her as a two-year-old, first standing on the couch, laughing as her father threw snowballs against the outside of the window, then inside her fort, her special hiding place on her grandfather's farm.

But those images were replaced by the fury boiling inside. "He's a monster," she said as she glared at the top of Rojas's skull. "Tortures people for information they do not have, rapes and murders women because he thinks it's fun."

"I know, Sweet Pea. But—"

"He enjoys power over women. He enjoys tying them up, making them beg for their lives, dominating them," Jana said as the shaking in her right hand intensified.

Though Rojas's eyes were still shut, he said. "Fucking little whores learned their lesson, didn't they?" He laughed until Jana jammed the gun into his head so hard that he winced.

"Learned their lesson?" Jana growled. "Well let's see if you can learn this lesson."

She straightened her arm into a shooting position and began to pull the trigger in earnest when her father said, "Bug? Buggie?"

Jana stopped and her head turned. "What did you say?"

"Bug," her father replied. "That's what I used to call you."

Jana searched her memory for something that would not come. It was a frantic effort to understand why hearing a simple name had tightened her throat.

Her father continued. "When you were little, I always called you Jana-Bug. Don't you remember?"

Jana swallowed. "I was only two years old when they told me you were dead." There was venom in her words. "They were just trying to protect me from the fact that you went to prison!"

He walked toward her. "You used to love it when I would read *The Very Hungry Caterpillar* to you. It was your favorite story. You pronounced it *calli-pider*. Then we would read that other one. What was it? It was the one about the zookeeper."

Memories gushed forth. They flickered in bits and pieces—sitting in her father's lap, the smell of his aftershave, the sound of coins jingling in his pocket, him tickling her before bedtime, and then there was something else, something she couldn't quite place.

"You pronounced it *zip-eee-kur*. Do you remember me from back then?" he whispered as he held his tightening voice in check. "You used to call me Pop-Pop."

"Pop-Pop?" she whispered as she placed her free hand over

her mouth. "That was you reading to me?" A tear eased onto her cheekbone as her inner turmoil boiled over. She turned to Rojas and her grip tightened on the Glock once again.

"Look at me, Bug."

Jana gripped the gun so tight she felt as though she might crush it.

Her father said, "Don't do this thing. Don't do it, baby."

"He—deserves—it," she managed to choke across clenched teeth and tears.

"I know he does, but this is something you can't undo. This is something you can't take back. And this is not you."

"I could have been one of those women," she said. "I could have wound up in his torture chamber. He's a monster."

Rojas laughed. "And we can't have monsters wandering the quiet countryside, now can we, Agent Baker?"

"Don't listen to him, Bug," Ames said. He waited a moment then added, "This isn't something they taught you at Quantico."

Jana's mind raced as images from her FBI training on the Marine Corps base at Quantico, Virginia, flashed before her eyes—running the obstacle course and its daunting final hill, *the widowmaker*; tackling a man playing the role of a bank-robbery suspect in Hogan's Alley, a simulated town designed for training; driving at high speed around the Tactical and Emergency Vehicle Operations Center as simulated bullets slammed into the driver's window, numerous flickers of classrooms, then back at the dormitories.

Jana's vision blurred and she shook her head. "Do you know what I see when I look at this piece of shit?" she said. "I see death. I see terror. I wake up at night and I'm screaming and all I can see is—"

"Don't you see what you're doing, Bug? When you look at

Rojas, you're not really seeing him. You're seeing Rafael, aren't you?"

Her head snapped at her father. "How do you know that name?"

"Cade told me. He told me the ordeal you'd been through, that Rafael had knocked you out with gas, then kidnapped you and took you to that remote cabin."

Visions of herself in the terrifying scene in the cabin exploded in her vision—stripped down to her undergarments, her arms and feet lashed to the chair, Rafael laughing as the then-most-wanted terrorist in the world, Waseem Jarrah, pressed a blade to her throat. "Oh, yeah?" Jana said. "Did he tell you what Rafael planned to do to me? Rape me, then cut my skin off while I was still alive? Did he tell you that?" she yelled.

"Bug, listen to me. No one knows the terrors you've been through. I don't blame you for shooting Rafael that day." He took a step closer. "But don't do this thing. Rojas may be the same kind of monster, but if you shoot him now, it will be murder. And you can't come back from that. The more things you do that aren't really you, the farther you drift from who you really are. Believe me, I know. That's exactly what happened to me. This will be something you'll regret for the rest of your life."

"I *have* to," she said. Yet the conflict within her flared again. Her mind flashed back to the FBI Academy graduation ceremony. She was on stage receiving the prestigious Director's Leadership Award from Director Stephen Latent, an honor bestowed on a single trainee per graduating class. She then returned to receive top honors in all three disciplines: academics, physical fitness, and firearms. She had clearly been the best trainee to complete the new agent training program in years.

"You and me, Bug," her dad said, "we're the same. Can't you

see it?"

"I've thought about it over and over. Ever since I found out you had committed treason. And I think back to shooting Rafael. I see how similar I am to you, a criminal! It's in the DNA, isn't it? When I joined the FBI, I didn't think it was, but I was wrong."

"No, that's where you *are* wrong," he pleaded. "Look at me. It's *not* in the DNA."

"What would you know about it?"

"It's not *like father, like daughter*. It doesn't work like that. Listen to me and listen closely. You are not the sum total of your biological parts."

"Oh really?" Jana yelled. "How does it work then?"

"You and I lost track of who we really are. The difference is, I've spent the last twenty-eight years trying to fight my way back, and you're doing everything you can to run further from yourself. You murdered Rafael and you've been running from it ever since." He paused a moment and his voice trembled. "I was in prison. But for you it's different. You're in a different kind of prison."

"What's that supposed to mean?"

"You carry your prison with you."

"Got it all figured out, do you?"

Ames went on unabated. "Your grandpa used to write me letters. He told me that the two of you would be on the farm and would hear the train whistle in the distance? There was that junction about a mile away and he said if you listened close enough, you could eventually tell if the train had taken the left fork or the right. He said you two used to make a bet as to which one it would take."

Jana's mind drifted back. She could almost smell the salted ham. Her voice washed quiet, and she spoke the way a person might speak at a funeral. "The loser had to wash the dishes," she said.

"That's us, Jana. That's you and me. We're on the same train, at different times in our lives. But if you do this thing now, you'll be taking the wrong fork and you can't get off."

"I'm doing what I know is right," she said as she fought back tears.

"There isn't anything *right* about doing something you'll regret for the rest of your life. Come on, baby. Put the gun down. Come back to the girl you knew growing up. Come back home."

She looked at the floor and began to sob, but a moment later raised again, readying to fire. "Oh, God!" she blubbered.

Her father broke in once again. "Do you remember the fort?"

Jana exhaled in a long shaky motion. *How could he know about that?* she thought. "The fort?"

"On Grandpa's farm. It was a cold fall morning. You and I were awake before anybody else. You were so little, but you used the word *adventure*. It was such a big word for someone so small. You wanted to go on an adventure."

The shaking in Jana's hand intensified as tears streamed down her face.

Ames started again. "I got you all bundled up, and we went outside and into the woods. We found this big stone," he said as his hands formed the shape of the large granite outcropping, "and we put a bunch of logs across the top, then pulled a big thicket of vines in front to make a door." He paused. "Don't you remember?"

It all flashed back, images of the logs, the feel of cold granite, rays of sun penetrating the canopy, then her and her father inside the newly constructed little hideout. "I remember," she whispered. "I remember it all. That's the last time I remember being happy."

For the first time, she realized it was her father that had built the fort with her in the first place. Her father was Pop-Pop. Her father was the one that had read books to her. Her father made pancakes for her. Her father had played with her. *Her father loved her.*

"Buggie, if you kill this man right now, you'll always regret it. Just like you regret killing Rafael."

She looked at him.

"I know you regret it," he said. "It sent you into a downward spiral. The same kind of downward spiral I was on. But for me, once I got started, things got out of control and I lost track of who I was. There were people that died because of the classified information I sold. And in the end, I went to prison. It doesn't have to be that way for you. And you know something? Prison wasn't the worst part. The worst part was that I'd lost you. You lost a father, and your mom was eventually murdered because of what I'd done."

"I've hated you my whole life," she said looking at him.

"And I deserved that. But this," he said as he motioned to Rojas, "this is your time. This is your choice." He walked to her and took the gun gently from her hand. "I've been waiting, Bug."

"Waiting for what?" she replied as her lower lip quivered.

His voice tightened and he pulled her into a hug. "Waiting for this."

71

A Knock at the Door

Rojas tried to stand but Ames thumped him on the head with the pistol. "I have him," he said as he pushed Rojas to the floor. "Go help Buck. Put pressure on that leg."

Jana rolled Buck over and leaned a stiff hand against the artery in his upper thigh.

Ames gripped the pistol.

Rojas said, "There is nowhere my organization cannot reach." It was an unveiled threat.

"Oh no?" Ames crashed his knee into the center of Rojas's back. He then removed his belt and secured Rojas's hands.

Jana heard something outside and turned to look. She found a heavily armed man in the doorway. He was dressed in black fatigues and held his weapon forward.

"DEA," his steely voice called out. "Team two," he said, "clear the building." DEA agents poured in. A few disappeared into the back rooms while another cuffed Diego Rojas. "Are you Agent Baker?" the commander said.

"I'm Jana Baker," she replied.

"Ma'am? You look like you need medical. Johnson? Martinez?" he yelled. "We've got two wounded here that need attention." He knelt next to Buck. "And this one needs an evac."

Jana released her hold on Buck as one of the medic-trained agents took over. Just outside, she heard one of them call for a medivac helicopter. Her eyes took on a distant quality. "I don't understand. Where did you guys come from?"

"Point Udall, ma'am."

"But how—"

"It was him," the commander said as he nodded to a man standing just outside the doorway.

Jana looked up. He was a short, round man with a massive beard. "Uncle Bill?" she said. She stood and hugged him. "What are you doing here? How did you know?"

His voice was grandfatherly. "It was Knuckles," he said as he pointed outside. The teenager stood in the stark sunlight, a flak jacket dwarfing his pencil-thin torso. "We couldn't raise you on the comms, but that didn't stop us from eavesdropping. We intercepted a lot of phone calls. Hacked every surveillance camera and computer on the island. We intercepted a lot of things, in fact. When I put two and two together, I finally knew what I think he knew." Bill looked at Pete Buck. "That a CIA air strike was inbound, and you'd be going after Kyle."

Jana gripped his arm, "Kyle, Stone! Where are they?"

He steadied her. "Fine, they're fine. One of the Blackhawks is with them. Stone's wounds are being tended to. Kyle looks to be in bad shape, but they'll get him into a hospital, then a rehab program. It will take a long time to break that drug addiction, but he'll be okay."

The medic-trained agent inserted an IV into Buck's arm and looked up. "He's lost a lot of blood. Chopper is inbound. Looks to have a concussion as well."

"Is he going to be okay?"

"We'll fix him up, ma'am."

"And the woman?"

Bill smiled. "Thanks to you."

"Bill?" Jana said. "Were we right? Al Qaeda is laundering money through the cartels?" She squinted at a tiny dot on the horizon—an approaching aircraft.

Bill said, "Since we shut down so many terrorist banking connections, it's no wonder they've turned elsewhere to move their money."

"But how do you know Al Qaeda isn't just getting into the drug business?"

Uncle Bill shook his head. "I have a feeling he's going to tell us," he said as he pointed to Pete Buck. "Anyway, somehow these terrorist scumbags find it perfectly okay to decapitate someone, or set off a bomb that kills innocent children, but to them, drugs are against the will of Allah. This has been a money-laundering operation from the outset."

The sound of a helicopter approaching turned both Bill's and Jana's attention.

Bill said, "Sikorsky SH-60 Seahawk, here for Buck."

The US Navy twin-turboshaft hovered just above the road near the house. A rescue hoist leaned over the edge. The T700 engines roared and dust flew in all directions. The aluminum-framed stretcher was lowered to the ground.

Two DEA agents detached the stretcher and ran it inside where they loaded Buck. Jana and Bill stood aside and watched as he was then hoisted aboard. The helicopter banked away and headed to sea.

"Where will they take him?" Jana said.

"The *George H. W. Bush*. Got a great hospital aboard."

"There's an aircraft carrier out there?"

Bill nodded. "That's where the CIA air strike originated. The president wasn't too happy when he found out. But," Bill shuffled his feet, "if truth be told, he wasn't all that upset either."

"Bill," Jana started, "they sent Kyle in there. They were going to leave him."

"It's called a throwaway, Jana. When a mission is deemed as having a high strategic value, certain sacrifices are made."

"Certain sacrifices? Kyle's a human being. And the president is okay with that?"

"Yes, he is. I hate to say it, but we're all expendable, kid. Nonetheless, when he found out it wasn't just some faceless CIA operative, and that you were involved, it kind of pissed him off."

"Me? The president knows who I am?"

"Same old Jana. You've got a particular penchant for underestimating your worth."

Jana smiled, then hugged him. She plucked a tiny orange crumb out of his beard. "Same old Bill. I thought Mrs. Uncle Bill wouldn't let you eat orange crackers anymore."

"Don't tell her, okay?"

Jana laughed. "Think we can catch a ride out to the carrier? I have a feeling Buck can fill in some blanks for us."

72

Here It Comes

Carrier George H. W. Bush, *seventy-seven nautical miles north-northwest of Antigua.*

When Jana and Uncle Bill walked into the surgical recovery room, Pete Buck nodded at them. As they drew chairs around his hospital bed, he started speaking. His throat was dry and raspy. "I know how this all started. You've got to understand the background. Otherwise, you're not going to believe a word I say."

"This should be fun," Bill said.

"It's beginning to look like the days of Pablo Escobar down there again, right?"

"You mean in Colombia?" Jana asked. "And you don't have to whisper, Buck. I kind of doubt the place is bugged."

"Very funny. They had a tube down my throat," he said. Buck shifted his position. "It started last year when a suicide bomber walked into a closed session of congress in the Capitolio Nacional building in central Bogotá. He had two pounds of C4 strapped to his chest. He detonated. It wasn't front-page news in the Western world because the meeting only consisted of four members of the Colombian government. Three senators and one other person. I guess the body count wasn't high enough for it to end up on WBS News."

Uncle Bill said, "I remember that. But refresh my memory. Who were these four Colombians and what were they planning to do?"

"You get right to the point, don't you?" Buck said as he grinned at Bill. "They were meeting to discuss the renewed drug trade. The Los Rastrojos cartel stood to benefit most from the death of one of those officials in particular."

"Now I remember. Juan Guillermo," Bill said. "Chief of the new drug police."

"That's right," Buck replied. "The assassination sent a message. With the support of the senators, Guillermo had cracked down on the new cartels. Broke up their truck transport system. Apparently, Los Rastrojos got a little pissed off about it."

Jana said, "Since when does CIA covertly track drug runners?"

Buck said, "When it's not just money laundering."

"Here it comes," Bill said.

Buck said, "The money was to flow to a new terror cell."

Jana thought about the implications. "A new terror cell? Where?"

The look on Buck's face spoke volumes and Jana knew, the new cell was forming in the US. "But what was the connection?" She paused a moment. "Let me guess, the suicide bomber in Bogotá was of Middle Eastern descent?"

Buck said nothing.

"With ties to known terror organizations?" Jana shook her head.

"You have a gift for this line of work, Jana. It's something you were born to do," Buck said.

"If I have to remind you one more time that I'm not going back to the Bureau, you'll end up with a fat lip. So you did a thorough background on the jihadist. Which terror organization was he tied to?"

"Al Qaeda."

"So CIA found out the suicide bomber was linked to Al Qaeda, and now the full-court press on the drug cartels."

"Yes, we've got to stop the flow of funding."

Jana stood and leaned on the chair. "There's one thing that doesn't add up."

"Just one thing?" Uncle Bill joked.

"Why would the cartels need the services of Al Qaeda? Why couldn't they just do the assassination themselves?"

"A gift, Jana," Buck said. "You've just forgotten who you really are." She moved on him as if to strike, but he knew it was a bluff. "That's just it," he said. "Los Rastrojos had tried and failed. When the cartel was unable to carry out the assassination themselves, they turned to Al Qaeda, who had already initiated an interest in partnership. Apparently, the key was to get all the players into a room at the same time. Before the suicide bomber walked in, these Colombian lawmakers believed they were going to greet a member of the Saudi consulate, for diplomatic purposes. It turns out he was a jihadist with explosives strapped underneath his business suit. It was the first time they had all agreed to be in the same place at the same time."

"Alright, fine," she said. "What about the other side of it? Was Al Qaeda's partnership interest simply them looking for a new source of funding?"

"Not so much that as a new way to launder their existing funds. Interpol had recently locked down several of their financial pipelines, so the terrorists had been scrambling for a new way to launder and move cash."

Jana said, "So Al Qaeda was looking for a financial partner, someone to launder money, and in return, offered assistance to assassinate the police chief and politicians. How very convenient. One of the organizations can move money, and the other can supply an endless stream of suicide jihadists who will do anything that is asked of them."

"And that's where we come in. For CIA, it's about the money trail. A good bit of this funding would flow right back to the terror cells. Particularly the sleeper cell Al Qaeda is planting inside the United States. God knows what havoc they could wreak on American soil."

Jana scowled. "Why are you looking at me like that?"

"We need you, Jana," Buck said.

"I'm never going back, so drop it. But getting back to the point, you're telling me CIA's response to the new terror cell is to obliterate the estate of Diego Rojas? Kill them all? Is that it?" When Buck didn't respond, she continued. "And what about Kyle? You were going to kill him too?"

"Not me, Jana," Buck said. "Kyle was going to be taken off the island."

She blurted, "What do you mean?"

"Kyle was icing on the cake. The cartel was going to make a money laundering deal with Al Qaeda, and Al Qaeda was going to get Kyle. He'd either be tortured for information or used as a bargaining chip. Or both."

"Are we too late?" Jana asked. "Has funding already made its way to the new terror cell building in the US?"

Uncle Bill glanced at her hand and said, "Don't you worry about that right now."

Jana glared at Buck as he sat up. "Yes and no. There was a trial run that apparently executed last month. We just found out about it. Sort of a test before moving forward with a full partnership."

"How much money slipped through?" Bill said.

"About two million dollars. That's paltry compared to what was about to happen, before we stopped it, that is." Buck looked over his shoulder. "You should go now." He shook their hands. "This conversation never happened."

73

Admission

Safe house.

"You've always been like a grandfather to me, Bill," Jana said as they walked back inside. "And I know you still think of me as that kid, that green rookie agent. But I'm not a little girl anymore. You don't have to protect me."

Bill followed her movements.

"Two million dollars is a lot of money," she added.

Bill's voice was choppy. "Yes, it is. To a small terror cell, it's a lifeline."

"Tell me the truth. Karim Zahir wasn't killed in the blast, was he?"

"DEA is combing the debris at the Rojas estate, looking for him."

She rubbed her temples. "I can't handle tracking down another terrorist."

Bill looked at her from out of the corner of his eye. "Are you saying what I think you're saying?"

"Bill," Jana said as she gazed out into the bay. "All of this is over now. My life here, I mean."

"You look . . . different."

"I feel lost. Where do I go? What do I do?"

"Do you remember what I told you the last time you asked me that?"

"You said, I go *on*."

He nodded.

"I don't think I know how."

"Sure you do."

A tear formed in Jana's eye and held. "I've lost track of who I am."

"Yes," Uncle Bill whispered. "But there's something in the way, blocking you from getting back. Am I right?"

"You do remind me of my grandfather."

"And what would he tell you right now?"

Jana thought back to her childhood. The farm, the wide porch, all the times her grandfather had given her advice. "I have to admit to myself I was wrong about shooting Rafael, don't I?"

"Were you wrong?"

Jana's gut swirled. It was as if she somehow knew her answer would determine the future course of everything she stood for.

She caught glimpse of Ames. He was down by the water's edge. Her lower lip quivered and her scar began to sting, but she was unabated. Her voice came out in a whisper. "I killed him, Bill. I killed Rafael in cold blood." She crushed a hand over her mouth. Uncle Bill put his arms around her. "I knew he was helpless. I knew what I was doing." She sobbed quietly as the emotional tumult spilled forth. Through the blur in her vision, she looked at Ames. "I even knew that my actions would be excused under the law, after the horror I'd been through. I knew what I was doing."

"Shhh," Uncle Bill said. He held her. "I've known you a long time. What happened in the past stays in the past." He turned and looked at Ames. "But sometimes we have to face the past to move forward. Telling me what you just told me? That's the bravest thing you've ever done. And it stays with me. I'll never speak of this to anyone."

Jana stood taller. The stinging in her scar abated and she took a breath. "And then there's him," she said. "My own father."

"Yes," Uncle Bill replied. He waited a moment. "He went through a lot of trouble to find you."

"I know he did. And he risked his life for me. I still don't understand how he didn't die in that explosion."

"I asked him about that. It was because of you. Once he knew you were clear, he headed into the woods after you. Apparently there were a few more motorcycles in that tunnel. He took out a few of Rojas's people who were coming after you."

"I know what you're going to say, Bill."

He grinned, though underneath his massive beard, it was hard to tell.

Jana said, "You're going to tell me to not do something I'm going to regret for the rest of my life. You're going to tell me I need to give my father a chance."

"Did I say anything?" he smirked.

She rubbed her scars. "You know, these have always bothered me. Every time I would look in the mirror, I'd see them and they would remind me. It's been like having a horrifying past I couldn't escape from. I kept wanting to go to a plastic surgeon to have them removed."

"And now?"

"I don't know," she said. "Maybe the idea of removing them was just my way of running away."

"You've been carrying that baggage for a long time," Uncle Bill said.

The edges of a smile emerged on her face. "These scars are a part of me. Maybe now they'll remind me of something else."

"And what's that?" Bill said as he grinned.

"They'll remind me of me."

74

A Future of Certainty

FBI Headquarters, J. Edgar Hoover Building, Washington, DC. Six weeks later.

Jana got out of the Uber car and stared up at the building. Somehow, it looked smaller than she'd remembered. The morning sun had crested and there was a bright reflection on the glass. Traffic was heavy and, in the crisp air, people moved with purpose on the sidewalk, some entering the building.

She smoothed the jacket of her new business suit and felt a little flutter in her stomach. Her fingers made their way just inside the top button of her white button-down until they found the trio of scars. She swallowed.

But then she heard a voice behind her—a voice from her past. "Are you sure you want to do this?" the voice said.

She turned. Without saying a word, she put her arms around him. "Hello, Chuck." It was Agent Chuck Stone, the father of John Stone, and the man that had started her on this path several years prior. Their embrace only lasted a moment. She smiled. "I can't believe you're here."

"I couldn't *not* be here. I got you into this."

"I may have been just an intern when you recruited me, but I made my own decision."

"I know you did."

Jana grinned. "You look old."

Chuck smiled. "Thanks a lot. But being retired from the Bureau has been good to me."

"How's Stone doing? I mean, how's John doing?"

"He's great. Healed up nicely from his injuries on Antigua. I can't believe you and my son met each other, much less were dating."

"He turned three sheets of white when I finally figured out he was your son."

Chuck's face stiffened. "That's your father over there, isn't it?"

"Yes. He shows up everywhere. He's really trying. He just wants to let me know he's close by, if I ever want to talk."

"I guess he figures he owes you that much. Do you talk to him?"

"Sometimes. I'm trying. There's still a lot of anger in there. But . . ."

Chuck nodded at the building. "Are you sure you want to do this?"

Jana looked at it again. "I'm sure. I feel good again. I'm scared, but I feel something I haven't felt in a long time."

"And what's that?"

She smiled. "Purpose."

"I've always known you belonged here," Chuck said. "Ever since I met you, back on the Petrolsoft case, I could see *agent* written all over you. Want me to walk you in?"

Jana looked into the reflection of sunlight on the glass. "No, this is something I have to do for myself."

****

CPSIA information can be obtained
at www.ICGtesting.com
Printed in the USA
LVHW01s0301120918
589891LV00021B/1090/P